PUFFIN BOOKS

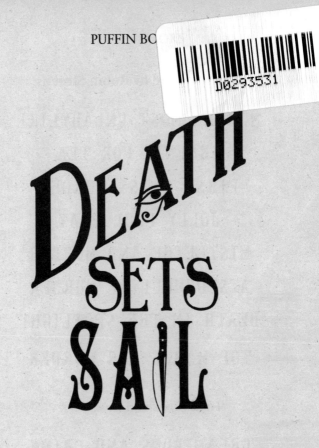

DEATH
SETS
SAIL

DEATH
SETS
SAIL

A MURDER MOST UNLADYLIKE MYSTERY

ROBIN STEVENS

PUFFIN

PUFFIN BOOKS

UK | USA | Canada | Ireland | Australia
India | New Zealand | South Africa

Puffin Books is part of the Penguin Random House group of companies
whose addresses can be found at global.penguinrandomhouse.com.

www.penguin.co.uk
www.puffin.co.uk
www.ladybird.co.uk

First published 2020

002

Set in 11/16 pt ITC New Baskerville Std
Typeset by Jouve (UK), Milton Keynes
Printed and bound in Great Britain by Clays Ltd, Elcograf S.p.A.

A CIP catalogue record for this book is available from the British Library

ISBN: 978–0–241–41980–9

All correspondence to:
Puffin Books
Penguin Random House Children's
One Embassy Gardens, 8 Viaduct Gardens, London SW11 7BW

MIX
Paper from
responsible sources
FSC   FSC® C018179
www.fsc.org

Penguin Random House is committed to a
sustainable future for our business, our readers
and our planet. This book is made from Forest
Stewardship Council® certified paper.

To my mother, Kathie Booth Stevens, my heroine

DEATH
SETS
SAIL

Being an account of

The Case of the Death on the Nile,
an investigation by the Wells and Wong Detective
Society, with assistance from the Junior Pinkertons.

Written by Hazel Wong
(Detective Society ~~Vice~~-President), aged 15.

Begun Wednesday 23rd December 1936.

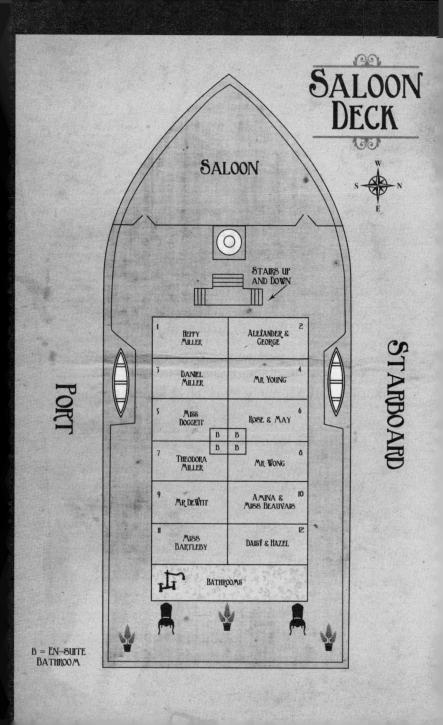

SALOON DECK

SALOON

W N
S E

STAIRS UP
AND DOWN

1 HEPPY MILLER	2 ALEXANDER & GEORGE
3 DANIEL MILLER	4 MR YOUNG
5 MISS DOGGETT	6 ROSE & MAY
7 THEODORA MILLER	8 MR WONG
9 MR DEWITT	10 AMINA & MISS BEAUVAIS
11 MISS BARTLEBY	12 DAISY & HAZEL

B B
B B

BATHROOMS

PORT

STARBOARD

B = EN-SUITE
BATHROOM

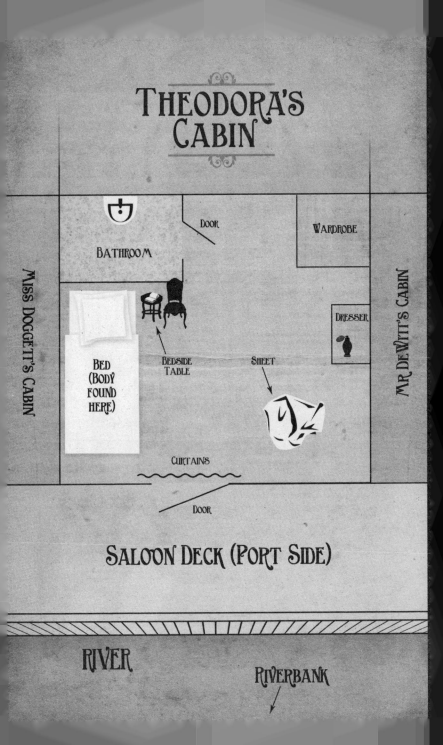

CHARACTER LIST

THE DETECTIVES

Daisy Wells – *the Wells & Wong Detective Society*
Hazel Wong (Wong Fung Ying) – *the Wells & Wong Detective Society*
Amina El Maghrabi – *the Wells & Wong Detective Society*
Alexander Arcady – *the Junior Pinkertons*
George Mukherjee – *the Junior Pinkertons*

THE SS *HATSHEPSUT*

Mr Mustafa Mansour – *the manager of the SS Hatshepsut*
Vincent Wong (Wong Lik Han) – *Hazel's father*
Rose Wong (Wong Ngai Ling, also known as Ling Ling) – *Hazel's half-sister*
May Wong (Wong Mei Li, also known as Monkey) – *Hazel's half-sister*
Pik An – *Rose's maid (also maid to May on this journey)*

Miss Adeline Beauvais – *Amina's governess*

Mr Joseph Young – *Alexander and George's tutor*

Ahmed – *a sailor, member of the SS* Hatshepsut's *crew*

Mrs Theodora Miller – *the leader of the Breath of Life Society and the reincarnation of Hatshepsut*

Hephzibah "Heppy" Miller – *member of the Breath of Life Society and Theodora's adopted daughter*

Daniel Miller – *ex-member of the Breath of Life Society and Theodora's adopted son*

Miss Ida Doggett – *member of the Breath of Life Society and the reincarnation of Cleopatra*

Miss Rhiannon Bartleby – *member of the Breath of Life Society and the reincarnation of Nefertiti*

Mr Narcissus DeWitt – *member of the Breath of Life Society and the reincarnation of Thutmose III*

Joshua Morse – *ex-member of the Breath of Life Society*

FALLINGFORD

Rebecca 'Beanie' Martineau – *the Wells & Wong Detective Society*

Kitty Freebody – *the Wells & Wong Detective Society*

Lavinia Temple – *the Wells & Wong Detective Society*

Bertie Wells – *Daisy's brother*

Harold Mukherjee – *George's brother*

Chapman – *the Wellses' butler*

Hetty – *the Wellses' maid*
Mrs Doherty – *the Wellses' housekeeper*
Toast Dog – *a dog*
Millie – *a dog*

PART ONE

TOWARDS ZERO

1

This is an account of the last murder mystery the Detective Society will ever solve together.

My name is Hazel Wong, and I am heartbroken. I used to think that nothing could ever change, not really, not with my best friend Daisy and me. The rest of the world could spin out of true and smash like a Christmas bauble on the floor, but still nothing would be able to touch us. We were Wells and Wong, after all. We were the Detective Society, and we always came out on top.

But I see now that I got caught in the trick of thinking like Daisy. Her voice in my head and my own have become so mixed up by now that I hardly know which is which unless I pause to think about it, and I never wanted to pause, not about this. And, besides, Daisy promised me – she promised—

I ought to be grown-up enough now to know that promises can be broken, that no one is safe, and that the myth of Daisy Wells, the girl who can walk through mortal danger without even a scratch on her cheek, is only that. A myth.

I am beginning this account on the day before Christmas Eve, at Daisy's home, Fallingford. The last time I was here for Christmas, there were enormous fires in every hearth, a gorgeously lit tree that stretched all the way up beside the great central staircase, and plates and plates of mince pies, carried spiced and steaming from the kitchen by the Wellses' maid, Hetty. But this Christmas is quite different. The house is cold, and somehow still dark, no matter how many lamps and candles Chapman and Hetty light. Mrs Doherty, the cook, has burned the mince pies, and even the dogs look miserable. My littlest sister, May, tries to feed them biscuits, but they ignore her, so she shouts at them.

'I think I hate English Christmas,' says my other sister, Rose, and I agree with her.

But it isn't England I want to write about now, it's Egypt: the wide light of it, the sparks of sun off the Nile, the hum and churn of our cruise ship moving under my feet – and Daisy. From the moment we stepped into the cabin and saw the blood, I thought that this was just another exciting adventure, another puzzle to solve, but I see now how wrong I was. I have held off writing up this case, but now, finally, I want to go back over those last days – our last murder mystery – to be with her again.

Perhaps that way I can bring Daisy back to life.

2

I suppose it all began during the autumn term at
Deepdean. Daisy and I were fifth formers now, which
sounds dreadfully grown-up and shiny with promise –
only the reality was as misty and confusing as the
English autumn weather.

Our fellow Detective Society members were out of
sorts, and it was not hard to see why. Our friend Beanie's
mother was still sickening by the day, and there was
nothing anyone could do about it. We realized, once
the initial shocking discovery in the summer term had
passed, that there really are no words in the English
language to explain how sorry you feel, and that grief,
outside books, is far less dramatic and far more
exhausting than you are led to expect.

'I don't want you to pity me,' said Beanie fiercely.
'Don't LOOK at me like that!' And so we all had to
pretend that we did not see her becoming thinner and

thinner until her big eyes stared out of her face like carriage lamps.

We all had to be very careful where mothers were concerned. Kitty had to bite off her complaining about her mother expecting a baby ('It'll be as dreadful as Binny! Worse, I expect!') whenever Beanie came into the dorm, and Lavinia threw away the thoughtful notes accompanying the beautifully wrapped packets of sweets and cakes from her stepmother, Patricia, so that Beanie would not see them.

Daisy, of course, was utterly Daisy about it all. She was the only one of us who really did forget most of the time that Beanie even had a mother. She threw herself back into lacrosse, and riding, and working creative mistakes into her essays – and she threw herself, with a vengeance, back into our quarrel with the other dorm, especially Amina El Maghrabi.

At first I was surprised at this. I had thought that, after the events of the summer term, we had agreed to be friends with Amina – and Amina was certainly being friendly to us. She waved at us in the corridors, she chattered to us at dinner and she waited so we could walk up to House together. Oddly, this meant that we spent far more time with Clementine Delacroix than we ever had before and, to my astonishment, I discovered that she was not as bad as I had always assumed. And I liked Amina very much – she was funny and clever and bold. I was determined to treat her kindly, for I knew how hard it was for anyone who did not look like the perfect English miss at Deepdean.

So I could not understand why Daisy met every one of her kind overtures with a snub. I was cross with Daisy over it, and rather embarrassed – and one morning, during the third week of term, I apologized to Amina at the breakfast table, while Daisy glared at us over a slice of toast.

'Oh, I don't mind,' said Amina. 'She doesn't mean it, do you, Daisy?' and she winked at Daisy as she licked jam off her thumb.

'HARDLY!' said Daisy nonsensically, and spots of colour appeared high up on her cheeks.

And I ought to have seen it then; only I did not.

I didn't see it when Amina passed Daisy notes in lessons, and Daisy tore them up and crushed them beneath the heel of her shoe. I didn't see it when Amina asked Daisy what she thought of her Sunday dress and Daisy told her, with a furious flush on her face, that she looked like an utter horror.

I didn't see it until I woke in the middle of one night during the fifth week of term to a tiny rustling, barely even a noise. A year ago, I would have slept through it, but my detective senses have been honed, and now I was alert at once. I kept my eyes carefully half-lidded, my breathing slow, and peered through my lashes to see

Daisy sitting up in bed. As I watched, she swung her feet down, cat-light, to press them gently against the dorm-room floor. There had been no Detective Society meeting scheduled – there was no case at all: the term had been quite crime free – so I could not think what she was up to. I made sure I did not move until she had slipped away to the window, and only sat up myself when I heard the squeak of the sash rising, then the gentle patter of feet and hands moving up the drainpipe.

I got up and crept across the dorm – although Daisy might not admit it, I have learned to move as quietly as her, and none of the others woke up – to stand by the window. I waited, peering after her, until she rolled over the lip of the roof high above me, and then I reached out my hands and climbed carefully upwards. These days I am good at that as well.

At last I pulled myself onto the slope of the roof. There was Daisy, crouched in the shadow of the eaves, the gold of her hair covered with a dark scarf. She was staring round a corniced chimney pot, as fierce as an owl, at something on the other side. I crept up behind her, holding my breath, putting one foot in front of the other as soft as silk.

'Hazel,' said Daisy, not turning round. 'How dare you?'

'How did you know it was me?' I hissed, startled. 'And – what are you doing? Why did you creep off without me? Are you on a case?'

'*Shush!*' said Daisy. 'I always know when it's you. You'd always know it was me, wouldn't you?'

I was level with her now. I peeped over her shoulder to see what she was looking at, and—

'Daisy,' I said, 'why are you watching Amina?'

For there Amina was, leaning on a roof peak twenty paces away, with her legs tucked under her, reading a book by torchlight. She had not noticed us – she seemed in a world of her own.

'She's behaving suspiciously,' whispered Daisy. 'She's a possible danger! Hazel, I—'

I saw it, then, the thing I should have all along. I knew, though, that I could not confront Daisy about it. Not yet.

'No, she isn't,' I said. 'She's not a danger at all! You – you're just looking for a mystery to solve this term, and you know there isn't one.'

It wasn't the truth, of course.

'Humph!' said Daisy crossly. 'There *might* be, Hazel! Constant vigilance.'

'I think you might be *too* vigilant in this case,' I said. I marvelled at my boldness. I was teasing Daisy Wells!

'Hazel, you are *not amusing*. But – oh, I grant you, there's nothing doing here. I just want a distraction! Everyone is being so mopey.'

'Because of Beanie's mother!' I said. 'Not everything is a fascinating mystery, Daisy. Some things are just sad.

Now can we go back to bed before we freeze?' It was almost November, and the night was flinchingly cold. Amina had a blanket, and Daisy her scarf, but I was in nothing but my regulation pyjamas.

'All right,' said Daisy. 'But – oh, if only something interesting would happen!'

So it felt like an answer to all of our problems when Amina came up to us after Latin a few days later and said, 'I've just had a letter from my parents. How would you feel about Christmas in Egypt?'

3

Daisy, of course, pretended to be quite uninterested.

'We shall have to see,' she said coolly to Amina.

'Thank you!' I added over my shoulder, as Daisy rushed me away back to the dorm.

'You shouldn't be thanking her!' Daisy hissed at me, her cheeks suddenly pink with excitement. 'We may be too busy to go, after all.'

'No, we won't!' I said. 'It's Egypt, Daisy! You've always wanted to see it!'

'Humph!' said Daisy, the crinkle appearing at the top of her nose. 'I – well—'

'Mummies,' I said. 'Pyramids. *Tutankhamun*. There are plenty of mysteries in Egypt!'

I saw Daisy's eyes sparkle despite herself. 'I shall have to ask Uncle Felix,' she said. 'He might say no.'

'Of course he won't!' I said. It is true that Uncle Felix is careful where Daisy is concerned – she is his only niece, and he is fierce about protecting her – but it was also a fact that Daisy and I had helped Uncle Felix and his wife, Aunt Lucy, by solving a problem during the summer holidays. He owed us.

'We shall have to get new clothes,' said Daisy. 'Our ones from Hong Kong will be too small. And what about your father?'

Truly, I was most worried about my father's reaction – but, when I telephoned him the next day, his voice sounded enthusiastic underneath the hiss of the line.

'What an opportunity!' he said. 'Hazel, I know I promised to come and visit you in England this Christmas, but what if we all met in Egypt instead? The history, the culture – it would be wonderfully improving for you all.'

I heard other-side-of-the-world shrieks at that and I imagined my father in his study, my little sisters dancing round him as their maids, Pik An and Ah Kwan, tried to pull them away.

'Really?' I asked, hardly able to believe it. 'Really – I can go?'

'Of course, my Hazel. We can all go.'

Daisy too came away from her telephone call beaming. 'Uncle Felix said yes,' she told me. 'He – oh, Hazel, I think we're going to Egypt!'

We clung to each other in the shabby House hallway, fizzing with delight – and, after that, Daisy gave up the pretence.

She bubbled over with Egypt, pharaohs and curses and floods. She did her prep in double-quick time so she could gaze at fat, cloth-bound books about Nile exploration parties and the Carter expedition to unearth Tutankhamun. 'There were *female* pharaohs, you know,' she told me, eyes gleaming. '*Women* ruled all of Egypt! Hatshepsut reigned for fifteen years and she wore a false beard so men would accept her. Just imagine! D'you think I'd look good in a beard?'

'No,' I said, sticking out my tongue at her, even though I knew very well that, if anyone could look good in a false beard, it would be the Honourable Daisy Wells.

'Yes,' said Amina from the row in front of us, turning back to grin at Daisy, who went red and ducked her head back down to her book.

'Of course, it *is* the pharaohs you're most interested in seeing,' I said to Daisy later.

'Of course,' said Daisy, straight-faced. 'Why else would we be going?'

That gave me an idea of my own. During our English lesson a few days later, I folded a piece of paper inside my English composition book, swapped my usual pencil for a rather less usual one that I kept in the bottom of my school bag, and began to scribble something that certainly was not the essay on Spenser that Miss Dodgson had asked for.

Dear Alexander, I wrote, my heart beating and the letters fading to nothing almost as soon as they left my pen.

How are things at Weston? Did you and George solve your problem with the dog? Things here are dull, mostly. No cases. We're all at a bit of a loose end without one.

Better news: we've been invited to Egypt for the Christmas hols. Daisy's terribly excited, though she pretends she isn't, and I am too. We've got special dispensation to leave school early since the trip will be educational. We're going to Amina El Maghrabi's family in Cairo first, and then Father's going to come and meet us with my sisters, May and Rose (remember I told you about them?), and take us to Luxor for a real Nile cruise on the thirteenth of December. Are you going back to your parents in Boston? Funny that we won't see each other at all until next year now.

Give my love to George — and you,
Hazel

I finished it before I could stop to think what I was doing. Those last two words – *and you* – had felt wildly daring in my head, but on paper they only looked vaguely embarrassing, like something an overeager shrimp would write. But, all the same, I turned the letter over as quickly as I could, swapped back to my usual pencil and wrote,

Dear Alexander,

Sago pudding twice this week! Disgusting. And Latin prep too, utterly dull. Hope you're having a better time of it.
In haste to chapel,

Henry

I folded the letter up and addressed it to Alexander Arcady, Weston School. It was a way of writing to each other that Alexander and I had made up years ago, after our first case together on the Orient Express, and had been using ever since.

I slipped it into the nearest postbox on our way up to House from school that evening, while Daisy was studiously ignoring Amina and Clementine as they giggled together, and then it was too late to worry about it.

A week later, I got a postcard of the front of the British Museum.

Georgina loves mummies. So do I. Alexandra x

That x lifted me like a kite through endless rainy Games lessons, through Kitty and Beanie falling out with each other, and Lavinia with everyone, through Prayers and French and Deportment. I tried very hard not to think of it too much, and then could not think of anything else.

We really were going to Egypt. I suddenly found I was almost too excited to breathe.

4

But somehow I had not considered the reality of Egypt before I stepped off the aeroplane into the Cairo heat. I was too caught up in saying goodbye to Kitty, Beanie and Lavinia, in my guilt at leaving them and the even guiltier thrill I had that I was leaving our troubles behind, for a few weeks at least.

I was also caught up in the shock of my first aeroplane flight. It had all seemed unimaginably glamorous when the three of us waved goodbye to Matron and climbed up into the airliner at Southampton – the stewardesses perfectly dressed and beaming, the seats comfortable and neatly upholstered. Daisy leaned back in her seat and sighed happily. 'It's just like *Death in the Clouds*,' she murmured. 'Oh, imagine if there *was* a murder, now, and we solved it before we even came back down to earth!'

'Not even Poirot could do that,' I said, rolling my eyes and grinning at her.

'We are far better than that old man!' said Daisy with a sniff. 'Why, he didn't solve his first case until he was *ancient* – and anyway *we're* real and *he's* not, and that gives us the edge.'

'What are you talking about?' asked Amina curiously.

'Nothing,' said Daisy. 'Never mind.'

The plane, which had been puttering along the tarmac, suddenly jerked forward and gave a howl that slid upwards into the most body-shaking, screaming whine. I reached out and clung to Daisy's hand, gasping, as we shook ourselves and shot up into the air. It was not at all like a bird taking off, I thought, as the plane bounced on nothing at all and my stomach bounced with it.

'I think I hate flying almost as much as boats,' I said through chattering teeth, squeezing my eyes shut. Amina threw her head back and laughed.

'Nonsense, Watson,' said Daisy, craning over me. 'Oh, look how small everything is! Just as though we were giants. I think I could reach down and pick that house up. It's like playing dolls with the world.'

I ought not to have been surprised that Daisy would enjoy the view so much, but I could only think how much I disliked it. The air smelled wrong, so high up, and my ears popped.

'See here,' said Daisy, 'if you're not going to look out of the window, can we swap seats?'

She was so on top of the world that she forgot to be cool with Amina and chattered with her all the way until we touched down in Marseilles – and that was when I truly understood the horror that was ahead of me. Up and down we bumped – Marseilles, Rome, Brindisi, Athens (where we stayed at a beautiful hotel owned by Amina's father's friend and Daisy pretended to be an American heiress), Alexandria (the Mediterranean below us, so small after we had heard so much about it in Latin lessons) and finally, bone-joltingly, down into Cairo.

I remembered the moment we had steamed into Hong Kong, in the spring, and realized at last how odd that must have felt for Daisy. Now it was my turn to arrive in a strange city, feeling as though I was swimming with a mile of dark sea below me. Cairo was foreign to me, even more foreign than London. But then I straightened my spine and reminded myself that, if I had made England feel like home, I could do the same with Egypt. I might feel nervous inside, but I would not let that show. I was a different Hazel Wong now.

Then Amina went rushing through the crowds, shrieking with joy, and threw herself on a man I recognized.

'Manners, habibti!' said Mr El Maghrabi – but I could tell he did not really mind. He beamed at his daughter, and Amina beamed back.

'Sorry, Baba!' she said. 'Baba, you remember Daisy Wells and Hazel Wong.'

'Welcome to Cairo!' said Mr El Maghrabi, shaking our hands. 'We are so glad to have you as our guests after what you did for us this summer. Insha'Allah, you will have a wonderful stay here. You are our guests, and anything you need you must simply ask for. You will be cared for by Miss Beauvais – Miss Beauvais! Over here!'

He gestured to a small European woman being buffeted by the throng of travellers. She had thinning brown hair and a regretful-looking face. When she saw Amina, her expression dropped even further into something very like alarm.

'This is Miss Beauvais. She is Amina's governess, and Amina is going to be *very* good to her this holiday – *aren't* you, Amoona?'

'Oh *yes*, Baba,' said Amina, and she turned her big, wicked grin on him, and then on Miss Beauvais, who took a handkerchief from her sleeve and pressed it to her brow. 'Now where shall we go first?'

That was the beginning of several days spent whirling round Cairo, drinking in the sights of it, the smells of it. I was delighted to realize that, in the furious pace of the traffic, the street-food smells rising, the shouts of people who either hated each other or were best friends, the children playing and the scrawny street dogs barking

21

in the twisty, dusty backstreets, Cairo was an echo of Hong Kong. But, where Hong Kong's heat is wet, so the air sits heavy and gorgeous on your skin, Egypt's heat is as dry as sand and bones. Cairo's buildings are all white and yellow and pink, boxes on boxes, dry bricks crumbling to parched mud, stacked balconies with rows of fat little railings, slim, graceful minarets rising behind them. The sky was blue above us, the palm trees were dusty-leaved, the air sang with prayers and voices I could not understand, and my tongue was heavy with spices I did not know. It *was* like Hong Kong, but also nothing like it at all, I thought.

And always, on the horizon, there was the astonishment of the Pyramids.

'Imagine!' said Daisy to me. 'I never thought they'd be just *there*. It's like going into a field and seeing a whale next to a herd of cows.'

It was not quite the analogy I would have used, but I agreed with her. The Pyramids had always been stories in my head – like the Hanging Gardens of Babylon – and suddenly there were those stories in the vista at the bottom of a street. It made me feel as though the whole of Egypt could not possibly be quite real.

But then I watched Amina scrambling out of our moving car to buy us sugar-cane juice from a street vendor, Miss Beauvais' cries of despair quite ignored, and I saw that I was not thinking properly. This was *her* ordinary. She took us to the Turf Club (for this Miss Beauvais had to reluctantly pretend to be the mistress, and Amina her servant, for no Egyptians are supposed to be allowed to use the club), and we had tea beside the tennis courts, our white linen table shaded by the trees and groaning with fruit meringues, chocolate tortes, spiced gateaux and creamy pastries. Amina sneaked bites of cake when none of the other members were looking, and shook with suppressed giggles. Miss Beauvais lay back in her chair and ignored us wanly.

'I make her do this quite a lot,' whispered Amina to us. 'Miss Beauvais never forbids me anything. She looked after my big sisters as well, and so her spirit is quite broken by now. She's never any trouble!'

'But why would you want to come here, when Egyptians aren't welcome?' I asked, glancing around.

Amina snorted. 'That's exactly why, Hazel – because I'm not supposed to be here! This is my home, after all. Why should the Europeans have all the nice things?'

We went to the Egyptian Museum (blessedly cool stone walls after the daze and heat of the Cairo streets) and pressed our noses wonderingly against the glass cases that held all the glow and gold of Tutankhamun. I stared and stared at the boy king's mask, trying to see the real person he had been underneath all the glamour. He had only been a few years older than us when he had died, after all. Did he like being king, or did it weigh him down?

Daisy, of course, was much more interested in looking at the cases full of unwrapped mummies. She stood in front of them, her eyes wide with curiosity. I tried to stand next to her, to see what she saw, but my eyes began to smart with sympathy. The mummies looked undressed, so sad and small. I did not think they belonged where people could stare at them.

'Poor things!' I said to Daisy and Amina.

'Oh, shush, Hazel! It's science!' said Daisy, but Amina nodded at me.

'I think so too,' she said. 'It's not how they wanted to be remembered, is it? They were real people, not decorations. Shown off like this, everyone thinks they own the pharaohs – there are even some dreadfully stupid foreigners who are always going round Cairo saying they're the reincarnation of them.'

'Yes, but they *are* remembered!' said Daisy. 'That's the most important thing.'

'Oh, do you think so?' asked Amina. 'I'm not sure I care whether anyone remembers me when I'm dead.'

'You have no ambition!' said Daisy. 'I'm never going to die, of course, but if I do I'm going to be remembered. Of course I am.'

*

That evening, once the sun had gone down, Amina stole a plate of cakes from the dining room and dragged us up onto the gorgeously tiled and gold-painted roof of her enormous house overlooking the Nile, giggling and shushing us. Out of her pockets she pulled a handful of brightly coloured rockets and, while I gasped, she set them up in a line and lit them. Trails of light spat into the sky, and Amina and Daisy stood on the roof edge, dancing and throwing handfuls of round firecrackers that cracked and popped noisily. I stood watching the lights in front of my eyes and the glitter of the river below.

Egypt, I thought, was wonderful.

5

The following evening, my father and sisters' train reached Cairo. We went to meet them at the hotel they would be staying at. Before they arrived, I felt mixed up when I thought about it, thrilled and nervous and sick all at once. They were home to me, but the last time I had been home, the last time I had seen them, was in Hong Kong, in circumstances I still hated to think of. And there was something else too: since Hong Kong, Daisy and I had solved three more murders. Would my father be cross with me for having been caught up in them too? He had forgiven me for the trust I had broken to solve the Hong Kong case, but, all the same, I knew he did not like the thought of me mixed up in mysteries.

I was worrying about all of this as we stood in the glittering gold lobby, guests swirling about us in pools and eddies, waves of conversation rushing over us. I looked around and saw us reflected in mirror on mirror, looking rather small and shabby (or at least I was) next to the velvet and marble and shine.

Then I was brought back to myself sharply when Daisy nudged me hard in the ribs with her elbow.

'Ow!' I cried. 'Daisy!'

'Don't make a fuss, Hazel! I hardly touched you. *Look*, over there!'

I turned where she was pointing, my heart speeding up for a moment in case she had seen my father. But the people she was gesturing at were a group of European men and women, wearing the sort of evening clothes and expressions of scorn and embarrassment that told me they were most likely English people on holiday.

I stared curiously, wondering why on earth Daisy had picked them out. One of the women, a tall, bony old lady with a pointed nose, was shouting crossly at a porter. The porter raised his hands in apology.

'Hazel,' said Daisy. 'Don't you know who those people *are*?'

'They're English,' I said. 'But other than that—'

'Hazel, you *never* read the papers! This is a dreadful failing in you – I've told you plenty of times before. They're—'

'They're the Breath of Life Society,' said Amina unexpectedly. I looked at her and saw that she was frowning angrily. 'Back again! They're the people I was talking about!'

'What do you mean, *again*?' I asked. 'Who are they? How do *you* know them?'

'They *think* they're ancient Egyptians,' Amina said, just as Daisy said, 'They're the most *fantastic* cult.'

Amina and Daisy eyed each other, and then Daisy said, 'Oh, go on then, tell her.'

'I almost don't want to,' said Amina. 'They're awful. Mama and Baba hate them. They come to Cairo every year and it's worse each time. They stand on street corners, giving speeches about how they're the pharaohs, brought back to life, and we all ought to join their society and worship them. Of course, they can't explain why the pharaohs would come back as English people instead of Egyptians, and so *we* all ignore them, but quite a lot of Europeans living in Cairo have joined up. Europeans think that ancient Egypt is *theirs*, after all, so they like what the Breath of Life says.'

'Yes, yes,' Daisy put in. 'They've pots of money. The more you donate, the more likely the Breath of Life is to say that you were a king or queen in a previous life, and that's what everyone wants.'

'Everyone?' I asked.

'Well, I *was* a queen in a previous life,' said Daisy. 'That's quite obvious. But, if I wanted the Breath of Life to tell me so, I'd have to pay them thousands and thousands of pounds. Those people there are the most important members of the society, and so of course they're all reincarnations of Tutankhamun and Cleopatra and so on. The society's led by a lady called Mrs Theodora Miller and, according to her, she's the reincarnation of Hatshepsut, and *the* most powerful person in the universe.'

'Which is a *lie*!' put in Amina. Her face was flushed with annoyance – I saw how it upset her. 'They've got everything wrong – that isn't what the ancient Egyptians believed at all.'

'Which one is Theodora Miller?' I asked curiously, staring at the Breath of Life members. They each looked like any English lady I might pass on the streets of Deepdean.

'That little dumpy one,' said Daisy, nodding with her chin at a small, round, middle-aged woman with sandy hair who was standing next to the tall, bony lady. I blinked at her. She did not look much like the queen of anything.

But then the porter said something, ducking his head nervously, and Theodora Miller suddenly drew herself up, bosom heaving with rage.

'That is NOT good enough! Don't you know who I am, man?' she bellowed, her voice carrying through the lobby – and I saw that appearances might be deceiving. This woman, small as she was, was fierce and frightening. I was fascinated.

And at that moment, just as I had finally forgotten all about my family, the doors to the hotel lobby were pulled open by the doormen and my littlest sister, May, dashed inside, skidding on the polished marble floor and wheeling her arms with excitement.

The Breath of Life would have to wait.

'BIG SISTER!' May screamed, and she skittered round several alarmed hotel guests in evening dress to throw herself at me and cling ecstatically to my waist. I leaned down to hug her – she smelled of travelling and dirt and *May*, which is bright, a little like oranges – and she turned her face up to mine and yelled, 'I'm SIX now, Big Sister! SIX!'

'You're *so* big, Monkey,' I said to her, smiling.

'Rose and Father and Pik An are coming, only they're SLOW,' said May. 'The ship took so *long*, Hazel. Rose was bored, but then Rose is *boring* and only wants to read books so she would be. I wasn't because I pretended to be a pirate and rushed the bridge to take it over – only the captain laughed at me and we had tea together and then he let me steer the ship for a bit.'

I looked up then and there was my middle sister, Rose, looking eager and graceful in a floral travelling dress, her hair in a careful plait, her maid, Pik An, puffing behind her with a heap of bags. She nodded at me, and I waved back at her, delighted to see her.

'Hazel, you look so old, like a grown-up. It's true, you do—'

'Oh, be quiet, Monkey,' I said, jostling May good-naturedly, and then Rose was hugging me too, slightly stiffly – or perhaps it was me who was shy. She had one of her favourite school storybooks in her hand, and it dug into me as I squeezed her.

'Hello, Wong Fung Ying,' said my father, and I looked up to see him reaching out to me, his familiar square hands with their heavy knuckles, pinstriped suit and shining golden cufflinks.

'Hello, Father,' I said, as shy as Rose.

'It's good to see you, my Hazel,' said my father – and I realized then that he was not upset with me, not in the slightest. I found myself crushed against his chest, clinging to him as tightly as May had clung to me.

'I missed you, Father,' I said, slightly muffled.

'I missed you too, my good girl,' said my father – and for several reasons I felt terribly guilty at that. 'Now tell me, how is school? Are you getting the best marks possible? I remember you did not win a prize in the summer, and I wanted to know why that was.'

And, as May dragged us all off to the cars waiting to take us to dinner at the El Maghrabis', I glanced back at the Breath of Life, assuming I would never see them again.

Of course, I was quite wrong.

6

The next day, we set off for the Nile.

We were driven in two of Amina's parents' smooth black cars to Bab al-Hadid station, emerging into noise and dust and smarting sun. Porters in turbans and galabeyas rushed back and forth, our cases piled up alarmingly high (my father and sisters had not travelled light), and Pik An and Miss Beauvais begged them to be careful. I looked at the enormous stone statue that stood in the square in front of the station. It was a creature with a lion's paws and a human head framed with a ferocious headdress, crouched next to a woman who stood gazing proudly into space, one arm raised to lift the shawl from her face. I thought it was beautiful, though very strange.

'Nahdat Misr,' said Mr El Maghrabi, nodding at it. 'Egypt's past – the Sphinx – and her future, her women.

Amoona, habibti, remember to tell the girls about your history. Be proud of it!'

'Yes, Baba,' said Amina, her face serious for once. 'I will.'

From Bab al-Hadid, we took the overnight express to Luxor. As the sun went down, I looked out of the train window to see rectangles of bright green grass and tall, spiky sugar cane, bordered by dark-fronded palms and thin strips of water that reflected the sky. Cows and donkeys stood beside mud-brick houses, and people sat in front of them, knees up and arms dangling as they laughed and talked together. The sky was rose and lemon and orange cream, smooth with only a few licks of darkening cloud.

The train was almost empty. As we waited for dinner, and for our sleeping berths to be ready, we had a carriage all to ourselves. May built a fort under the seats and burst out at us from time to time, being an ancient sea creature (Pik An had to pretend to be surprised), Rose read *Millie of the Fourth Form*, my father did the crossword, Miss Beauvais snored and Daisy paced back and forth restlessly. I knew she was remembering the last time we rode on a train together, and the things that had happened on that journey.

'Are you excited?' Amina said quietly, looking at me sideways. In Egypt her hair was even glossier and more glorious than ever, and she was wearing an impossibly lovely travelling suit and a little hat and veil of the sort that all the Egyptian women seemed to wear.

'Yes!' I said, and I truly was. Everything was so strange and wonderful. Although I kept on seeing flashes of the real Egypt through Amina's eyes, a country where people still had to bother about dull, ordinary things like prep and train tickets, I could not help feeling as though I had stepped into a story, as if I had dropped through space and time. I felt oddly convinced (perhaps I was thinking about the Breath of Life again here) that I might turn my head to see the boy king Tutankhamun, sickly but regal, sitting next to me in the train carriage, or as if the woman I could hear shouting in the next carriage along might turn out to be the pharaoh Hatshepsut, her eyes (as fierce and clever as Amina's eyes in my imagination) painted dark and thick with kohl, and a little wooden beard tied to her chin with a strap.

'I can't wait,' said Amina. 'I've never been before, not on a proper cruise. I know all the stories, though. That's what Baba meant when he said goodbye – he wants me to make sure you hear the real stories. Sometimes they don't tell them properly to westerners.'

I breathed in the bare, hot smell of the carriage around me, and the smell of sweat and Amina's perfume, something as light and pretty as she was.

'Why did your parents send you to Deepdean?' I asked. 'Wasn't Miss Beauvais enough?'

'Miss Beauvais is quite useless, really,' said Amina with a glance over at her sleeping form. 'We only keep her about because French things are fashionable. I told Baba I couldn't learn from her, and so I had to go to school. And then there wasn't much choice, once I'd gone through all of the schools in Cairo. King Farouk was at school in England before the old king died – they had to fly him back to Cairo to take the throne, you know. So it's the done thing at the moment. The aunties and my older sisters bullied Baba into it too. Mama was cross, but she knew I wanted to go. I like adventure, you know.'

'My mother didn't want me to go to school in England, either,' I said quietly, so that Rose and May would not hear me mentioning Ah Mah. 'She – she doesn't like Western things.'

'Why is your mother not here?' said Amina, looking at me more searchingly than ever.

I shrugged. I could not bear to explain it, not to Amina, whose mother was so proud of her.

'I asked to go, though,' I went on quickly. 'I wanted to see England for myself.'

'Hazel Wong!' said Amina, grinning at me. 'I think we're a little alike, you and me.'

'But I'm not – I'm not adventurous, not like you and Daisy,' I said.

'You're one of the most adventurous people I've ever met!' said Amina. 'You travelled halfway round the world on your own when you were only a shrimp, you've done all kinds of wild things – you're friends with *boys*. Baba would kill me if I even looked at one—'

'*Shh!*' I said urgently, as my father stretched and turned the page of his crossword book. That reminder had made me come out in an uncomfortable sweat.

'All I'm saying is, don't let Daisy make you think you're dull,' said Amina. 'Perhaps you were once, I don't know. But the Hazel Wong I know is quite the opposite. I'm glad I'm friends with you.'

'We're glad we're friends with you too,' I said.

'Hmm,' said Amina. 'Are you sure that's how Daisy feels?'

I looked up at Daisy. She had come to a stop in her pacing and was standing like a marble statue in a museum, staring out of the window at the high hills as they were lit pink by the sunset. I knew, though, that she was listening in on what we were saying.

'You ought to ask her,' I said, blushing a bit.

'Well,' said Amina, tossing her head and raising her voice so Daisy was certain to hear, 'she ought to like me – I'm brilliant.'

It was such a Daisyish thing to say that I laughed out loud, and Amina laughed too.

*

36

We had dinner in the candlelit dining carriage that made me feel as though I was inside a star. But we had barely sat down when we were startled to see some very familiar faces – the men and women of the Breath of Life Society. There was plump Theodora Miller, berating one of the waiters, and I realized that her voice was the one I had heard in the other carriage. That gave me a strange feeling. I had been comparing her to Hatshepsut, and that was how she saw herself.

As I watched, the waiter stepped back from Theodora's fury and bumped into her bony companion, who shouted at him. The waiter looked quite horrified.

'They're following us!' hissed Daisy, prodding me with her salad fork.

'I hope not!' I said. 'They're awful!'

'Awfully *fascinating*!' said Daisy, and she listened in so frantically to the Breath of Life table next to us that she only half replied to all of my father's questions.

I had to admit that I agreed with her. I kept hearing snippets of conversation that made me want to lean in further – reincarnation, followers, money, pharaohs, and then—

'Now, Ida, really, you can't mean that.'

'But I do!' said the bony woman sharply. 'It came to me in a dream last week. I have been mulling it over and really the only answer is this: I am the reincarnation of Hatshepsut.'

'Ida, you *can't* be Hatshepsut!' said a fluffy-looking little old lady, very short and almost circular, her hands clasped in front of her in distress. 'There is only one Hatshepsut at one time and—'

'And it is ME,' said Theodora Miller, drawing herself up. The other Breath of Life members – a tall, gangly young woman with curly hair, a dark-haired young man and an old, wrinkly man with a surprisingly yellow head of hair and a cane – all sucked in their breath and stared at Theodora and bony Ida. '*I* am Hatshepsut,' Mrs Miller repeated. 'You are Cleopatra, Ida. We've discussed this before.'

'Cleopatra was a poisoner,' snapped Ida. 'A poisoner and a coward. I have felt for a long time that I have no connection to her, but, on the other hand, I have the most intimate connection with Hatshepsut. I understand her. I feel her. She is ME.'

'SHE IS *ME*!' said Theodora Miller furiously.

'Oh, please don't argue!' said the fluffy little old lady, at the same time that the gangly young woman cried, 'Mother, don't, please!'

'Heppy, do NOT call me by that name!' gasped Theodora, swinging her head towards the woman. 'That's another black mark in your Book – the fourth today! You will *never* discover your reincarnation with that attitude. And Rhiannon, do be quiet or I shall reconsider your being Nefertiti.'

'Sorry, Theodora dear,' said the fluffy lady, Rhiannon.

'I'm sorry!' said gangly Heppy, tears in her eyes. 'I am trying!'

'You are certainly trying my PATIENCE!' said Theodora – and then May knocked over her glass of lemonade onto my skirt, and I lost the rest of their words.

But the group stayed with me, swirling about in my head all night, so that my dreams were full of old ladies wearing crowns and false beards and sentencing people to death. I was quite glad to wake up the next morning and find the train almost at Luxor.

7

The sun rises sharp and hot in Egypt, and so it was already up as we stepped off the train in Luxor, warming our shoulders and making the hairs on the back of my neck prickle. There was dust in the air, a stampede of porters and a bewildering press of men all trying to make us buy things. Woven scarves in bright colours, cups of water, fly whisks, clattering strings of beads, carved stone statuettes and smooth round things like tokens that I realized after I had one pushed into my hand were, in fact, carved scarab beetles, just like the ones Daisy and I had seen in the British Museum all those months ago. I remembered that case, and suddenly thought of Alexander.

'No thank you,' I stammered to the man who had given it to me. 'Shukran.' But that was obviously not the right thing to do, for he held out his hands to me with a wounded look. 'Lady!' he cried. 'Only fifty piastres – for you a good price. Please, lady!'

Fifty piastres seemed expensive to me, but he was so insistent that I felt I had to scrabble for my purse, only to have Amina push me aside. 'Hazel, you have to haggle!' she hissed. 'He's told you a dreadfully wicked price – that thing's not worth five. Here, let me!' She began to speak very loudly and dramatically in Arabic, and the man shouted back, looking mortally offended.

I had never felt more miserably like a tourist in all my life. 'It's all right!' I whispered to Amina. 'Please, I can pay him.'

Amina ignored me. At last she turned, holding two scarab beetles and looking extremely pleased with herself. 'Two for thirty,' she said. 'Of course, they're not worth it, but that's not the point.'

'What is the point?' I asked.

'The argument mostly,' said Amina. 'And thirty piastres is nothing to us, but quite a lot to him. So we both got a good deal, if you think about it. The other beetle is for Daisy.'

'Oh, I suppose,' said Daisy, looking uninterested – but I saw her tuck her beetle securely into her pocket.

'Thank you,' I said to Amina. I held up my new scarab beetle, which shone as blue-green as the sea, and put my arm through Daisy's.

Then my gaze was drawn along the platform to where the pack of sellers had re-formed round the Breath of Life Society. Without someone like Amina to help them, they were not faring well. Fluffy little old Rhiannon cowered, and bony Ida – today wearing a magnificent pale green dress – glared and brandished her parasol. 'Go away!' she shouted. 'We don't want anything! Get out of it!'

'Really!' said Amina. 'There's no need to be rude. The thing is to ignore them if you don't want to buy.'

I saw the old man waving his shiny gold-tipped cane threateningly, his matching, shiny golden hair glinting in the sun. I was worried that he might hit someone. And then a furious voice cut through the noise and made the sellers freeze.

It was Theodora Miller – and again I saw exactly why she was in charge. She might be built like an overstuffed sofa or like Miss Lappet, our Latin mistress back at Deepdean, but she carried herself like a ruler, her eyes boring into the sellers she was glaring at.

'MOVE ON!' she bellowed at them, and they staggered backwards, looking quite horrified. Her voice was clearly not what they had expected from someone her size and shape. 'GO ON, GET OUT! You horrid people! Get away from us! We don't want to buy and we shan't be tricked by you!'

'But, madam!' tried one. 'The lady, your friend – she still has my scarf, and she has not paid for it.'

'Then that is YOUR FAULT!' shouted Theodora Miller. 'You should have thought of that before you gave it to her! Go on, go away!'

I was shocked. That was simply not fair. If you take a thing, you ought to pay for it. I saw my father shake his head, and Amina purse her lips.

'Excellent work, Theodora,' said the old man in a cheerful voice, waving his cane. 'Well said. Can I have that scarf if you aren't using it, Ida?'

'Certainly not, Narcissus!' snapped Ida. 'It's mine. It goes with my dress.'

'Do stop squabbling, you two,' said Theodora Miller. 'Ida, hire us some appropriate carriages. NOT the ones with silly ornaments all over them – I can't bear the jingling noise. And make sure the horses aren't white. White horses are too restless in temperament; they will cause a bumpy ride.' Ida nodded and started forward. The young woman, Heppy, made to go after her, but was stopped with another almighty bellow from Theodora.

'No, Heppy, NOT you!' she roared. 'You stay here with me where I can keep an eye on you. I don't TRUST you!'

Heppy flinched and trembled, tugging at her curly hair where it was wriggling out from her long plait. This seemed to enrage Theodora further.

'HEPPY! STOP trying to chew your HAIR! How many times MUST it be entered in your Book of Life before it gets into your head? That's two black marks today, and it isn't even lunch time!'

At that, Heppy twitched all over and pulled her hands down to her sides. I could see her chest rising and falling as she stuttered, 'I'm sorry, M—Theodora, I really am. I didn't even notice—'

'I notice!' roared Theodora. '*I* notice, Heppy – how many times must I tell you? Now be a good girl and go and look after Miss Bartleby, won't you?'

With that, Theodora Miller's demeanour changed so quickly that it startled me – and made me realize how closely I was watching this scene play out. The rage in her eyes died away and she suddenly looked like nothing more than a plump little old lady again. I might have thought I had imagined her fury if it were not for Heppy, who went stumbling over to fluffy little Rhiannon – Miss Bartleby – vibrating with nerves like a plucked harp, and held out a slightly shaking arm to her.

Miss Bartleby patted her comfortingly. 'There, there, dear,' she said. 'You know you bring this on yourself. You mustn't be such a trial to Theodora.'

I was shocked. Heppy, as far as I could see, had done nothing at all. But, all the same, Ida and Narcissus made a hum of agreement.

Off Theodora went towards the station entrance, and everyone else followed in a procession after her. Then they were lost in the press of the crowd.

'They're awful!' said Amina. 'I think I hate them even more than I did before. What horrid people, behaving as though everything is Heppy's fault when it's not!'

Out through the columns of the train station we went, under the outspread wings of the painted vulture above our heads, and into a stamping, sweating, yelling group of taxi drivers, all leaning out of their carriages to shout at us.

'They're dreadful people. They're also going quite the wrong way to be on our boat, thank goodness,' said my father. He was clearly as against the Breath of Life as we were. 'Pik An, hurry up, and bring Rose and May. Let's go and take the perfectly nice white horses and carriages that those foolish ladies left behind.'

My father handed me into the nearest one, its cracked leather rough under my hands and its canopy curving over me like the wings of a scarab beetle. Daisy, Amina and Miss Beauvais squeezed in beside me and, with a jingle and a jolt, we were off, the wheels spinning, the poor thin horse's shoes clicking and the driver's whip cracking.

We rattled down a long, wide, dusty street, past square, light-coloured, box-on-box houses, fruit sellers and children who ran along beside our carriage, cars and carts and blond, skinny dogs, rubber trees and pink, papery flowers, then turned past a mosque and – Amina gasped – an enormous ruined temple, rising high on our right, its stone glowing in the sun.

'That's Luxor Temple,' said Amina excitedly. 'Those statues are of Rameses the Second – he was an awfully important pharaoh. Oh, I've always wanted to see it!'

She dangled out of the carriage as we turned again onto a wide front, lined with lovely hotels on our left, and on our right – and now it was my turn to gasp – the Nile river, shimmering the softest, palest blue, the far shore only a line, and behind it mountains so distant and vague that I thought at first they were clouds.

And floating on the Nile like a swan was our boat.

8

The SS *Hatshepsut* was white, with blue trim, a white-and-blue smokestack and curving white paddles. It had cabin windows studded along two long, low decks, and a third covered roof deck with little white basket chairs and tables dotted about on it. Its white was lit almost gold by the morning sun, and I could see uniformed figures waiting for us at each end of the long, thin gangway.

I could smell the river, as thick and rich as the green soup we had been served in Cairo – or perhaps that was the laden donkeys, the horses pulling carriages like ours, the dust kicked up by hooves and bare feet.

Our carriages stopped, and my father jumped out and offered me his hand. I stepped down, followed by Amina, Miss Beauvais, Daisy (she took my father's hand like a queen, her chin lifted high and her golden hair blowing back in the breeze), Pik An, Rose and May.

Suddenly we were surrounded by a group of helpful men, all reaching for our cases.

'So many daughters!' said one of them to my father admiringly. 'The fair one, is she married?'

The glare my father turned on him made him step backwards, his hands raised.

'I shall never marry!' said Daisy haughtily.

'I thought you were going to marry a lord?' I asked.

Daisy glared at me. 'Hazel, I *told* you I have reconsidered. I shall be far too busy to marry anyone.'

'Oh, what a pity,' said Amina, and she winked at Daisy.

I rarely saw Daisy at a loss for words, but at this she opened her mouth several times and closed it again. Her nose wrinkled, and a flush appeared at the tops of her cheeks. And I was certain, then, of what I had guessed before. Daisy was not in Egypt for adventure at all, no matter what she had said to me.

She was here for Amina.

'Humph,' she said at last. 'Hurry up and get on the boat, someone!'

I was desperate to talk to her, to ask her how she felt – but I knew perfectly well that you cannot ask Daisy Wells something like that. I had to wait for her to admit it to me.

My father was already halfway up the gangplank, May skittering round him excitedly. As I watched, she bobbed dangerously close to the edge, and my father reached out a hand and grabbed her by her pigtail.

'You aren't a tightrope walker, Mei,' he said to her as she grumbled, and passed her over to Pik An, who held her tightly.

I followed them, the thin tongue of the gangplank bouncing and teetering under me in a way that brought the taste of breakfast back up in my mouth. I had not really thought of it, but this of course was a boat – and I do not do well on boats.

At last, either a moment or an eternity later, I stepped onto the polished wooden deck of the *Hatshepsut*, helped by a dark-skinned man with tightly curling hair who was wearing a smart uniform that matched the *Hatshepsut*'s blue-and-white trim.

'Good morning, miss!' he said to me, and turned to say the same to Daisy.

'I am an *Honourable*!' said Daisy proudly. I made a face at her. Daisy is so funny about her title.

I could see the man hesitate at the sight of all of us together. We were an odd group – May, Rose, Pik An, Father and I like no one else I had seen in Egypt, the golden blue-eyed Daisy, tired Miss Beauvais and finally Amina, quite clearly not a tourist. But he smiled politely at us and said, 'You are Mr Wong's party, I presume? Welcome, honoured guests!'

Another man in livery put a drink into my hand, something dark red and sweet. It looked a little like blood, I thought to myself, and then told myself how silly I was being.

'They are not *all* my daughters,' said Father, and the curly-haired man laughed in relief – and then tried to pretend he had not.

'I am Mr Mansour,' he said, nodding his head to Father. 'I am the manager of the *Hatshepsut*, and my crew and I will be attending to all your needs while you are onboard. Anything you require, anything at all, you must ask for immediately. Please do not hesitate! Our porters will now carry your bags to your cabins, which are all on the starboard side of our saloon deck. Mr Wong, sir, you are in cabin eight, a room with a bathroom ensuite. Miss Rose Wong and Miss May Wong are in cabin six, Miss El Maghrabi and Miss Beauvais are in cabin ten and Miss Hazel Wong and Miss Daisy Wells are in cabin twelve, as agreed. The maid is in cabin twenty-four, on the lower deck.'

'Good,' said my father. 'Now, Hazel—'

But then he paused, staring over my head at some more passengers who had just begun to climb the gangplank.

'Goodness,' he said. 'I think – I think I know that boy. Hazel, wasn't he on the train with us last year? I could have sworn . . . but it can't be, can it?'

Suddenly I was barely able to breathe, tingling from head to toe with excitement and dread, all at once. I wanted to look, but I couldn't.

Daisy, though, was looking. 'Oh heavens,' she said, and her face was alight with mingled amusement and annoyance. 'I do believe you're right. We know him.'

9

I turned round – and there was a tall blond boy next to a dark one, walking up the gangplank in front of a harassed, sunburnt man who was carrying a pile of books and luggage.

'*Hazel Wong!*' hissed Daisy in my ear, and I knew I was in the most dreadful trouble. I also knew, as the blond boy caught my eye and beamed at me, that I did not care.

My letter had worked.

Alexander raised his arm and waved, and I waved back.

'Wong Fung Ying, what on earth is this?' said my father.

I felt myself blushing red to the very tips of my fingers.

'What a coincidence,' I said stiffly. 'It's the boy from the Orient Express – Alexander Arcady. He seems to be here with his friend George.'

'Good morning, sir,' said George to Mr Mansour politely. 'We are here for the Nile cruise. We are George Mukherjee and Alexander Arcady, and this is our tutor, Mr Young.'

'Good morning, sirs,' said Mr Mansour. 'Welcome to our honoured guests, Mr Mukherjee, Mr Arcady and Mr Young! Mr Mukherjee and Mr Arcady, you have room two, and Mr Young has room four, both on the starboard side.'

'Starboard!' cried Mr Young, his face flushed with the heat. 'But I have been told never to accept a starboard cabin on the way to Aswan. It gets the afternoon sun – it's no good for learning! As you can see, I do not – I do not do well in the heat. I must be in a condition to impart knowledge to these boys. I am their tutor, you see, introducing them to the sights of Egypt. Their parents have entrusted me with their care, and they expect them to come back full of learning, not heatstroke.'

'I'm afraid these were the last available cabins on the saloon deck,' said Mr Mansour. 'I do apologize – you see, there has been quite a lot of interest in this cruise. There is another party – they booked the port side months ago, whereas your booking was quite last-minute. I was only able to accommodate you because of a late cancellation – a lady novelist and her companion were booked into your rooms, but she changed the reservation to February next year.'

'This is simply not good enough,' said Mr Young. 'I shall be making a complaint, mark my words.' Then he noticed us all staring and coughed awkwardly. 'Good morning,' he said loudly and slowly. 'How do you do?'

I could tell that he expected us not to be able to understand English. My father glared at him. 'Good morning, sir. I must confess that I am surprised to see your party here,' he snapped. 'I know one of your charges – Mr Arcady. Mr Arcady, can you explain yourself? Why are you here on this ship today? Or, even better, perhaps my daughter can illuminate this curious occurrence. Wong Fung Ying, *explain*.'

I suddenly found myself very short of breath. I twisted my hands together and tried desperately not to look at Alexander, who was uncomfortably red. Daisy was digging her fingers into my arm in suppressed glee.

'Mr Wong, sir, I think I can explain what happened,' said George unexpectedly.

I jerked my head up to look at him in shock. Was he about to ruin everything?

But then George glanced at me – one quick flicker of his eyes – and I knew that everything would be all right.

'You see,' George went on, smooth and smiling, 'we all met last Christmas, in Cambridge. My brother's at St John's College – my father went there, and I'm expected to go as well. We became friendly, and while we were in London in the spring we spent some time together at the British Museum. We were all quite fascinated by the Egyptian collection, and the mummies in particular—'

(I flinched, Alexander coughed and Daisy looked quite unconcerned – she is as good at pretending as George.)

'—and, after that, all we could talk of was seeing Egypt itself one day. So Hazel must have spoken to you, sir, and Alexander and I to our parents – and the result is that we're all here at once! It's the most incredible coincidence.'

'Coincidence,' said my father slowly, looking from me, to Alexander, to Daisy, and finally back to George. 'Aren't you the boys – Hazel, aren't *these* boys the ones who were there at that mur—'

'They were there,' I said hurriedly. 'Just like us, but that's all. Everything just happened, Father, really – you know I've told you that sometimes things *just happen* to us—'

'Hum!' said my father. 'WELL! The thing is done, the ship has been booked and it is about to sail. I can't exactly get off it with five girls in tow. BUT, Wong Fung Ying, I am saying this now. Things had better not *just happen* to you on this holiday.'

'Of course not, Father,' I said – and, for a moment, I almost believed myself.

10

The boat's horn sounded, a long-drawn-out howl that made us all jump.

'Almost time to set sail,' said Mr Young to Mr Mansour. 'I do not see any sign of that other party, so I shall be asking for the portside cabins, if you please.'

'I wish I could, sir,' said Mr Mansour unhappily. 'But I believe that is them now.'

He pointed – and there, to my amazement, were the carriages commandeered by Theodora Miller and her group, pulling up in a cloud of dust. I could hear Mrs Miller bellowing at her driver, a man with an absolutely desperate look on his face.

'YOU'VE TAKEN US THE LONG WAY ROUND! YOU HAVE! WELL, I *SHAN'T* BE PAYING YOU! HEPPY, GET OUT! NO, NOT LIKE THAT! MORE REFINEMENT! DANIEL, HELP HER!'

The young man – Daniel – jumped easily out of the second carriage and reached up his hand to the struggling Heppy, her curly hair spilling awkwardly out of its plait down around her face, and her legs quite tangled up in her dress. For a moment, Heppy glanced up at the ship, and us, her expression just as lost and frightened as our friend Beanie's when she is being told off. She caught my eye, and she must have seen the horror on my face for she ducked her head again quickly.

The group approached the gangplank. Theodora Miller sailed up it like a ship herself, and came face to face with Mr Mansour.

'*I* am THEODORA MILLER,' she told him. 'I am here with my party to connect with ancient Egypt. You see, we are *originally* from this country. In our *first* lives.'

'Greetings, honoured guests,' said Mr Mansour, rather weakly, glancing from Theodora Miller's firm face to his clipboard and back again. 'You are welcome onboard. If there is anything you need, you have only to ask us. Now let me see. Your party—'

'I take it I am in one of the cabins with a bathroom?' Theodora asked. 'Hurry up, man – tell us!'

'Yes, er, madam, of course,' said Mr Mansour, now thoroughly thrown. 'You are in the ensuite cabin on the port side, number seven. Your daughter, Miss Hephzibah Miller, is in cabin one, your son Mr Daniel

Miller is in cabin three, Miss Ida Doggett is in ensuite cabin five, Mr Narcissus DeWitt is in cabin nine and Miss Rhiannon Bartleby is in cabin eleven.'

'But I require an ensuite bathroom as well,' said wrinkly old Narcissus DeWitt. 'This is simply not good enough, man!'

Up close, I realized that Mr DeWitt's gold hair was so shiny because it was dyed. It was an odd, almost greenish colour, and it clung to his head like a helmet. It was hard not to stare at it, and at his wrinkles – he was even older than I had assumed.

'But one was not booked,' said Mr Mansour soothingly. 'I am sorry—'

'Theodora!' cried Mr DeWitt. 'How can you do this to your Thutmose?'

'Narcissus, do be quiet,' said Theodora Miller. 'You were only confirmed as Thutmose last week, far too late to have booked you a bathroom.'

'Um,' said Mr Mansour. He dabbed at his temples with a handkerchief. 'Forgive me, I'm not sure I understand—'

But now Heppy was speaking, brushing her hair out of her face and blinking up at Mr Mansour.

'You see, Mr Mansour,' she said breathlessly, glancing at Theodora Miller as she spoke, as though she was looking for approval, 'these are all very important people. Mr DeWitt was Thutmose the Third in his past life, Miss Bartleby was Nefertiti and Miss Doggett was Cleopatra. They are all here to learn more about themselves, so you must help them in every way you can. And M—Mrs Miller is the most important of all. She is the reincarnation of the pharaoh Hatshepsut; the daughter of Amun Ra. She is a god on earth.'

11

As we changed for lunch in our wood-panelled cabin, the door firmly shut and the two neat little white beds tidily made, I was still full of what we had seen on deck. We were on the Nile with the Breath of Life Society – I felt that something astonishing and mysterious was about to happen.

'It's just like the Orient Express!' I said to Daisy. She was brushing her hair, staring into the mirrored panels along one wall and pursing her lips thoughtfully. 'It really feels like the beginning of that adventure. Only George is here too, and Amina – and Pik An, May and Rose.'

Daisy was silent for a moment. Then she put down the brush, swung round and fixed me with her blue stare.

'Hazel Wong, did you write to Alexander?' she asked.

I should have known that this would be on her mind, just as much as Theodora Miller and her followers.

I wriggled uncomfortably – but I cannot lie to Daisy the way I can to my father. She is too close to me. Sometimes I forget that we are really two people instead of one.

'I never thought he'd actually come!' I protested, feeling myself flush again. 'But yes. I wrote a letter saying we'd be here.'

'And he *did* come!' said Daisy. 'Which says something, doesn't it, Hazel? And I don't quite like it.'

'What do you mean?'

'You know precisely what I mean. He crossed a continent – and I don't think he did it for *me*. He barely looked at me, up on deck. I started to think so in the summer, and I'm sure of it now – he's quite done with me. On the one hand, how lucky that he's finally got *that* idea out of his head! I was quite tired of telling him to go away. But, on the other, Hazel, I must say one more time that he is simply *not* good enough for you. His arms are too—'

'Too long, I know!' I snapped at her. Daisy really has used that argument far too often, and it's not even true. When we met Alexander the summer before last, he happened to have grown out of his shirts, and he stood at an awkward angle because of that, but these days he wears perfectly nicely fitting clothes and is hardly awkward at all. 'I wish you wouldn't say that. And he isn't *not good enough* for me. He's nice and I like him. Why shouldn't I? Anyway, I don't ever tell you that people aren't good enough for you. I wouldn't say a single bad thing about Amina! I think she's *lovely*.'

The words were out of my mouth before I could stop them. I froze, staring at Daisy, who was frozen, staring back at me, as though we were mirror images of each other.

'What are you *talking* about?' gasped Daisy. 'I am NOT in love with Amina! I – I – why would you say that, Hazel?'

Her trembling fingers clamped round my wrist so tight my bones clicked.

'I didn't mean to!' I protested. 'I'm sorry, Daisy. It's only that – well, she didn't invite us to Egypt because of *me*. That's obvious.'

Daisy shook her head, her cheeks pink with emotion. 'Hazel, I – I will not be drawn into this conversation. It's not relevant or important and – I don't want to hear you mention it again. Can't we talk about something more interesting, such as the fact that we're on a boat with at least *four* pharaohs, one of whom thinks she is also a god?'

'They're not really pharaohs, or gods,' I said. 'They're just ordinary people.' I was glad to be moving away from the awkwardness of our talk about Amina and Alexander. The Breath of Life felt easy in comparison.

'Of course they are. As if the pharaohs would decide to come back as *them*! As, um, Amina says' – here Daisy blushed again – 'they're not even Egyptian. It makes no sense. But isn't it fascinating? We're on a ship with a cult! Oh, Hazel, how delicious! Do you think they'll do dark rituals with human sacrifices, and summon Satan, and things?'

'Of course not,' I said. 'The ancient Egyptians didn't do human sacrifices, Daisy, and they didn't believe in Satan.'

'Oh, all right, Osiris, then,' said Daisy.

I opened my mouth to say that I was sure Amina would have some cutting things to say about the way Daisy was inventing facts about ancient Egypt, but reconsidered.

'Isn't Egypt wonderful!' said Daisy, sitting down on her bed and bouncing happily on it. 'All the rules have gone out of the window!'

'They haven't! It's still a country, just like England. It's like being in Hong Kong, Daisy: there are still rules, even if they aren't the ones you're used to. That's what Mrs Miller and the Breath of Life don't understand.'

'I know,' said Daisy, sighing. 'I was teasing. But it is thrilling. Strange things will happen on this trip, you'll see!'

Her eyes were sparkling – but, all the same, I don't think she had even an inkling of how strange things were about to get. I certainly did not. I remember that moment now – before anything had happened at all – when we were still happy, and with our friends, and bowling beautifully along the bright-coloured river under the sun, and my heart aches.

It was Sunday the thirteenth of December, and Theodora Miller had one day left to live.

And Daisy Wells had two.

PART TWO

APPOINTMENT WITH DEATH

1

We were to stay in Luxor until the evening, so after lunch (more of the sweet dark-red drink – which Amina told us was hibiscus juice – jewel-like salads of fruits and meats and herbs served on generous platters, followed by plates of tiny cakes that tasted of dates and cinnamon and almonds) we wobbled our way back down the gangplank and were led in a dusty string of carriages to Karnak Temple.

I am not quite sure what I was expecting when we reached the temple. Ancient Egypt is always a place that has lived for me in my books. I had imagined its ruins only the size of the bigger buildings in Hong Kong, which were the largest things I could picture. But it only took one look at the cliffs of stone hanging above me to realize I had not really understood them at all. These ruins were not built for people, with human-sized windows and doors. They were built for gods, and humans were meant to cower in front of them.

'This is Karnak!' announced our guide. 'Twenty-seven rulers took more than two thousand years to build it. The highlight is the Great Hypostyle Hall, which contains one hundred and thirty-six beautiful columns. Ladies and gentlemen, follow me and be amazed!'

I looked and looked and looked, shocked breathless by the height of things, the blunt, staring faces of the half-ruined statues, the stark shadows and glaring bright walls. And then we slipped into the shadow of the great pillars themselves. It was like stepping into cold water, or perhaps a forest at twilight – suddenly everything was hushed, and smooth, and mysterious.

The guide talked on, about the god Amun Ra and his wife and son, fainter and fainter as I walked away through the pillars, mesmerized. The sky was blue and far away, and the sun cast vivid streaks on the very tops of the columns. I looked at the carvings at my eye level – sharp-faced people, curving symbols, strange animals – and felt fingernail-small, so brief. This had stood for more than 3,000 years. I tried to imagine someone like me carving that bee, chiselling that goose into the stone the way I write our adventures down in my casebooks, and I could not. The thought of my words remaining years after I am dead gave me a very wobbly feeling, and I had to put it out of my mind.

Daisy stopped in front of a half-obscured frieze of a god holding out an ankh like a gift or perhaps a weapon. She looked rather like a picture herself – and, as I looked to my left, I saw Amina watching her too. I wondered if she was having a similar thought.

'I don't know if I like this,' said George, suddenly next to me, and I turned to him in amazement. 'I don't see why I should!' he said, shrugging. 'We're looking at temples supposed to be built by kings for gods – but the work was really by a lot of people who've never been given credit for it. It's all about the pharaohs, isn't it, even though they didn't lift a finger to make it?'

I felt half exasperated and half – well, the way George always makes me feel, as though he has expanded my mind in a direction I'm not entirely grateful for.

'But we can still see what they made,' I said. 'Isn't that important? It's all so beautiful, and it's lasted.'

'Just because it's beautiful doesn't mean it's good,' said George – and he looked over at Daisy too. 'Some beautiful things are good, but it doesn't necessarily follow that they will be.'

'George, come off it!' said Alexander, popping round the edge of a pillar and elbowing him in the ribs. 'Enjoy it, can't you? We're in Egypt!'

'So we are,' said George. 'And that's why we're all here, isn't it: to look at the ruins of Egypt?' And he looked straight at Alexander, and then me, and I felt my face burn. 'Now I'm going to go over there and examine that interesting wall. Have fun, you two.'

Alexander and I were left alone.

We both stared straight ahead, at the carvings – and I *felt* him next to me, even though I was not looking at him, as though I had gained some sort of second sight.

'I, er, I think it's nice,' said Alexander after a while.

'Oh, me too!' I said, and I turned my head just as he turned his to me.

That was somehow even worse, unbearably so, and we both looked away from each other again.

'I like Egypt so far,' I said stupidly, as though I was May's age.

The silence between us seemed to burn and stretch like a lit thread – and then a man in a turban came round the side of one of the pillars and said, 'Lady! I can sell you a mummy's finger? A real finger! The best price! Here, boy, you could buy it for your girl! Maybe she will love you then!'

'No thank you!' I cried in horror.

And then, of course, Daisy was there, saying, 'A real finger? Can I see? Which mummy? What happened to them exactly?' and I had to drag her away. It took a long time for the blush to fade from my cheeks – not until we were back on the boat, and Daisy and I were sitting side by side on the top deck, watching the sun race for the far horizon and turn the sky bloody orange.

'D'you know,' said Daisy, leaning against me, 'I heard something back at the temple that I forgot to tell you about. It was just before that man tried to sell us the finger – which you should have let me buy, Hazel, really!'

'No, I shouldn't!' I said. 'It was disgusting! What did you hear?'

'Mr DeWitt and Mrs Miller. They were staring at those . . . obelisks – the needle things, you know. Mr DeWitt said, "You won't regret this, Theo." Mrs Miller said, "Whatever do you mean?" and Mr DeWitt said, "Naming me your Thutmose. I know you've been ruling alone, but you don't have to any more. I'm here to help you now, just as in our past lives Thutmose helped Hatshepsut and ruled after she was gone." He said it so grandly, as though it was a gift to her, but then Mrs Miller burst out laughing. She said, "But it doesn't mean anything, Narcissus, you idiot! It's just a title. You didn't think that I'd let you get your hands on the society, did you? No, I carry on running it, no matter *who* your reincarnation is." Then she kept staring at the obelisk, but Mr DeWitt – well, Mr DeWitt looked like he wanted to murder her.'

2

We set off then, cutting through the darkening water and churning it white. I was bracing myself to feel sickened, like I usually do on boats – but the Nile is as calm as a bath, and there was only the gentlest rocking motion. I could eat dinner, and even pudding, without any trouble at all. It was quite night when I went outside afterwards, the moon rising red and odd-looking across the water. I could not think what was wrong with it, until I realized that it was turned sideways from the shape I was used to.

'Blood red!' said Daisy gleefully when she saw it. 'What does that mean? Perhaps there'll be a mur—'

I nudged her hard, for my father was walking by us to his cabin, and giving Daisy a very suspicious look.

After lights out, once the boat had been moored on the east bank next to a thick forest of palm trees, Daisy and I slipped bolsters down our beds in case anyone should look in on us, wrapped scarves around ourselves against the night-time chill and climbed up the steep stairs to the top deck. We had barely settled into our little basket chairs when Amina appeared, followed by George and Alexander.

'Evening!' whispered George.

'You weren't followed?' asked Daisy suspiciously.

'Miss Beauvais snores,' said Amina, unfolding her handkerchief to reveal some extra cakes from dinner. 'So I know she's asleep. And I locked her in, just in case. Isn't it useful that the keys work on both sides of the cabin doors here!'

'And Mr Young is falling asleep over his notes,' said George. 'He doesn't know anything about ancient Egypt, really, so he has to spend all his time in his cabin, studying things to teach us. That's why we chose him! He's one of Harold's Cambridge acquaintances. He's failing History, so I thought he'd be perfect. He won't look in on us until breakfast tomorrow.'

The five of us talked and talked, the stars flickering overhead as though the world was lit with candles. The wicker of my chair prodded the skin of my arms and the cold licked at my cheeks and my fingers and I felt utterly grown-up and daring. I was out at night, with boys. I stared at the shape of Alexander in the dark and wondered whether he was *really* here because of me. It had not seemed likely in the heat of the day, but up here, at night, thrilling with something that was either chilly air or excitement, I almost believed it.

The clock in the saloon below us rang the hour, and Amina giggled. 'Two o'clock!' she whispered. 'Let's do something – come on!'

'What do you want to do?' asked Daisy curiously.

'Oh, I don't know,' said Amina, shrugging. 'Switch the numbers on the cabin doors. Get into the dining room and swap all the breakfast cutlery about. *Something.*'

'What if we—' Alexander began, but then Daisy held up her hand.

'Shush!' she hissed. I thought she was just being rude to Alexander, as usual, but then a moment later I caught the sound that had startled her. A soft, regular noise like a heartbeat – the sound of footsteps on the deck below us.

Daisy rose out of her seat like a ghost and stepped to the port side of the ship. We all followed her and peered over the railings. My own heart was thumping, and I clutched at Daisy's arm.

The deck below us was lit softly by the moon, which had faded to creamy white and hung almost over our heads now. In its glow, we could see something drifting along the saloon deck, moving with a strange, eerie gait.

I do not believe in ghosts, I have told myself that a thousand times, but—

I gasped, and Daisy elbowed me.

'Ghosts don't have footsteps, Hazel,' she whispered in my ear, and I came back to myself. How could I have been so ridiculous? What I was seeing was only a person in a white nightgown – a pale person with long, curling hair, their hands outstretched before them a little, as though they were reaching for something.

'It's Heppy!' whispered Amina. 'What's she doing?'

'Going for a walk!' said Alexander. 'How weird. It's two in the morning!'

His voice must have carried, for below us Heppy twitched and turned her face up towards us. And we saw something that made me shudder. Heppy's eyes glinted in the nearest lamp, but they were quite expressionless.

'She's sleepwalking!' whispered George and Daisy together, glancing at each other in delight.

I was too busy trying to calm my breathing to feel anything but horror. Heppy's cold, blank face, her reaching hands – it was like watching a nightmare from the outside.

As we stared, she drifted down the deck, paused and pushed open the door directly below us.

'Whose cabin is that?' whispered Alexander.

'Either Miss Doggett's or Theodora Miller's,' Daisy whispered back. 'Oh, how strange!'

We waited, breathing carefully, and, five minutes later, Heppy floated back out, closing the door quietly behind her. Her eyes, as she moved away, were still empty. It was one of the eeriest things I had ever seen, and our party lost its fun after it. We drifted off to bed, feeling prickly and uncomfortable.

We had no idea how important what we had seen that night would prove to be.

3

In the morning, I woke to find that the sun was already high and the sky bright, although it was barely eight o'clock. Breakfast was glittering fruits and flaky pastries on the top deck, along with tiny cups of black coffee. I decided to drink one to look grown-up, but had to put it down in disgust at its gritty, thick taste.

We were sailing again past low green palm trees and high yellow mountains, the wide river around us smooth dark blue. Feluccas drifted by, their sails billowing, ducks paddled in the water and on the shore a man in a white galabeya chased his donkeys who had got loose from their tethers. We went through Esna lock, most of our party going out on deck to watch as the ship floated upwards magnificently. Rhiannon Bartleby wandered by, wringing her hands and looking for her glasses (which were on her head), and Theodora snapped at her about it. Heppy was hard at work, fetching and carrying things for the rest of the Breath of Life. She looked tired, I thought, and I pitied her even more.

Then we were off again, May leaning over the railing and trying to throw things into the paddle as it spun. Pik An, looking rather green (she had eaten salad on the train, and it had not agreed with her), dragged her away.

In the afternoon, when the sun hung heavy and hot in the west, the ship moored at a dusty little town, and we jingled off in a procession of horses and carts to another temple. Pik An did not come – she was greener than ever with food poisoning, and could not leave her cabin.

The dry heat of Egypt was dazzling, and the stark, sunlit walls and columns overwhelmed me. Everywhere I looked there seemed to be another pharaoh smiting his enemies, another god with a crocodile or jackal or lion face. This temple was covered over, and the rooms were dark. I began to get an exceedingly creepy feeling in the pit of my stomach. Of course, I am not sure whether I am only making this feeling up because of what happened later – but I really do remember standing under a vast frieze and feeling so unsettled I was almost trembling.

'See here,' Amina was saying to Daisy, her eyes sparkling with excitement. She was not afraid at all, of course. 'This is Osiris. He was killed by his brother Set—'

'What motive?' asked Daisy.

'Oh, jealousy, I think,' said Amina with a shrug. 'Anyway, Set cut Osiris into fourteen pieces and scattered them all across Egypt. But Osiris's wife, Isis, went flying up and down the Nile until she found them all, and she put Osiris back together again. Then she made their son Horus go looking for Set, to get revenge for chopping up his father. See here, this is Horus. He's got Set all chained up.'

'Isn't that marvellous!' whispered Daisy in my ear. 'Even the ancient Egyptians had murder mysteries! D'you think Isis was the first detective?'

'She wasn't a detective,' said Amina, looking at Daisy a little oddly. 'She was a goddess.'

'Yes, yes, of course,' said Daisy. 'Come on, Hazel, there's a man over there who says he can sell me a mummified snake!'

And then dusk was falling, and it was dinner time again (that was a lovely thing about the *Hatshepsut*, how very much food there always was), and that was when Theodora stood up and announced that she would be holding a ritual in the saloon that evening.

Of course, being Theodora Miller, she said it very rudely.

'I want you all to clear out of the saloon this evening, do you hear me?' she said to Mr Mansour. 'I want to hold a ritual.'

'But, madam, the other guests—'

'The other guests do not matter,' said Mrs Miller, and I felt Father bristle beside me. 'I must hold the ritual of the weighing of the heart immediately, do you understand?'

Mr DeWitt, Heppy and Miss Bartleby beamed – but I saw Daniel throw up his hands in annoyance, and Miss Doggett press her lips together and flare her nostrils.

'Theodora,' she said. 'A word?'

'Not *now*, Ida,' said Theodora Miller. 'The ritual will be performed in the saloon at ten tonight. As we are MISSING our sacred objects because ONE OF OUR NUMBER left them at the customs house in Alexandria' – here she looked hard at Heppy, who flushed, shiny-eyed – 'we shall just have to make do. We shall need a pair of weighing scales, a feather, a knife and, of course, the Cup of Life. Rhiannon, if you would be in charge of sourcing them?'

'I can do it, Mo—Theodora,' Heppy said hopefully.

'*No*, Heppy,' said Theodora. 'You'll only ruin it, as you did last time.'

Heppy sagged.

'Theo, if I *could* have a word!' said Miss Doggett.

'WHAT?' snapped Theodora, and she swung her head round bullishly to glare at Ida.

They whispered together – next to me, Daisy leaned forward like a creeping vine to listen in, but alas our table was too far away. We only saw Mrs Miller shake her head vigorously, Miss Doggett narrow her eyes, and then leap up and stalk out of the room.

Everyone stayed frozen for a moment, not sure how to pretend that they had not witnessed the scene – and then Miss Bartleby clapped her hands and said cosily, 'Now, who can find me a knife?' and the spell seemed to be broken.

'Oh, whatever did she *say*!' hissed Daisy to me.

'*I* heard!' said a voice at our feet – and we looked down to see my little sister May, panting and rather creased. 'I hid under her table,' she told us, pushing her hair away from her eyes. It had got out of her pigtail again.

'However did you!' I cried.

'I'm practising to be a spy,' said May. 'Don't you want to hear what I heard? The bony white woman—'

'—Miss Doggett,' I translated for Daisy's sake.

'*Her*, she was saying to the horrible white woman—'

'—Mrs Miller.'

'—HER, stop being so grown-up and *listen*, that this was not the time for the ritual and she was making a mockery of the gods and so they would – *mite* her. I don't know that word – what is it?' May was slipping back into Cantonese, which she did whenever she was annoyed or confused.

'Do you mean *smite*?' I asked in English.

81

'Probably – English is a stupid language. What's it mean?'

'It means *kill*,' I said, thinking of the temple walls. 'It's a thing kings do when they're cross with people.'

'Ooh,' said May, 'I hope someone gets smit. I'm going to go and spy again. Bye!' And she was off, wriggling away across the dining room from table to table.

Daisy put her chin on her hands. 'Just like we used to do,' she said wistfully. 'I wish we were still small enough to fit under tables. That's the only problem with growing up.'

Alexander laughed – and then glanced guiltily at us, his hand going up to his hair. I knew he was thinking about how Daisy and I had once hidden on the Orient Express.

'We've got to watch the ritual!' said Amina. We all stared at her in surprise – apart from Daisy, who looked very admiring and then saw me looking and haughtily tried to pretend she was not. 'I want to see what these fools will do. The weighing of the heart's part of the afterlife, you know – when the dead person's heart is weighed by the gods against a feather to see if they did wrong in their life.'

'A *feather*?' asked Alexander, pulling a face. 'Against someone's heart?'

'I've always thought it must have been a very big feather,' said Amina, grinning.

George looked at her thoughtfully. 'But won't it upset you?' he asked.

'Not any more than I already am,' said Amina. 'And it's not as though I *believe* in it. I'm Muslim. It's more that – well, they're making a mockery of my country's history. And—'

'And?' asked Daisy.

'And,' said Amina, 'if something were to go wrong . . . well, it would be funny, that's all.'

She sparkled around at all of us – and that was how we all found ourselves pressed against the outside of the saloon windows that evening at 10 p.m., spying on the Breath of Life's mysterious ritual.

4

As always, the reality of our missions was more awkward and annoying than the fantasy of them. We had told Miss Beauvais, Mr Young and Father conflicting stories about where we were off to, and I was terribly worried that they would realize our deception. I was also very aware that my heels were teetering on the edge of the narrow walkway around the saloon, and just as aware that there was a river flowing below my feet. Most of the others had to turn sideways to fit on. We clung together, Daisy's arms digging into my shoulders, George's left shoe pressed against my ankle, and Amina's fingers clinging to my left arm. I was doing my very best not to touch Alexander at all.

The net curtains were lowered for the evening, turning everything inside the saloon misty and indistinct – and giving us the perfect spying opportunity. I knew that the people in the saloon would be cushioned by the warm pink glow of their shaded lamps, able to see nothing but the light – certainly not the blurry faces of five people pressed against the second window from the left on the port side.

'Your hair's in my way, Hazel,' hissed Daisy in my ear, writhing to the left and almost overbalancing me.

Amina squeaked and said, 'Hey!'

'Shush, everyone,' whispered George, his voice so quiet that I more felt the rumble of it than heard it. 'It's about to begin.'

And it was. The followers of the Breath of Life Society were ready, wearing what I supposed were versions of the galabeyas that the Egyptians wore – but these robes were gaudy and cheap-looking, hung about with shiny stones and embroidered with gold thread. On their heads were crowns, cheap gilt paper ones.

Amina snorted. 'Their crowns are all wrong for pharaohs,' she said crossly. 'Well! I'm gladder than ever that I—'

Here she stopped, and grinned to herself.

'What?' asked Daisy curiously.

'Oh, you'll see,' said Amina, smirking more than ever. 'You'll see.'

There was a small, round pharaoh with a flash of white hair that must be Miss Bartleby, the yellow-haired helmet of Mr DeWitt, bony Miss Doggett, and a taller, curly-haired person who stood as if in an unhappy dream – Heppy. There was no sign of Daniel. Then everyone shifted and rustled and swayed aside as one more robed figure, this time in gorgeous gold and deep blue, proceeded in from the doorway that led to the cabins. It was Theodora Miller, clutching in one hand a large carving knife that had clearly been pilfered from dinner and – I clapped my hand over my mouth to stifle a laugh – a small feather duster in the other, of the sort that the maids used to tidy the cabins every morning.

There was a lull within the saloon, then Heppy jumped, shook herself and cried, 'The great pharaoh Hatshepsut returns! She has triumphed over death, and now she comes to weigh us all in the balance and bring us too to eternal life. Welcome her!'

'Welcome!' intoned everyone. Now Daisy was giggling too – big, shaking gasps that almost threw me off balance into the river below. I prodded her, holding my breath.

'I AM HERE!' cried Theodora Miller. 'REJOICE! *Heppy, that delivery was quite off – you must apply yourself more. And where is Daniel? I thought he'd be here.*'

'*Sorry, M—Theodora,*' said Heppy. '*Daniel said that he didn't want to come. I did ask, I promise I did.* Lo, she weighs our hearts on her scales against the feather of truth. But beware: the unworthy will face the Knife of Destiny!'

Theodora raised her arms dramatically.

Miss Doggett stepped forward, palms up, looking as though she was expecting to receive something, but Theodora turned away from her, handing the knife to Mr DeWitt. I saw Miss Doggett start and scowl, and a smile break across Mr DeWitt's wrinkled old face.

'I will weigh your hearts,' said Theodora Miller theatrically. 'I will WEIGH YOUR HEARTS on the SCALES – *Heppy,* are *you listening? Where are the scales? Didn't Rhiannon give them to you?*'

Heppy jumped again. '*Oh – yes – sorry, of course,*' she stammered. '*They're just down here – oh, wait, I was sure they were here—*'

'*Ida, help her!*' snapped Theodora Miller.

Miss Doggett shoved Heppy aside and went ferreting about one-handed under the saloon table, emerging a few moments later with a large, battered weighing scales that looked as though they had come from the kitchens.

'*Excellent, Ida,*' said Theodora. 'Now I shall sit, and—'

But, as she lowered herself dramatically into one of the saloon chairs that had been draped with gorgeous fabrics, the room was filled with a long, loud, very rude sound. Mrs Miller leaped up again, scarlet in the face, and from under her seat pulled out a whoopee cushion.

Beside me, Amina was in paroxysms of laughter. 'It's perfect!' she wheezed. 'Perfect! Did you see her face!'

Theodora was looking about her at the other Breath of Life members. Mr DeWitt was bewildered, Miss

Doggett disgusted, Miss Bartleby embarrassed and Heppy horrified. But Theodora must have misread Heppy's expression, for she hissed, '*Another black mark! I shall talk to you afterwards!*', her eyes screwed up with pure rage.

And I got an uncomfortable feeling. Amina's joke – for I knew it had been her – was funny, but Theodora Miller could not see the funny side at all. She had been humiliated, and she thought she knew who was behind it. Would Heppy have to pay for what Amina had done?

5

But the ritual, after a pause, seemed to be back on track. Intoning mysterious words ('They're nonsense!' hissed Amina in annoyance. 'She's just pronouncing Arabic words wrong! How silly!'), Theodora Miller took the feather duster in both hands and began to make the most extraordinary movements around the room. She spun, she leaped, she reached up and crouched down, waving the duster in front of her.

Daisy was properly laughing now, and even Alexander was making a guilty sniggering noise. I looked over at him and he mouthed – '*I can't help it! It's just* so *funny!*'

At last Mrs Miller put the duster reverently on the scales.

'It is time for the Reckoning,' she intoned. 'Come forth, and place your hand here.'

Miss Doggett and Mr DeWitt stepped forward together, and then glared at each other. Once again,

I saw that they were vying for the role as Theodora's second – and, once again, Theodora made her choice.

'Narcissus,' said Theodora. 'Come and be weighed.'

Mr DeWitt moved over to the scales, Miss Doggett hissing furiously behind him. He placed his hand lightly on the opposite side of the scales to the feather duster. It wobbled gently, and then held.

'Well, of course it's not going down. He's not putting any weight on it!' said George scornfully.

'I see your good deeds these past few days have lightened your soul,' said Theodora approvingly. 'You remain a worthy Thutmose. Go now, and do likewise.'

It was so odd to watch this ceremony – it felt like a strange mixture of the Christian services I knew in Hong Kong and England, and the things I had read about ancient Egyptian beliefs. Neither one was done right, though, and nothing about this felt real. It was like looking at worship in a funhouse mirror, pulled out of shape and ridiculous.

Miss Doggett was next. She put her left hand down confidently, but Theodora reached out a finger and tapped it. The scales dipped, the feather duster rising, and Miss Doggett gasped.

'You have work to do,' said Theodora to her. 'You have erred lately, Ida. You have not been faithful to me and my orders. You must step away from the darkness and move back towards the light, otherwise you may no longer be worthy of Cleopatra's name.'

And the look that Miss Doggett gave her was so fierce that I almost thought I could feel it through the window and the curtains.

Miss Bartleby was pronounced good – I saw her flinch a little, and wondered why – and then it was Heppy's turn.

She stepped forward, and I could tell she was trembling. She placed her hand on the scales, and before Mrs Miller could even lean forward her shaking made it dip, the side with the feather duster rising upwards sharply.

'Wickedness,' breathed Theodora. 'Sin. Heppy, you have done wrong yet again. You are not following my orders. You are rude, you are lazy, you are hopeless, and you still sleepwalk constantly. I know you were in my room again last night!'

'But I didn't mean it! I do try!' whimpered Heppy. 'It's just that I have such bad dreams.'

'You are not trying hard enough. You disappoint me, and you disappoint the gods. Reincarnation continues to move further away from you. At the moment, you are an entirely unsuitable vessel for the spirit of any great person.'

'But – but—' gasped Heppy, a sob in her voice.

'No buts. Do better. And bring me the Cup of Life so we can at least finish the ritual.'

'Yes, of course,' said Heppy miserably.

There was a pause, in which I saw Heppy look around in mounting panic.

'Where *is* the Cup of Life?' asked Theodora Miller. 'Heppy! Where is the cup?'

'Um – you asked – you asked Miss Bartleby to get it,' said Heppy at last.

Theodora swung round to Miss Bartleby, who had been standing, looking vaguely around, as though she hoped the cup would appear from someone else's robe. Her face changed as I watched – through surprise, to confusion, and at last a sort of sick horror.

'But I'm sure I asked *you* to get it, dear,' she said.

'I – I – but I told you an hour ago!' said Heppy. 'You were standing just outside, and I came up to you and asked—'

'I'm sure you did NOT!' snapped Miss Bartleby, in a sharper tone than I had ever heard her use. 'Nonsense! You've forgotten it, Heppy, and you're making up excuses, just as Theodora said!'

'She does that,' agreed Mrs Miller. 'It is one of her many failings. Heppy, go and get a cup!'

Heppy gasped, her eyes filling with big tears, and then she fled from the room, crashing the door open and making everyone jump. There was another further-away crash as her cabin door opened, a spilling sort of rattle, another crash, pounding feet and then she was back, the tooth mug from her cabin in her hands.

'Here,' she said thickly. 'Take it. It was my fault.'

But I was looking at Miss Bartleby, whose face had resumed its haunted, horrified expression, and I was not so sure about that. It seemed as though everyone in the Breath of Life was determined to pin their mistakes on Heppy.

Theodora blessed the water in the tooth mug by blowing on it, Mr DeWitt took it from her and passed it round, and everyone took a thin little sip (I suspected it still tasted faintly of toothpaste).

'Rejoice, you are all blessed,' said Theodora briskly, picking up the duster again and taking the knife from Narcissus. 'Well done, Narcissus and Rhiannon. You have pleased me. Ida, Heppy, you will do better tomorrow.'

I looked at Miss Doggett again, and saw her vibrating with fury at that. Her bony knuckles were clenched. Next to her, Heppy looked crushed. Mr DeWitt was smirking, and Miss Bartleby still had that blank panic on her face.

I got a very uncomfortable feeling. It had been a joke, to watch the ceremony. But what we had seen was not really funny at all.

6

Then the saloon door opened once again. We craned to see who it was. I could feel the same nervous detective excitement that was in me (for it *was* detective excitement by then: I was certain that something dreadful was going to happen) in everyone else as well. We were all hooked in, the five of us, like a line of fish.

'This is the best adventure I've ever been on,' murmured Amina quietly beside me.

Daniel Miller stood in the doorway, his arms folded.

'Have you quite finished?' he asked. 'Can I come in for a drink, or are you still messing about with your nonsense?'

'*Daniel*,' said Mrs Miller, and for the first time that evening her face softened. 'Come in. I wish you would listen to me – if only you would let me welcome you back into the society.'

'Never,' said Daniel, his expression full of disgust. 'It's all fakery! You tricked me in your letters – you told me this would be a family holiday. It's the only reason I came.'

'The Breath of Life *are* my family, Daniel dear. And they can be your family once again, if you come back to us. There's a place for you here. I have had powerful messages from the Beyond in the last few months – I am more sure than ever that you are the reincarnation of Tutankhamun.'

Daniel staggered as though he had been pushed. 'How could you?' he gasped. 'That was – that was what you called *him*. That's how you tricked *him*!'

'We don't trick anyone! It is true that Joshua Morse was our Tutankhamun once – but Joshua made the decision to leave us.'

'And then he *died*!' cried Daniel. 'You never mention that detail, do you, Mother? He died within a day of leaving your disgusting society.'

Beside me, I heard Daisy's sharp intake of breath.

'Don't use that word!' Theodora Miller's face twisted in pain. 'I am not to be referred to as your – your – and, as you know, we in the society do not *pass away*. Joshua's body is gone, but his ba, his soul – the great soul of Tutankhamun – is still present, and I believe it has settled in your body.'

'You're ridiculous,' said Daniel, fury on his face. 'You can't just *pretend* that we aren't your children because it isn't *convenient* any more. Well, I'll give you what you want. After this trip is over, I never want to speak to you again. This was your last chance to be rational, but I see you can't ever be. I want you to know that I blame you utterly for Joshua's death – and you have given me no reason to believe otherwise. You'd got all his money, hadn't you? You had no need of him any more!'

'Daniel!' said Theodora. 'You're wrong! This is the true way! You must – you *must* come back to the group! Please – if we could just talk—'

She sounded quite desperate.

Daniel said something to her that I cannot repeat. The door slammed so loudly behind him that it shook the railings we were balanced against.

'Poor troubled boy,' said Theodora, her voice unsteady. 'I pray he will see sense in time. Rhiannon, come with me. I need to get ready for bed. Heppy, you come too in a bit. It can be a good deed for your Book. Narcissus, tidy up. Ida, think on your errors.'

She stormed out, passing Mr Young in the doorway.

'Er, hello,' he said to the others. 'Have you – have you seen the boys? I seem to have lost them.'

'Certainly not,' said Miss Doggett, and then she and the rest of the Breath of Life stood, not quite looking at each other, the way British people do when they have seen something embarrassing that they want to pretend was not real. At last they filtered away. Mr Young wandered back towards his cabin, seemingly quite unaware of the scene that had just preceded him.

'Rats!' said Alexander. 'George, we'd better go find him.'

'Gosh!' sighed Daisy. 'To think that we were there for *that*! Now hurry, let's go before he notices us here. Alexander, George, go and pretend to have been downstairs or something.'

As George and Alexander slipped away, we all felt rather pleased with ourselves. It felt like the beginning of something mysterious. We were sure we had seen many important things.

But what we did not know, of course, was that the most important moment of the night was yet to come.

7

Daisy and I lay in our beds, unable to sleep, staring at the ceiling and listening to the crackle of insects and the splash and call of night-time birds. A mosquito had slipped its way into our cabin and was circling, its hiss louder and softer with every spin past my ear.

'Wasn't that fascinating?' said Daisy after a while.

'It was awful!' I replied. 'I really think something's up with the Breath of Life.'

'I know!' said Daisy, sitting up with a bounce. 'And it's about time that something happened. At last! We're in Egypt, on a boat with a religious cult, and something's afoot. Who is Joshua? Did Mrs Miller really have something to do with his death? That seems to have been what Daniel was getting at, wouldn't you agree? What's up with Miss Doggett and Mr DeWitt's rivalry? Why is Miss Bartleby behaving so shiftily? Why is everyone so determined to pin things on Heppy? It's thrilling. Don't you feel it, Hazel?'

'Yes, all right, I do,' I said. 'Only – it feels a bit wrong to hope something awful will happen. We shouldn't be wishing for crimes, Daisy.'

'Don't be po-faced, Hazel. Why shouldn't we wish for danger and adventure and excitement? Unravelling mysteries is the most important thing we do. Why, we're only half ourselves when we don't have a crime to solve. Hazel, school – even Deepdean – is not quite enough for us any more. I would do anything for it, but we need adventure, danger, *action*. Thank goodness we only have two and a half years left.'

'But then we'll go to university,' I said.

'We will NOT!' said Daisy. 'As I've told you before, we can't wait any longer to accept our life's mission, Hazel. There's so much to do! We can't mess about with learning things for ever, not if we want to become the world's greatest consulting detectives before we're old and dull. Don't you feel it? We need to do things with our lives *now*. We need to be – *big*.'

'I think I'm going to stick at this height,' I said.

'Don't be facetious. I mean the *other* sort of big. The sort that gets us into books. You know, like Alexander the Great, or Napoleon.'

'Except we're not men, or kings.'

'Now I know you're teasing me!' said Daisy, getting up and throwing herself on my bed. She sat on my stomach, squashing the breath out of me. 'If you want to get silly about it, then like Cleopatra, or – or Lucrezia Borgia. *Heroines*.'

I almost pointed out that both of those women were, strictly speaking, poisoners, but thought better of it, not with Daisy squeezing me so crossly. 'So we're going to be heroines,' I said, slightly breathlessly.

'Yes!' said Daisy. 'We're going to be famous, so people in one hundred years' time will say, "I wish I was like Daisy Wells and Hazel Wong, the greatest detectives ever!" Of course, we will still be alive in one hundred years to hear them say it. I have promised never to die or leave you, and I mean to keep that promise.'

She said it with such conviction that I really believed her, then. Daisy and I would be detectives together, for ever, and we would never die. Perhaps it was Egypt, or the Breath of Life and their strange beliefs – or perhaps it was Daisy's clear blue gaze staring me down with absolute confidence.

'All right,' I said. 'We will.'

Of course, I was quite wrong.

8

We woke up the next morning to screaming.

I remember it backwards somehow. I had thought I was having a nightmare where I was struggling against hands that were holding me as I tried desperately to get to the screamer – who might have been Daisy, or one of my sisters, I was not sure. But then I sat up with a tearing jump and a gasp and discovered that the screaming was outside me, outside our little cabin, high and shrill and terrified, and filling the air like black ink spilling over a white sheet.

'What is it!' I said. 'Who is it?'

Daisy, of course, was up on her feet, pushing open the white curtains and our door, braced and ready to run. She was still wearing her floating white nightie and her feet were bare. Behind her I could see the wide, misty river, and the far streak of darkness that was the greenery of the west bank of the Nile. The rest of the world looked very far away.

'Come on!' she snapped at me, holding out her hand and beckoning. 'We have to find out what's happened. Oh, hurry up, Hazel – come *on*.'

And I scrambled out of bed, head still blurry and afraid, caught hold of Daisy and stumbled out onto the deck after her. The moon was still high and pale in the sky, and the sun was not up. Everything was a soft haze of pinks and blues. White birds took off from the river like elegant ghosts, and the air was cold enough to make me flinch.

Heads were popping out of cabin doors all along the starboard side – there was Rose, my father, George, Alexander, Amina and Miss Beauvais. The screaming was coming from the port side, and I breathed out in relief. But Daisy, of course, was not interested in people who were all right.

'Come ON!' she hissed. 'Don't *dawdle*, Hazel! Something's HAPPENED!'

I glanced back at the boys' cabin. Alexander's blond hair was rumpled with sleep and his striped pyjamas were, I noticed, slightly too short for him. He looked at me, and I was suddenly very aware that my pyjamas were fraying at the cuffs and slightly greyish after a term being put through the Deepdean wash.

'Hazel, come here!' said my father.

'HURRY UP!' Daisy bawled over her shoulder, and I got a shot of boldness. I turned away from my father and followed Daisy as she went running across the wooden deck floor. I heard feet behind me, and knew that George and Alexander were coming after me.

'Hazel! Come HERE!' Father cried, but I ignored him.

Daisy darted round the back of the boat, dodging the empty cane chairs and little tea tables. In my haste to follow her, I tripped over something on the deck and went sprawling, knocking into a potted fern. It fell over with an enormous clatter, spilling dark soil across the deck.

I looked down at the thing I had stumbled over. It was a small lump, wrapped in blankets. I thought for a second that it might have something to do with the screaming, but then the blankets stirred and a tousled little head popped out of them, glaring at me crossly.

'OW!' said my sister May.

I gasped. 'What are you *doing*, Monkey?' I asked her.

'Sleeping on deck like a pirate,' said May, as though it was obvious. 'Or I was until someone started screaming. Make it stop!'

'May!' I said in frustration. 'Go – go to Father. There's no time to be a pirate. Something's *wrong*!'

By this point, Daisy was already halfway up the port side of the *Hatshepsut*, and I rushed away from May and her bundle of blankets to where she was standing. It was by the cabin the scream was coming from. Daniel Miller was already in front of it, along with Daisy, staring inside. Its door was open, and its white floating curtains were pushed aside, so we could see the whole scene in front of us.

9

We have seen plenty of dreadful things in the past few years, Daisy and I. Being detectives means looking at horror without blinking, not even when you would give anything to. But all the same I was not prepared for what I saw.

Theodora Miller was lying on her bed, and she was dead. That was quite clear, from her waxy pale face and the heavy spread of blood high up on one side of her white ruffled nightdress. Her bedsheet had been cast aside, and lay crumpled and bloody on the floor to the right side of the cabin door as I looked through it.

'A struggle!' breathed Daisy in my ear. 'A stabbing!'

But that was not, somehow, the worst thing.

Next to Theodora, standing in the middle of the cabin floor, was Heppy, and she was the person screaming. She had her hands up to her face, and her hands were rusty with dried blood. There was blood on her cheeks, and blood was spotted and smeared down her sensible, plain pyjamas and on her hands. Next to her feet was the carving knife I remembered from the ritual the night before, its blade gleaming, and Heppy was staring at her hands and the knife, and screaming, screaming, screaming.

'Heppy!' shouted Daniel. 'What did you do, you idiot? What did you DO?'

I suddenly smelled the blood in my nose, hot and iron, and my head buzzed like a swarm of mosquitoes.

'Breathe through your mouth,' George whispered. I thought he sounded awfully assured and grown-up, but when I looked back at him his face was as pale as anything.

'What do we do? What do we do?' Alexander kept on asking. He had gone quite pale too, and I thought he might faint. George put out his hand to steady Alexander, and they clung together.

Amina came running up, Miss Beauvais still pulling at her and bleating.

'Do go away!' cried Amina. 'Let me see – oh! Inna lillahi wa inna ilayhi raji'un!'

My father had arrived too, Rose and May by his side. He hung back a few paces as May strained to go forward. 'Hazel!' he called to me. 'Hazel, what is it? Come here!'

'I – I can't!' I called back to him. 'I – take Rose and May away. They shouldn't see this!'

'Ooh, what *is* it?' cried May, surging forward again. Father grabbed hold of her by her pigtail. His look at me was sharp and worried.

'Are you sure you know what you're saying, Hazel?'

'Yes,' I said, trying to keep my voice steady. 'Something terrible's happened. They shouldn't see.'

And – quite incredibly – my father nodded briefly at me and pulled May and Rose away. I could hardly believe it. It took quite an effort for me to drag myself back to the scene of the crime.

'She's dead!' Amina kept on repeating. 'Oh! She's dead!'

Of course, I thought. She had never actually seen a murder before.

Miss Beauvais simply screamed and fainted. She lay on the boards of the deck, and everyone ignored her.

'Pull yourselves together!' Daisy snapped at everyone. Her face was white, but I knew that had nothing to do with nerves. It was pure excitement. Daisy manages to think clearly in the worst situations – I sometimes suspect that she likes nothing better. 'Move out of the way, Hazel, and stop swooning. You aren't a silly girl in a book!'

She pushed past us into the cabin, stepped over the knife without touching it and very carefully slapped Heppy across the face twice.

Heppy's screams stopped as though a tap had been turned off. She fixed blurry eyes on Daisy and blinked slowly.

'I woke up,' she said in a voice that we had to strain to hear. 'I woke up in my bed and there was blood – blood all over me! *So much blood*. And then I came in here, and Mother – there's so much blood!'

'Do you mean you came in and found her like this?' asked Daisy sharply.

'Yes,' whimpered Heppy. 'The blood was already on me when I woke up. And I had a dream, one of my sleepwalking dreams – I had a dream that something terrible happened. I – I think I killed Mother. I THINK I KILLED MOTHER!'

Her voice was rising again, unbearably. It seemed quite clear to me what had happened. We had seen Heppy sleepwalking the night before, after all, and heard Mrs Miller herself say that she did it regularly – and here Heppy was, covered in blood, saying she had sleepwalked again. And I almost felt – disappointed. It was such an easy and obvious explanation. After all the rivalries and jealousies we had witnessed between the Breath of Life Society members, this death was not mysterious at all. Poor Heppy was responsible.

At least, that is what I thought until Miss Bartleby peered round us into the cabin, rubbing her little eyes in panic, and turned the case on its head.

'This is terrible,' she said. 'He's *dead*!'

I thought I must have misheard her – after all, it was very noisy, and everyone was in shock.

'Miss Bartleby,' I said. '*Mrs Miller* is dead.'

Miss Bartleby's face crumpled. 'Oh no,' she said. 'Not Theodora too?'

'Are you all right, Miss Bartleby?' asked Amina. She had pulled herself together, and looked so earnest and sweet as she said it – like George, Amina is good with grown-ups.

'No!' bleated Miss Bartleby. 'He's dead! *She's* dead! And I think – I think *it was me*!'

I always assume we have seen everything, Daisy and I. But, all the same, this was the first time we had ever been faced with a murder that not one but two people confessed to as soon as they saw the body.

10

But that was not all. For as we all stood there I turned to see bony Miss Doggett watching what was going on, wrapped tightly in a gorgeous bathrobe. Her expression was horribly *wrong* somehow. She did not look afraid, or disgusted – on the contrary, she looked almost as excited as Daisy. She peered inside the cabin, her eyes darting about, and I heard her give a little sigh. She clenched her fists and her thin lips twisted into a nasty smile.

'So it has happened,' she said. 'She's dead.'

It was such a clear, calm thing to say and, after Heppy and Miss Bartleby, I felt dizzily that anything was possible. Were we about to hear a third confession?

'She was unworthy,' said Miss Doggett. 'I have been saying it ever since her ridiculous decision to make Mr DeWitt Thutmose. Last night my ba flew out and witnessed her death, and now it has happened just as I saw it. She proved herself unworthy of being Hatshepsut, and now she has been punished for her overreaching.'

'Punished by who?' asked Daisy sharply, coming to stand next to me, one hand on my shoulder.

'Isn't it obvious?' asked Miss Doggett. 'The gods.'

Amina snorted.

'*The gods* stabbed Mrs Miller?' Daisy could not keep the scorn out of her voice. 'How d'you explain Heppy, then?'

'The gods work through mortal hands sometimes,' said Miss Doggett. 'Ancient magic is strong.'

'The gods?' cried Mr DeWitt. He had come out of his cabin and was standing in a pair of mismatched silk pyjamas, wringing his hands. His shiny hair was disarranged, his trouser buttons done up wrong and his wrinkles looked deeper than ever, as though they too had been cut with a knife. 'Are you calling Heppy a god?' And he glared at Miss Doggett.

'At least *some* people haven't confessed on the spot,' whispered Daisy in my ear.

'She's not dead too, is she?' cried Mr DeWitt, noticing with a start that Miss Beauvais was slumped on the deck.

'She's only fainted,' said Daisy.

'Good grief!' said Mr DeWitt. 'She must be moved – she gave me a terrible shock. I think – Ida, your cabin is best. You, boy, help me.'

'No!' cried Miss Doggett, but George and Mr DeWitt were already dragging Miss Beauvais away.

'I shall go and get Mr Mansour!' shouted Daniel, who had been standing, wringing his hands. 'Oh my God, Heppy, you've done it this time!'

I saw him running away down the deck so quickly he seemed to be flying, his feet in soft white slippers. He appeared upset – but then I thought of the scene we had witnessed the night before, and felt uncertain. Daniel had seemed quite unrepentant and furious then. Was he simply realizing now that he loved his mother, after all? Or was he trying to cover something up?

Alexander was breathing quickly through his nose – he dislikes corpses even more than I do – and Amina's eyes were big and her lips were trembling again. In the distance, I heard the ring of a bell.

'Hazel!' called my father, and I turned to see him striding towards me once again, alone, his face very serious. 'Hazel, come here. I need to talk to you.'

My heart was beating as I stepped away from the others and went over to him. I knew he was about to try to remove me from the scene of the crime.

'You and Miss Wells have a real talent for placing yourselves near dead bodies, Hazel. What am I to do with you? What am I to do now?'

'Please don't take us off the ship,' I stammered. 'Please. I need to stay here. I need to help.'

'If you stay, do you promise not to do anything dangerous?'

'I'll be good, I—'

Then I heard what he had said and paused in confusion.

'Pik An is still ill in her cabin. I have locked May and Rose into *their* cabin for the time being, but you know your littlest sister. She'll be out through some crack like the monkey she is if I'm not there to watch her. So, as I see it, I have two options: I can forbid you to have anything to do with this mystery, an order I know you will ignore, or trust you to remain out here without me.'

'Father!'

'You seem to have solved a number of murders without my consent. It seems tiresomely inevitable that you will investigate this one too. So I choose to give you my consent this time. Only, Wong Fung Ying – *promise* me you will come to me at once if you ever feel yourself in real danger?'

'I promise,' I whispered. My ears were ringing and my mind was spinning. I could not believe what was happening – but my father, when I blinked several times, still stood before me, as solid and sensible as ever.

'Now go to Miss Wells. I will be in my cabin with your sisters, and the door locked.'

And with his astonishing blessing echoing in my head I ran to find Daisy.

PART THREE

THE SECRET ADVERSARY

1

'There you are, Hazel,' said Daisy when I came rushing into our cabin, my mind in turmoil, to find the others gathered in a huddle. 'You're late! Really, I do expect more from you by now!'

'I had to talk to my father,' I said, still feeling rather disbelieving. 'He – I don't think he's going to stop us detecting.'

'No,' said George. '*Really?*'

Alexander beamed at me. I blushed. 'Really,' I said. 'I mean – he still doesn't like it, but he has to stay with my sisters. I think he's just going to pretend it isn't happening.'

'So he's finally come round to our brilliance,' said Daisy, as though she had not been fighting to keep the Detective Society secret from grown-ups for years. 'How useful. Now, Hazel, can we get on with it, or are you going to have to go and talk to anyone else?'

'See here, what's wrong with you all?' asked Amina. 'Why aren't you – why aren't you more *surprised*?'

The four of us looked at each other a little guiltily. I saw Daisy freeze in horror.

'Oh, er, yeah,' said Alexander. 'The thing is . . .'

'Should we tell her?' asked George.

'Tell me what?' asked Amina.

'We're detectives,' said Alexander. 'All of us.'

Amina burst out laughing. 'Of course you are,' she said.

'No,' I said. 'We really *are*. Daisy and I are the founders of the Detective Society. We've solved nine murder cases so far, and Alexander and George have solved—'

'Well, three murders with you, and lucky Alex did the Orient Express case too – and more mysteries on our own,' said George, grinning at Amina. 'The Junior Pinkertons, at your service.'

Amina's face flickered from doubt to amazement. 'You're *not* joking!' she said. 'Is that – is that what happened at the gala weekend at school? I thought that was just a one-off.'

'The gala weekend case was our *eighth*,' said Daisy, speaking up at last. 'And see here – we're only telling you this because we *have* to. Our detective societies are secret, and they must remain that way. You have to *swear* not to compromise us! Promise! Can you do that?'

Suddenly I saw real worry in Daisy's eyes. She was very still, watching Amina ferociously. This was a test, I knew it – and I hoped quite desperately for both their sakes that Amina would rise to meet it.

'I swear not to tell anyone,' said Amina. 'I promise, honestly – I'm only smiling because I'm nervous. There was really a murder! You're really detectives! This is really *real*! Brilliant!'

For one unguarded moment, Daisy glowed with happiness. She caught Amina's eyes and they beamed at each other. Then she snapped back to her usual self.

'Of course it's real. And now we must stop chattering and get down to business. A murder has occurred, and we must detect it. There's no one else onboard who can, after all. This crime may look quite simple – but is it really? For we have heard not one but two confessions. Is there more to this case than meets the eye? And is this the first murder that has occurred in the Breath of Life, or the second?'

2

'It's funny, isn't it?' said Alexander. 'Usually all of our suspects say they haven't done it. I don't think we – or you – have ever had a case where they all say they *have*.'

'It isn't *funny*,' said Daisy, sniffing. 'And it's not all of them – as I said, it's only two. It *is* fascinating, though, I must admit. Now, Hazel, casebook out, please! We need to write down the facts in the case. Amina, you see this is what we always do: logically put down everything we know, so we can begin to see the pieces of the puzzle we don't yet have.'

'*We* always do it a bit differently,' said George. 'And Alex is our stenographer. He knows shorthand.'

'Shush!' said Daisy. 'Irrelevant. Hazel, CASEBOOK.'

I bent down beneath my bed and pulled open my little travelling case, more battered than ever, and with several shiny new customs stamps overlapping one another on its surface. These days, I never go anywhere without a new casebook ready and waiting in my bag. It seems a superstition to do that – as though by it, I am inviting death in – but I would not dream of doing anything else, for every time I think we have finished with our detective lives and become nothing more than ordinary fifteen-year-old girls, the world tilts and suddenly we are facing the problem of yet another body.

'The Case of the – what are we calling this one, Daisy?'

'The Murder on the *Hatshepsut*!' said Daisy. 'No, the Death on the Nile? That does have a nice ring to it, doesn't it?'

'The Case of the Death on the Nile,' I said. 'Present: Daisy Wells, Hazel Wong, Alexander Arcady, George Mukherjee and Amina El Maghrabi.'

'See here,' said Amina, 'am I a proper detective, then? And, if so, which society am I joining? I quite fancy being a Pinkerton.'

'You are absolutely *not* a Pinkerton,' said Daisy decidedly, just as George said, 'You're always welcome to join us, isn't she, Alex?'

'No, you are a Detective Society member, *thank* you *very* much,' Daisy went on, shooting George a dark look. She is always so funny with George – they are really so similar that sometimes she cannot bear him. 'You can be an assistant detective for this case, just until you find your feet. Now recite after me: *I swear to be a good and clever member of the Detective Society . . .*'

121

I looked at her sideways as Amina said the words with a smile in her voice. Daisy only stared back at me, eyebrow raised, as though daring me to say anything.

Once the oath was complete, I began.

'Facts in the case: Theodora Miller was discovered dead in cabin seven on the port side of the saloon deck of the *Hatshepsut* at ten past six this morning.'

'Really, Hazel, that's too late!' said Daisy. 'Heppy's screams began at exactly five past six. We got to the cabin at six minutes past, and I saw you check your wristwatch at ten past. Now that's the time of the discovery – but not of the death, I should say, from the old appearance of the bloodstains.'

At this, I could not avoid making a face of disgust, and Alexander said, 'Ugh!'

'I noticed that too,' said George, as unfazed as Daisy. 'The blood all looked quite rusty.'

'It was at least a few hours old,' said Amina unexpectedly. 'Don't look like that – I know bloodstains too! I spent a lot of time when I was younger getting into scrapes and having to be patched up. When you properly cut your arm or something, it comes out all bright, and then it dries and goes that dull colour. So she must have been dead for a while.'

'Very good,' said Daisy approvingly. Amina twinkled at her, and Daisy glanced away. 'What else can we deduce?'

'She was stabbed,' said George. 'Obvious, but we might as well say it.'

'And stabbed by the knife that was on the floor next to her,' agreed Alexander. 'Pretty obvious too. I mean, it's all pretty obvious, isn't it?'

'Is it?' asked Daisy.

'I think it is!' said Amina. 'Isn't this all' – she gestured round at us, and then pointed at me with my casebook – 'a little unnecessary? We know who did it! She was standing there, covered in blood, and she confessed.'

'That's what I was going to say!' said Alexander. 'I've heard about this kind of thing before. People sometimes commit crimes while they're sleepwalking, and they don't know it till they wake up again. My mom told me about one case that happened in Boston, a hundred years ago. A man killed his girlfriend while he was sleepwalking – he didn't wake up till the morning.'

'It's psychology,' said George, nodding. 'You know – buried wishes. Mrs Miller was horrible enough to Heppy, wasn't she, for Heppy to resent her and want to hurt her?'

'You really think Heppy was telling the truth?' I asked. 'She's the one whose confession is the real one, and Miss Bartleby was making it up?'

'Isn't it the simplest possible explanation?' asked Alexander. 'Miss Bartleby gets confused sometimes – we saw that last night. But I believed Heppy. Her confession was the real one.'

'STOP, all of you!' said Daisy. 'You are not being rigorous!'

'But I think they're right, Daisy,' I said. 'She was the only person with blood on her, after all!'

'Hazel! When it was clear that Mr DeWitt had just put on a fresh pair of pyjama trousers that didn't match his top? When Miss Doggett was wearing a bathrobe over her nightie? How do we *know*! You're not being rigorous at all. And then there's the knife. Even – even Amina should be able to tell me what was wrong with it!'

'Rude!' said Amina. 'But I'll bite. The knife blade should have been covered with blood, shouldn't it?'

I thought back to the scene of the crime. Theodora Miller, lying in bed, her arms at her sides, the bloody sheet on the floor and the knife between them, glinting in the lamplight.

'OH!' said Alexander and I together.

'The knife was clean!' I gasped. 'Why would Heppy have cleaned it?'

'There you have it,' said Daisy. 'And, come to think of it, what was that sheet doing on the floor? It must have been on the bed during the murder, or it wouldn't have been stained with blood. Did Theodora push it off during the crime?'

'No, she couldn't have done!' I said, remembering. 'I saw Theodora's hands – they weren't bloody. She couldn't have touched the sheet. I suppose she might have kicked it off, but it was so far across the room, I don't see how she could have.'

'You see?' said Daisy. 'It doesn't make sense.'

'Are they always like this?' Amina asked, amused.

'Always,' said George. 'Alex and I are almost as bad, though. But I have to admit that they have a point. Heppy's confession assumes that she sleepwalked into her mother's room, murdered her, and then went back to her bed, as usual. But would a sleepwalker clean a knife like that? How did the sheet get onto the floor? And why didn't we hear Theodora screaming last night? Because we didn't, did we? There were no loud noises like that.'

He looked round at all of us. We shook our heads.

'I heard people moving about a couple of times,' said Daisy. 'A few thumps, at about two. But no screaming. And the cabin walls are thin enough that we would have done. We heard Heppy this morning, didn't we?'

'Well then,' said George, 'if Theodora didn't scream, it's because someone stopped her screaming. And *that* suggests someone who was very much awake.'

'So,' I said. 'Something's wrong, isn't it?'

'Oh yes!' said Daisy. 'I agree. Something is not what it seems at all. And that means that we most certainly do have a case. We cannot simply accept Heppy's confession until we have ruled out everyone else definitively. Detectives, the game is afoot!'

3

I could feel the tension humming in the air, sparking between us like an electrical charge. Daisy's, George's, Alexander's and Amina's faces were all bright with excitement – although in Alexander's case it was mixed with uncertainty, and Amina's with open curiosity. Daisy's and George's, though, were sharp and purposeful, their minds on nothing but the case.

'So what are we saying?' I asked. 'That we don't think it's Heppy? All right, then, what did happen? How did she get all that blood on her?'

'Whatever did happen, it convinced her *she* did it,' said George. 'Which is a problem! She's already confessed, and she'll confess again as soon as the police get onto the ship. Amina – what are the police like here?'

'They're all right,' said Amina. 'I don't know what you want me to say exactly – they're good enough, and so are the people who control them, the Parquet.

They're the ones who question witnesses and decide whether a case should go to trial. They're not stupid or backward. But, if they got a confession, I don't know that they'd look much further. The Parquet are in every big city – let's see, I suppose we're in Aswan Governorate now. Well, that's good for us, I suppose.'

'Why is that good?' I asked.

'Mr Mansour will order the ship to keep heading for Aswan,' said Amina. 'I would, if I was him, and I was surrounded by Europeans. They'll want high-ups, not just town policemen, and they'll want the Consul too. That's all in Aswan. And Aswan's hours away yet, almost a full day's sailing.'

'So we've got time!' said Daisy, eyes sparkling. 'Oh, *wonderful*! Now, Detectives, before we move forward with our investigation, we must consider our suspects, and do so rigorously. No one on this ship can be ruled out, not even us.'

'Of course we can rule ourselves out!' said Alexander. 'We don't have to waste time on us. George couldn't have got out of our cabin without waking me, and I couldn't have got out without waking him. And I bet you two are the same.'

'We are,' I said, thinking back to Daisy and the Deepdean rooftop.

'Well, what about me?' asked Amina, shaking back her hair and quirking her lips into a smile. 'I hated

Theodora Miller, and I know how to get past Miss Beauvais without her waking up. What if I'm a murderer?'

I saw Daisy freeze, and I knew why. '*Don't* joke,' she snapped.

Amina's smile faltered. 'I was only teasing! Look – my cabin's next to yours. You said earlier you heard thumps. Wouldn't *you* have heard me leave? Check my clothes for blood if you like.'

'That sounds like something a murderer would say!' said George, and Amina stuck her tongue out at him.

'All right, so it *wasn't* us,' I said. 'We didn't hear you, Amina. And it can't have been May or Rose, either, as they're too little to have caused those wounds. But it could have been anyone else on the ship. Mr Mansour or the crew, Mr Young, Miss Beauvais, Pik An – *Father* even.' I felt sick to say it, but I had to. It would be poor detective work for me to leave him out.

'HAH!' shouted a voice from underneath my bed. It was so loud and sudden that we all jumped, and I yelped. 'YOU'RE WRONG! I can rule out almost EVERYONE!'

After the initial shock, I discovered that I knew this voice – and the person who owned it – extremely well. I threw myself flat on my stomach and stuck my head over the edge of the bed. I saw an upside-down view of the tidy floor of our cabin, my suitcase and the posts of my bed – and a fierce little face with button eyes and an enormous grin.

SUSPECT LIST

1. **Hephzibah Miller.** The victim's daughter. She was first on the scene, and was found covered in blood. She says that she woke up with no idea how the blood got onto her, and only realized her mother was dead when she went into the victim's cabin. We know she is a sleepwalker, and she believes that she murdered her mother while asleep. But can this be true?

2. **Ida Doggett.** The second in command in the Breath of Life Society. Theodora believed Miss Doggett was the reincarnation of Cleopatra, but Ida wanted to be Hatshepsut instead, Mrs Miller's reincarnation! We witnessed many disagreements between the two — they have clearly fallen out since Mr DeWitt joined the group. Miss Doggett mentioned being pleased that Theodora was dead this morning, and blamed the gods for the crime — a strange thing to say. She appeared on the scene wrapped in a bathrobe — could she have been hiding blood on her nightdress?

3. **Rhiannon Bartleby.** Another member of the Breath of Life Society. Theodora believed she was

the reincarnation of Nefertiti. She seems sweet and gentle, but she made a suspicious confession when the death was discovered this morning.

4. *Daniel Miller.* The victim's son. He has been estranged from her, but was temporarily reconciled with his mother to come on this holiday. However, we know he was extremely angry with her last night. He mentioned Joshua Morse, an ex-member who is now dead — we must learn more about him.

5. *Narcissus DeWitt.* High up in the Breath of Life Society, and seemingly on Theodora's side. It's clear that he is fighting with Miss Doggett to become second in command. Mr DeWitt was wearing mismatched pyjama trousers when we saw him this morning — why?

PLAN OF ACTION

1. Take a closer look at the scene of the crime.

2. Investigate the other cabins on the saloon deck for clues.

3. Re-create the crime: work out why no scream was heard in the middle of the night and pin down the time of death.

4. Discover who Joshua Morse is and what happened to him!

5. Investigate our suspects, gain their trust and begin to rule them out.

6. Discover more about Theodora Miller. Who was she?

7. Get in to see Heppy!

4

'HELLO!' said my sister May.

'What are you *doing* here, Monkey?' I hissed at her. 'I thought Father had you and Rose safe in his cabin!'

'I escaped while he was out talking to you! Rose is reading again – *boring*. Father hasn't found me yet so he must still be looking. And your door was open. You shouldn't leave it open, especially when there's been a *murder*. Anyway, I know something important, something that you don't.'

'It's May,' I said furiously, twisting my head to look up at the others. 'She says she knows something important. May, come out here and speak English!'

'ALL RIGHT!' said May, wriggling out from under the bed and beaming round at everyone. '*In English*, I *still* know something important. Do you want to know what it is?'

'Yes,' said George.

'No,' said Daisy.

'I'll tell you if you let me be a detective,' said May.

'NO,' several people said at once.

'I'll ask again in five minutes and you'll say yes,' said May. 'All right, here's the first thing I know. I spent all of last night out on the deck, being a pirate.'

'Mei!' I gasped. 'So that's why – you mean you were there *all* night? I thought you'd just got up a bit before us.'

'Yes, all night. I waited until Father said goodnight to us and then I got out – just like you did the night before! I know you did! It was colder than home is at night, so I had to bring my blankets, and I had to hide once because Mr Young was walking about, talking to himself, but he didn't see me. Anyway, being a pirate is difficult. Decks are hard to sleep on, even with blankets. I woke up every time I heard a noise, and I woke up four times. The second-to-last time there were lots of noises, and a few people moving about, and the last time there was a splash, like someone throwing something into the water. But it was all on the other side of the boat to our cabins. After the splash, I fell asleep beside the chairs, and that's where you stood on me.' May glared at me accusingly.

'I didn't do it on purpose!' I said – and then I realized what she was telling us. She had heard more than Daisy or I had, and she had been watching the starboard side of the ship. 'May, are you saying that, if anyone had gone out of their cabins on the starboard side, you'd have seen them?'

'Yes!' said May. 'And I didn't, so they didn't. I'm sorry I didn't go and look on the other side now, because I might have seen the murderer, but I was worried about being told off. But that's only half of what I wanted to tell you. When I decided to sleep outside, I *didn't* want to risk silly Pik An beginning to feel better and coming up to our deck during the night to tuck us in. So I set up an alarm. I tied strings over the top of the stairs to the other deck below us, and I hung a bell on them, so that if anyone came up the stairs the bell would go off and wake me. The strings were extra-thin thread, and no one going up in the dark would see them before they walked into them. So, you see, it was perfect. And it didn't go off! Not once, not until after the screaming. I heard it just now. That's how I know that none of the other guests came up, and it can't have been any of the sailors, either.'

I hated to admit it, for May is my little sister, and I still half see her as an angry, wriggling red baby and not a real person, but I realized that this was very clever of her (the thin strings especially), and she had done two very useful things. I remembered the bell I had heard when Daniel had run to get Mr Mansour, and I knew she was telling the truth. I also knew that she had helped narrow down our investigation significantly, and helped give us a timetable for the murder.

'The only people who could have killed Theodora are the ones with cabins on the port side of the saloon deck,' I said. 'That's Heppy, Daniel, Miss Doggett, Mr DeWitt and Miss Bartleby. But, May, you shouldn't have done that! It was dangerous!'

'Hah!' said May. 'It helped you, didn't it? Now, do you want to let me be a detective? I helped you on a case before, didn't I?'

She had, but – 'No!' I said. 'This is different!'

'Oh, let her!' said Amina.

'*You* don't have any little sisters,' I said. 'You don't understand.'

'I *am* a little sister!' said Amina.

'And so am I,' said Daisy. 'Or have you forgotten about Bertie, Watson?'

'Well – she's too young!' I said, floundering. 'Why should we, May?'

'Because I'm little!' said May. 'You're all too big now, like grown-ups. You can't creep any more. But you didn't notice me coming into the room, did you? And nor will anyone else. See, I've already been doing some detecting, and I found out something else important – which I'll tell you about only if you let me be part of your Detective Society!'

We all looked at each other. At last George sighed. 'She's right about us being too big to hide anywhere and listen,' he said. 'May, what did you hear? If it's good, we'll say yes.'

'There were two people standing on deck when I was coming to your cabin,' May said. 'The bony woman and the old fat one.'

'Miss Doggett and Miss Bartleby,' I translated. 'So?'

'Well, the bony one said something like, "As Joshua, so Theodora!" And then the old fat one said, "I didn't mean it! I didn't mean to hurt either of them!" Then the bony one said, "Well, now she's gone, we can take our rightful places. We must be ready. We can't let a man take over!" And then the old fat one started crying. You see? I can be useful – you wouldn't have heard that if it wasn't for me!'

Despite myself, I felt a prickle of real excitement. This seemed very suspicious indeed. Here was Miss Bartleby, still convinced that she was behind not one but two murders, and Miss Doggett, gloating over Theodora's death. I looked around and saw that the others were as fascinated as I was.

'We have to let her in,' said Alexander. 'Come on! She could be really useful.'

'Temporarily,' said Daisy. 'Like we did in our Hong Kong case. She's been useful before, after all.'

'Oh, all RIGHT!' I said. 'But you have to do what we tell you to, May.'

'Obviously,' said May, and I had the suspicion that she was crossing her fingers behind her back. 'So, what are we doing first?'

5

'YOU,' said my father furiously, throwing open the door to our cabin, 'aren't doing anything at all, Wong Mei Li! Come here at ONCE, and if I catch you out of my cabin one more time you – shall go without dinner for a week.'

'*No, I won't,*' whispered May to me, as she was seized by the shoulder and dragged away. '*He wouldn't!*'

Remembering the times I went without dinner when I was May's age for being far less naughty, I had to bite my tongue at the unfairness of being the oldest.

'Do this WITHOUT May, Hazel Wong!' snapped my father, and he slammed the door behind him.

'Er,' said Alexander, glancing at me. 'What – what are we doing first?'

'It's quite obvious,' said Daisy. 'It's still chaos outside if May could escape so easily. While everyone's running about like frightened rabbits, we need to get back to the body and the scene of the crime – and we can look into the other rooms too, while we're at it. We only have a limited amount of time before Mr Mansour takes control of the *Hatshepsut* once again – or until Miss Beauvais and Mr Young start bothering us – and we need to use every second of it! All right, to arms! Detectives, ready?'

I nodded at her.

'Ready,' said George and Alexander.

'Ready,' said Amina, tossing her hair.

'Then let's go and solve a murder,' said Daisy.

Outside our cabin, the sun was rising behind the east bank of the river, birds calling from the dark palm trees on the shore, the sky lifting and brightening. I looked at my wristwatch and saw it was almost seven o'clock. Above us the moon was still high, and in front of us the ship was still in chaos. The crew were pelting up and down in a panic, and the Breath of Life were huddled round Heppy as she sobbed.

'Heppy, please don't cry. It'll be all right. You just have to explain what you did to the police,' said Daniel. I watched him – his panic of earlier seemed to be almost gone. Was he *too* calm, I wondered? His sister had apparently just murdered his mother, after all.

'It was not your fault,' said Mr DeWitt solemnly. 'You didn't know what you were doing.'

'It was the gods!' cried Miss Doggett. I saw that she had her free hand on Miss Bartleby's shoulder, and as she said this she squeezed so tightly that Miss Bartleby flinched and gasped, tears starting in her eyes. 'It was punishment from the gods.'

'Absolute nonsense—' Daniel began, just as Mr Mansour marched onto the deck.

'Please! Everyone! Please! A word!' he said.

'Let's leave them to it,' whispered Daisy. 'Come on! To Mrs Miller's cabin!'

But we were stopped by the trembling figure of Mr Young, still in his pyjamas and dripping with nervous sweat.

'Boys!' he called in a shaking voice. 'Boys! Come here! It isn't safe! You must come with me!'

George groaned. 'He's such an annoyance,' he murmured to the rest of us. 'Here, hold on a moment, I'll deal with it. Mr Young! Mr Young, you need to get back in your cabin immediately.'

'What do you mean?' quavered Mr Young. 'I'm here to take care of you!'

'But it's you who are in danger,' said George, leaning forward confidentially. 'We've heard that Heppy killed Theodora *because of her knowledge of Egyptian history and myth.* The murder – why, it was committed by someone with intimate knowledge of Egyptian lore, that's clear enough – done because of Mrs Miller's connection to ancient Egypt! She was stabbed in the heart – and, as you know, the heart was most important to the ancient Egyptians in their afterlife. That proves that Heppy was punishing her mother for her connection to the pharaohs – and she is a danger to anyone who knows too much about ancient Egypt! She may seem subdued now, but you never know when she might strike again!'

'But – but—' Mr Young stammered.

'Of course, we're quite safe,' said George. 'We hardly know anything, do we? But you – why, you've studied it for years! The only thing you can do is keep your door locked until we arrive in Aswan.'

'But boys – I can't just leave you!'

'You must, sir, please. We're only thinking of you. We're going to look after the girls, and make sure they're safe—'

'Oh yes,' said Daisy, nodding. 'We're terrified. In fear. Helpless.'

I nudged her. This seemed to be laying it on a little too thick – but then I saw Mr Young's face. It was papery with terror.

'—but you can't risk being outside for a moment longer!'

'She doesn't look dangerous,' faltered Mr Young, peering along the deck at Heppy's slender figure.

'That's the trick she uses!' said George. 'It's always the most unhinged criminals who look the most ordinary. Please, sir – you must get inside!'

Mr Young nodded and fled. We heard his lock being turned, and something heavy being moved in front of the door. Alexander covered his mouth to stifle a laugh, and George winked at us. 'That's him dealt with,' he whispered. 'It'll take him ages to start to realize that what I said made absolutely no sense at all.'

'But are you sure?' I asked. 'That thing you said about the heart – what if it's right? That would help prove that only a member of the Breath of Life could have done it, wouldn't it?'

I saw Alexander look at me admiringly, and blushed.

'Not bad, Watson,' said Daisy. 'A very interesting thought! But now for the body! Hurry up, everyone, come on!'

We went rushing round the side of the ship, and down the port side. It was quiet here, doors left hanging open, curtains blowing in the slight breeze. The sky was hot yellow and pink, the sun just behind the tops of the trees.

But when we reached Theodora's cabin, number seven, and looked inside, it was quite empty. Only blooming halos of red left on the white undersheet and the pillow to show where the body had lain, scuffed footprints and kicked-aside furniture.

Theodora Miller's body was gone.

6

Daisy hissed. 'It's gone!' she cried. 'Those clodhoppers! How dare they move it before the police have even had a chance to examine the crime scene!'

'At least Mr Mansour is doing *something*,' George said. 'He's moved the body before it has a chance to heat up and spoil its evidence. That's rather better thinking than most of the English policemen we've met.'

'That is hardly relevant!' said Daisy, who hates to have the truth pointed out when it is inconvenient. 'You – we – oh bother!'

'Alex and I will go and look for the body,' said George. 'They'll have it downstairs in the cold-storage room, where the food is kept. You know they won't like it if you girls are wandering about on your own – but they won't worry as much about boys.'

From the look of pure annoyance on Daisy's face, she knew as well as I did that this was revenge for the trick she had played on the Pinkertons during our last investigation with them. 'Oh, all *right*!' she snapped at last. 'But take Amina. She can speak Arabic, after all. And Hazel and I will look at the crime scene. We'll move on to Mr DeWitt's in cabin nine and Miss Bartleby's in cabin eleven once we're done. If you get back in time, take a look at Heppy's in cabin one, Daniel's in cabin three, and Miss Doggett's in cabin five. Of course, if any of our suspects are in their cabins, exercise caution. Don't let them know what we're doing!'

'Wait,' said Amina. 'But can't I—'

'Detective Society President's rules,' said Daisy. 'Go on, go!'

I saw Amina's face as she followed the Pinkertons away – it was hurt and confused.

'Daisy!' I said. 'She wanted to stay with – er – us.'

'I have no time for that!' snapped Daisy. 'We have a murder to solve!'

I sighed. Daisy, I saw, was coping with her feelings as well as she ever did. 'All right,' I said. 'Let's look at the scene of the crime.'

We stood in the doorway, staring at the cabin in front of us. The door was opened outwards, and the white curtains that every cabin had behind its door, tinged a little pink from the rising sun, moved gently on their rail. There were a few smears of something dark on their edges, and I nudged Daisy. We both bent forward and peered at them. They were only little smudges, as though someone or something had brushed against them.

'D'you think this happened just now?' I asked. 'When they were moving the body?'

'No, it couldn't have!' said Daisy, reaching out delicately and tapping one of the marks. 'This blood is dry. It's been here for hours. It must have happened at the same time as the murder! Draw it, Hazel, draw it at once!'

She was back to being Daisy, I thought as I sketched, as though Amina had never existed. It always made me marvel, the way she could do that. No matter how interested in a case I am, I can never forget the other parts of my life.

Then we stepped into the crime scene itself, looking about at the damage done by the crew. The mattress of the bed was half off its frame, and there were dusty boot prints on the floor.

'Clodhoppers!' snarled Daisy. 'Moving the victim! Destroying evidence! What nonsense!'

'We are in Egypt, Daisy,' I said. 'It gets warm here so quickly – as soon as the sun's up. George was right – they did have to move the body. And they didn't exactly know we'd be coming to investigate, did they?'

'Well, they should have done. I suppose it's just lucky we saw the room earlier. There's the sheet, and the knife – oh, Hazel, they've left the knife! Look at the way it's been wiped – its blade is quite clean of blood. I suppose we can agree that it is the one used in the ritual last night?'

'Yes!' I said, kneeling to peer at it. 'Mr DeWitt was holding it, I remember, and then Mrs Miller took it away. So she must have brought it back to her room – wait, does that help Heppy or harm her case? After all, if it was already here, she might have just picked it up in her sleep.'

'I wonder if it has fingerprints on it?' asked Daisy. 'Here, there's a powder compact and brush on the side table. We can dust it for – oh!'

For the brush, as she shook powder over the knife's handle and twirled it expertly, revealed nothing at all. The handle was quite clean – smeared, as though it had been wiped, but with no prints whatsoever.

'There should have been at least four sets of prints on it, if it was Heppy sleepwalking!' I gasped. 'Mrs Miller's, Miss Bartleby's, Mr DeWitt's – and Heppy's. We saw Mrs Miller and Mr DeWitt holding it during their ritual last night. But someone's wiped them all off!'

'Which certainly does *not* seem like a thing someone would do in their sleep,' said Daisy, eyes shining with excitement. 'Now, Hazel, onto the next clue. Let us observe this discarded sheet on the floor. What can we say about it?'

We were both crouched down, heads together over the crumple of white. It had been kicked to the opposite side of the room to the bed, on the right of the door, and it was bundled up quite tightly. The drips and stains of brown blood across it made it stiff, resisting us as we carefully tried to pull it apart.

'There are cuts in it,' I said quietly. 'Look, there, there – and there again. Three stab wounds. It must have been tucked round Mrs Miller when the crime happened, just as we thought. How horrid!'

'Don't be a weakling, Hazel!' said Daisy, unmoved. Her nose was so close to the sheet that it was almost touching it, her eyes narrowed. The truth is that the body is always the worst part of an investigation for me. I hurt for the victims, so much so that my mind goes almost white with pain and I cannot act like a rational, calm detective. But Daisy can see even the worst gore and be unmoved.

'Hazel, look at this. What does it look like?'

I stared where she was pointing. 'Bloodstains,' I said.

'Hazel! Don't be silly or I shall replace you. Look *properly*!'

'You can't replace me!' I said. 'You couldn't detect without me!' But I looked again, and then I had it. 'Those stains look like – well, like drips.'

'Which is odd, isn't it?' asked Daisy, breathing carefully, still not looking at me. 'The blood has dripped in long, straight lines down the sheet. And I'm quite certain that scientific principles do not allow for long, straight drips on a sheet that has been crumpled on the floor in a heap.'

'So perhaps the sheet was on the bed, and the blood dripped down there,' I suggested – but I knew, as I said it, that this could not be right.

Daisy, as I had expected, looked at me with a withering glare.

'Nonsense, Hazel. Where on that bed there can you see drips down the side? Nowhere! The sides of the bed are quite clean. The blood remained on the *top* of the bed, soaking around the place the victim lay. So that means that at some point, quite soon after it was first stained, this sheet was not positioned like this. It was *hung up*. But where?'

I looked round the cabin. It had the same tidy white walls and small mirror as ours. The only difference was a small bathroom through a door behind the bed on the left-hand side.

'The bathroom?' I suggested. 'No! Daisy! Look!'

In turning back to Daisy, I had glanced beyond her, to the open door to the deck with its blowing curtains – and the curtain rail on which they hung. The rail was shiny brass, but marring that shine was a long, rusty smear.

'Blood!' hissed Daisy. 'Oh, Hazel, oh, Watson – that's it! When you combine the evidence of this sheet with the stains on the curtains, and the wiped knife – we have the beginnings of *proof* that this murder is no mere case of sleepwalking. Do sleepwalkers wipe their weapons and hang up sheets in the doorway to rooms? I think not!'

I suddenly saw it, and I was horrified. Hands carefully reaching up to hang a bloody sheet over an open doorway, and waiting – waiting – for a sleepwalker to blindly push her way through it and implicate herself in a crime she had never committed.

'Someone *did* frame Heppy!' I whispered. 'And we're on our way to proving it!'

7

'Yes!' cried Daisy. 'Exactly, Watson! Write it down, write it all down!'

I did, and I drew a plan of the room in this casebook with all of our clues carefully marked. I felt more and more certain that what we were facing was a truly wicked murderer. So many small things did not add up with what Heppy believed had happened – but, if we had not been here to notice them, they would already have been lost. All the Egyptian police would hear, once we docked in Aswan, was that a woman had been murdered, and the murderer had been her sleepwalking daughter.

'We ought to go,' I said, staring at the doorway anxiously. 'Mr Mansour is bound to send someone to guard the cabin soon.'

'Well, obviously, Watson,' said Daisy. 'Time is always of the essence, but in this case even more so. But before we leave this cabin we must make sure we have examined every inch of it. This may well be our last chance to look at the scene of the crime. I shall stay in here. I know you, Hazel – you won't look at a room properly if a dead body was in it recently. You can go into the bathroom, where it's less gory.'

This, of course, was Daisy at her most Daisyish – she loves to give orders, the more outrageous the better – but I did not complain.

I stepped through the little half-door into the bathroom. Theodora's cabin was one of the nicer ones, with not just a ewer and basin as in our room, but a proper bathroom. It had shelves for fat glass bottles of pills and tonics, her tooth mug with her toothbrush sitting in it, and a marble sink with gilded taps. And these taps, I saw, were smeared with rusty marks. The white sink itself was spattered with pale pink flecks, and there were prints of hasty fingers on the marble top.

Someone had washed blood off in this sink.

But I remembered Heppy's bloodstained hands, and I knew that these marks could not have been made by her. She had not washed herself at all. I got a prickle of real excitement. I knew then that we were on the right scent. *Someone else* had been in here, cleaning themselves in the sink.

'Daisy!' I cried. 'Daisy, come here!'

'Is it important, Hazel?'

'Yes! Quick!'

'It had better be,' grumbled Daisy, but when she stepped into the little bathroom space she gasped. 'Blood! Watson, this is fascinating! It means that—'

'That someone was here who wasn't Theodora or Heppy! I know! Daisy, this is additional evidence that the case is more complicated than it seems.'

'*Very* interesting,' whispered Daisy, peering deeply into the sink. 'This is excellent detective work, Watson. We have the evidence of the bloodstained sheet and curtain rail, and now the bloody basin. And, if you come with me, I believe I have discovered more things of note.'

She beckoned me back out into the main cabin, where she had been ferreting through the wardrobe and drawers.

'Luckily for us, Theodora was very organized, but terribly bad at hiding things. Look, her accounts book was tucked under her stockings.'

'Is she rich?' I asked.

'Oh, immensely, I should say. The amount of donations coming in from people who want to discover that they're really the reincarnation of ancient Egyptians! As far as I can tell, Theodora could have bought fifty houses if she'd wanted to. She's absolutely rolling in it. So that's a motive to kill her – which, at first, seems excellent for someone in her family, like Daniel or Heppy. But the interesting thing is who the accounts are registered to.

It's the Breath of Life account. Theodora is the only person authorized to draw money out – but there are *two* people who are also listed on the accounts, who will be able to access them now that Theodora's dead: Miss Doggett and Mr DeWitt. So—'

'—so they might be able to take all that money!'

'Well, technically, it's the society's money, but yes, there's no reason why Miss Doggett or Mr DeWitt couldn't now draw it all out and flee to Outer Mongolia. Which is very interesting, Hazel! It reveals a most excellent motive for them both – especially Miss Doggett, who as we've seen has expensive taste in clothes. Mr DeWitt's name was only recently added too – it's in different ink, much less faded. But that's not all. Look at this!'

Daisy brandished something at me, so enthusiastically that she hit me on the forehead with it.

'Ow!' I said, for the thing was heavy glass, as round as a stone, on the end of a chain.

'Hazel, your reflexes are still not what they ought to be,' said Daisy unrepentantly. 'Look at it!'

I looked, and recoiled. The round thing was a glass locket, very old-fashioned and rather dusty, and inside its clear glass dome was something that looked like – 'Fur?' I asked.

'Close enough,' said Daisy. 'It's *hair.*'

'How do you know?'

'Well, on the back of the locket it says *Alfred 7.5.1915 RIP* and *Gabriel 31.7.1917 RIP*. Now Alfred and Gabriel might be dogs or cats, of course, but it's rather more likely they're people, especially when you consider that these dates coincide with the sinking of the Lusitania and the Battle of Passchendaele. And don't you know about the disgusting habit old people have of taking hair from people they loved and keeping it? Horrid. It seems at least *likely* that Theodora lost two men who were important to her.'

'Poor Theodora!' I said. 'How awful for her!'

'Poor nothing!' said Daisy. 'She was an awful person – look how she treated everyone she was with before she died! If you ask me, it's not a surprise at all that someone's done away with her. Now I believe that we have discovered all we can from this cabin. Let us move on quickly before we're compromised.'

8

We stepped carefully out of Theodora's cabin, looking around to make sure we had not been seen. The deck was still clear, becoming brighter and brighter – but from cabin number eleven we heard the sound of sobbing. It was so lost and broken that it made my skin tingle with uneasiness.

'It's Miss Bartleby!' I whispered. 'It has to be!'

'An excellent opportunity!' Daisy whispered back.

'Daisy!' I said, but Daisy had already reached out her hand and knocked.

'Who is it?' asked Miss Bartleby's voice tremulously. 'Please, I want to be left alone!'

'I'm sorry, Miss Bartleby!' said Daisy, as charming as she can be. 'We only wanted to see if you were all right?'

'Quite all right! Oh, do leave me *alone*!'

She sounded so upset that I drew away from the door. 'We can't go in!' I whispered. 'She doesn't want to see us!'

'Watson!' hissed Daisy. 'Clearly we can't *listen* to her! She is one of our suspects, and she is also in a weakened emotional state. We need to observe her room, and observe her, and she is giving us the perfect opportunity to do that. Go on, go in!'

Daisy, of course, never does bother about people. To her, they are merely pieces moving about on a board where the only real players are she and I. I made a frantic face at her, for Miss Bartleby really did sound distraught – but she was already pushing me forward, opening the door, and I had no choice but to step into Miss Bartleby's cabin. There were no bloodstains that I could see, at least, although the room was untidy.

Miss Bartleby was curled up in a little heap on her bed, in her nightie, a handkerchief draped over her face, howling.

'Oh dear!' cried Daisy, all sympathy. 'Whatever's the matter!'

'Please!' sobbed Miss Bartleby. 'Oh, do please go away!'

'But we heard you crying,' I said. 'We wanted to make sure you were all right.'

And I really was worried. Miss Bartleby looked so harmless, so upset. But I knew Daisy wanted me to take my true feelings and use them to trap her further, trick her into saying anything that might help us shine light on this case. I reminded myself sternly that Miss Bartleby might be the murderer.

'Please go away!' gasped Miss Bartleby again. 'Death! Death, everywhere!'

I glanced around, and Daisy elbowed me crossly. 'Not *literally*!' she said under her breath. 'Bear up, Hazel!'

'I'm so sorry, Miss Bartleby,' I said.

'*I'm* sorry!' Miss Bartleby said. 'I – I ought to be ashamed of myself. That's what she said. I ought to pay more attention, only I can't.'

This seemed to be rather sideways to the matter at hand. Daisy and I exchanged a quick, confused glance.

'Do you mean about the objects for the ritual?' Daisy asked.

'Did I forget them?' asked Miss Bartleby. 'I didn't mean to!'

'I – er – well – you helped Mrs Miller to bed last night, didn't you?' asked Daisy, trying not to look bewildered.

'Yes, I do that,' said Miss Bartleby. 'Dear Theodora lets me serve her. Such a thrill. I help put on her night things, and tuck her tightly into bed just as she likes. She tells me that, if I continue my good work, she may be able to tell me my reincarnation soon. She says it may even be – so exciting – *Queen Nefertiti*.'

'But—' I began. We knew perfectly well that Miss Bartleby had been confirmed as Nefertiti already.

Daisy's fingers closed over my wrist.

Miss Bartleby's eyes clouded. 'But what are *you* doing here? Where's Joshua? What's happened?'

'Miss Bartleby,' I said, pulling my hand out of Daisy's grasp, 'Joshua isn't here. It's Mrs Miller. Something's happened to her.'

Miss Bartleby flinched. 'No!' she gasped. 'No, surely not!'

'I'm afraid it's true,' said Daisy. 'She was found dead this morning.'

'Oh no!' said Miss Bartleby. 'It's happening again! I can't stop it!'

'Stop what?' I asked.

Miss Bartleby sat up and fixed her eyes on me. 'Things keep on *going missing*, you see. Sometimes I put things down, and they're not there when I turn to pick them up. Sometimes my mornings go missing, and it's two afternoons in a row. Or people – they move about, and it's all wrong somehow. Like – like you. Are you new members? Do I know you?'

'We're Miss Wells and Miss Wong,' I said. 'We're on this ship with you.'

'A ship? No, that can't be,' said Miss Bartleby. 'We're in Humbleby, dear, at home.'

Then I saw her eyes change. She leaped off her bed. 'What are you doing here?' she cried. 'Who let you in? Help! Help!'

'Miss Bartleby!' protested Daisy, staggering backwards as Miss Bartleby charged at us, shrieking. She was tiny, even shorter than me, but in her current state she was quite alarming. 'Miss Bartleby! OW!'

'We're leaving, aren't we, Daisy?' I said. 'We're so sorry, Miss Bartleby – we only wanted to help.'

'HELP!' shouted Miss Bartleby. 'You wanted no such thing! Get out! Get out!'

Daisy lunged at me and, clinging together, we backed out of the cabin and closed its door behind us. We gripped each other for a moment longer, staring at each other in shock. Things on the *Hatshepsut*, I thought, were getting odder and odder every moment.

9

And we were still reeling from the strangeness of the encounter when we walked straight into another alarming scene. Miss Doggett was standing at the end of the row of cabins with her back to us, beside the cane chairs and potted plants where I had found May. Her arms were outspread towards the Nile river and her eyes were closed, her face tipped back. Her gold-embroidered bathrobe was still tied tightly round her waist.

She did not look like someone at all concerned with what had just been discovered – although, I thought, sometimes people do hide their grief. She seemed to be quite in a trance – but, when she heard the sound of our footsteps, her eyelids flew open and she spun round and glared at us. We both froze.

'*Good* morning,' said Daisy, recovering as quick as a blink, and oozing politeness.

'I'm sorry for your loss,' I added, trying to be charitable.

'Loss?' said Miss Doggett, closing her eyes. She spoke in a strangely deep voice that I had never heard before, as though she was pushing it down into her chest. 'There is no loss. The Breath of Life teaches that there is no true death. The ba flies out of the dying body in the shape of a bird, and it can settle into another when it finds a true heart. Theodora's imperfect body may be gone, but the great spirit of Hatshepsut is already in flight, seeking another body to inhabit with the rising of the sun.'

'Will Hatshepsut land soon, then?' said Daisy, nudging me at this mention of hearts.

Miss Doggett's eyes flew open again. 'That is not for you to know!' she cried. 'It is only for society members to learn.'

'Oh, I see,' said Daisy. Then she took my arm and began to pull me past Miss Doggett, so that she was forced to turn sideways to look at us. I could not think what Daisy was doing – until there was movement to my left and I caught a flicker of blond hair ducking out of one of the cabins and then back in again.

George, Alexander and Amina, I thought – and I knew that Daisy and I had to work to make sure that Miss Doggett did not notice what was happening.

'But – but could it be anyone?' I asked. 'How is the, er, body chosen?'

'Again, that is not a question to ask!' said Miss Doggett, annoyed. 'These are mysteries, girls, deep mysteries that cannot be revealed to simply anyone.'

'But what if *we're* reincarnations of someone?' asked Daisy, still shuffling round so that Miss Doggett had to spin after us. We had almost got her turned all the way round, with her back to the cabins – and, as I watched, I saw Alexander edge carefully out of one, George creeping behind him. 'What if I had – er – Queen Elizabeth's ba in me – or Boadicea's?'

'It's quite clear that—' Miss Doggett began, and then a red ray of sun rose up above the trees and caught the top of Daisy and Miss Doggett's heads, lighting them like fire.

Daisy said, 'OH!' and stumbled forward, as though she had been dazzled by it. She brushed against Miss Doggett, knocking the tie of her bathrobe loose.

Miss Doggett made a hissing noise like a teakettle and staggered backwards, thankfully no longer interested in the deck behind her.

'Clumsy girl!' she cried.

I looked over her shoulder, and saw the door to the next cabin closing gently. The boys and Amina were safe.

'Terribly sorry,' I said, reaching out for Daisy's elbow and tucking my arm through it. 'We'll go. Come on, Daisy.'

'It's supposed to be me who says that to you!' said Daisy as we trotted away towards the starboard side. 'And you're trembling, Hazel! Goodness, it's all right. The others are safe, if you're worried about that.'

'It wasn't the others!' I said. And it was not. It was Miss Doggett. It had been such a strange little encounter, but somehow it felt quite enormous and unsettling.

'Oh, do calm down!' hissed Daisy. 'Good heavens, Hazel, who's *this* now? Another suspect!'

A figure was hovering just round the corner of the starboard side. I saw his cane, upraised, and the glint of metallic greenish gold on his head in the sunlight, and knew that this was Mr DeWitt.

'Good morning!' I said, and Mr DeWitt jumped.

'Hello – er – young ladies,' he said. 'What are you doing here? Shouldn't you be in your cabin? I was – er – just keeping an eye on Miss Doggett. What's she up to?'

He gestured towards Miss Doggett, who had her eyes closed once more and had turned back towards the rising sun.

'Er,' I said, 'I'm not sure. She said some things about Mrs Miller's spirit – er – her ma?'

'Her ba, you mean. She thinks Hatshepsut is going to rise again in *her*!' said Mr DeWitt with a snort. 'That woman understands *nothing* about the niceties of reincarnation. She's got quite the wrong kind of personality to be Hatshepsut. She's a natural

Cleopatra – although I guess it's in Cleopatra's nature to be dissatisfied with her lot.'

That was the oddest thing about the Breath of Life – the way they would say things in such an ordinary tone. Mr DeWitt might have been talking about his next-door neighbours instead of two long-dead pharaohs.

'If you ask me,' said Mr DeWitt, still staring at Miss Doggett, 'that woman is not just useless, she's a danger!'

'Oh!' I said, shocked.

'She only has herself to blame if she's feeling shut out. She was a useless second in command, always pinching society money to buy herself clothes and hoping Theodora wouldn't realize – I'm already turning the fortunes of the society around, and she's furious about that.'

Mr DeWitt seemed hardly to notice we were there, so wrapped up was he in his own thoughts. 'Well,' he went on, 'I think that's one of the first things I'll do. Get rid of Ida. Oh, things will change around here.'

I tried not to shudder. I could smell Mr DeWitt under his cologne, sour and slightly off, and I could see the gold caps on his back teeth as he talked.

'Do excuse me, ladies, I must go to my room.'

He bowed to us both and hurried away to his cabin, his cane tapping on the floor.

Daisy and I looked at each other.

'Bother!' said Daisy. 'Now we've missed the chance to check his room for clues.'

'But, Daisy – wasn't that awful!'

'Everyone on this ship is quite mad,' said Daisy. 'Quite mad, Hazel! I believe either of those two could have done it. And – wait, who's that?'

10

The sun had come up fully by now, and was floating hot and yellow just above the trees. The day was beginning to get warm, but the heart-rending sobs coming from the other end of the saloon deck made me shiver.

Miss Doggett, still wrapped in her bright bathrobe, turned and hurried away towards the noise, and Daisy, eyes wide with excitement, grabbed my hand and towed me after her. Mr DeWitt, I noticed, pointedly went on towards his cabin.

I remembered the screams this morning, and my feet stumbled against the boards of the deck, but Daisy's grip was firm and sharp, and before I could do anything much we were on the scene.

Daniel was standing at the top of the stairs on the starboard side, his arm round Heppy, who was weeping, her rusty hands up against her face, so her cheeks were becoming more and more smeared with blood. 'Ruining evidence!' hissed Daisy.

Next to Daniel and Heppy was Mr Mansour, one foot on the second step of the stairs. He had an extremely determined look on his face, his suit jacket absolutely impeccable, although his hair was not quite combed.

'Sir,' he was saying. 'Mr Miller. Please.'

'See here, you can't do this to her!' Daniel snapped. 'Look at her! She's terrified!'

'Sir, if you please – there has been a crime—'

'You simply don't understand! She doesn't know what she did, poor girl. Heppy's always been mentally delicate, and cooped up with our mother and her hideous group she was bound to come to grief. I should have got her out sooner!'

Heppy's shoulders shook. 'I'm so sorry!' she wailed. 'Oh, poor Mother!'

I felt a pang of pity. Heppy reminded me more and more of our friend Beanie. She was so upset, and she seemed so helpless. I knew we had to save her.

But Mr Mansour cleared his throat and said, in a tone of voice that told me that he had said it at least five times before, 'Sir, madam, if a crime has been committed, it is my duty to take the suspect into custody and keep them there until we reach the nearest town. Miss Miller, you cannot remain in your cabin, and you cannot bathe until the police have taken your picture. I will make you comfortable in a cabin on the lower deck, and you will be entirely safe there. I will have one of my men guarding you at all times until we reach Aswan, where you will give your statement. I trust that this matter will be cleared up soon, but you must see that I cannot allow you to wander about the ship. I have the other passengers to think of. There is breakfast to serve. The ship must sail. *Please.*'

Aswan! I thought. So Amina was right!

'Mr Mansour, Heppy is no danger to anyone! Look at her, man! This is barbarous!'

'On the contrary, our police service is very advanced,' said Mr Mansour, bristling a little. 'As good as anything you'll find in England, as you'll see when we reach Aswan. Now please let me take Miss Miller to her new quarters.'

'Daniel,' gasped Heppy, and she seemed to be trying to pull herself together. 'Let him. Please. It'll only be for a few hours. And – and I can't be trusted.'

'Nonsense!' said Daniel. 'You know you're not a danger.'

'Oh, this is infuriating!' whispered Daisy in my ear. 'I thought Mr Mansour would be a clodhopper, but it's worse – he seems quite competent! If he has Heppy locked up, we shan't be able to get in to see her easily. And we still need to question her!'

'But isn't it good that he's trying to preserve evidence?' I asked.

'Humph!' said Daisy, the crease appearing at the top of her nose.

I rather thought that she was jealous. I felt quite impressed by Mr Mansour. I could see how shaken he was – after all, unlike us he was not used to dealing with dead bodies – but he was not giving in to it. He turned to us and Miss Doggett.

'Ladies,' he said. 'I apologize unreservedly for this. Once I have conveyed Miss Miller to her temporary quarters, I will be on the upper deck, should any of our honoured guests wish to express their displeasure and ask questions. But I would advise that everyone return to their cabins immediately. I will arrange service of breakfast to your rooms, so you will not need to venture out. Again, I do apologize unreservedly on behalf of the owners of the *Hatshepsut* for this terrible event. A death of this nature has not happened in the twenty years I have been working on this ship.'

And we all stood watching as he led Heppy downstairs.

11

'*Psst!*' said a voice.

We turned and saw that George, Amina and Alexander were gesturing to us from the port side of the ship.

'*Come on!*' mouthed George. '*Come here!*'

We scurried round the side of the ship, out of Miss Doggett's view.

'Thanks for helping us earlier,' George said, as soon as we were standing with them, squinting in the sun. 'She nearly saw us! Did you manage to get into Theodora's cabin?'

'Obviously,' said Daisy. 'And we found some brilliant things.'

'So did we,' said George, shrugging.

'I bet it won't be as good as what Hazel and I found, though.'

'Bet you it will.' They glared at each other, chins high.

'Have you been in all of the cabins yet?' I asked. 'Mr Mansour's going to start going round and getting everyone back into their cabins as soon as he's put away Heppy – so shall we finish up investigating rooms, or would you prefer to keep staring at each other?'

'Hazel Wong!' said George, laughing and turning away from Daisy. 'All right, you win. We've been in Heppy's, and Daniel's, but not Miss Doggett's.'

Daisy raised an eyebrow.

'We couldn't!' said Alexander. 'You saw – she nearly caught us.'

'*Good grief*,' said Daisy, squinting at him like a cross cat. '*Well*. We had better go and look at it, then.'

'I don't know why you're upset!' I whispered to her as we padded across the warming boards of the deck towards Miss Doggett's cabin. 'She's an excellent suspect! Aren't you pleased that we get to search her cabin?'

'Of course,' Daisy whispered back. 'It's the *principle* of the thing, Hazel. It doesn't do to be too excited.'

We were all rather shocked to realize, when we pulled open Miss Doggett's cabin door, that Miss Beauvais was still in it, lying propped up wanly on the scarf-draped bed. She was the sort of person you forget about – and obviously no one had remembered she was there.

She struggled up onto her elbows, a look of alarm crossing her face. 'Amina, what are you doing here?' she gasped. 'I'm quite comfortable here, really. I shall go back to my cabin in a bit.'

I wondered then whether Miss Beauvais had been rather enjoying being forgotten about.

'I've come to look after you, of course,' said Amina cheerfully. From Miss Beauvais' face, I could tell she thought that idea was nightmarish.

'Really, no, that won't be necessary,' she said in French. 'I'm feeling much better. I only wanted to rest here a little while.'

'I'll take you back to your cabin,' said Amina. 'Come on. Really, I promise I don't have any mice in my pocket this time—'

'*Amina!*' I said, and Amina looked guiltily pleased with herself.

'Hey, I can take you, Miss,' said Alexander, catching my eye. Miss Beauvais sagged with relief.

'Oh yes, an excellent idea!' she cried, and leaned on Alexander as she stumbled out of the cabin.

The sound of their voices receded, and the four of us looked at each other.

'If Miss Doggett comes in,' said George in a low voice, 'we'll just say we came in here to get Miss Beauvais and now we're tidying up after her. All right? Now this is a Pinkerton investigation, so we'll take the room as Alex and I would usually. Hazel, you look under the bed and on the floor; Amina, look at the bed and wardrobe itself; I'll search on the desk; and, Daisy, you investigate the top of the wardrobe. All right?'

I looked at Daisy warningly, and she gritted out, 'All *right*!'

As the search began, I got down on my hands and knees and shone my torch about under the bed to see what I could find. It was chaos – sandy shoes, loose earrings, bits of bunched-up waste paper and a black case that I pulled open to find full of heavy dark books. They smelled of dust and crumbling pages. I sneezed.

'More books?' asked George from above me. I backed out from under the bed to find him staring down at me, a fat, leather-bound book in his hand. 'The desk's full of them. They're – well, a lot of them are hieroglyphic, I think, but there's Greek too, and Latin—'

'Here, let me see that!' said Amina. She bent her head to the book in George's hand, pushing back her long hair, and then she looked up again in indignation.

'I know what this is!' she said. 'It's – it's the – well, I didn't understand what they were saying about that Book of Life thing before, but now I see it. They've made a *horrible* mistranslation of the Book of Going Forth by Day.'

My skin tingled. 'Oh!' said George. 'Right!'

'What's that?' I asked.

'It's – well, it's lots of spells to help ancient Egyptians avoid the gods and demons that they thought were waiting for them in the afterlife. It's nothing to do with recording silly little things you've done wrong in your life at all, but of course they don't understand that! That's what all of these books are.'

'Yes, but why has she got so many copies, then?' asked George. 'And look – she's written notes all over this one.'

Amina took the book from him and began to look through it, and her face scrunched up in disgust. 'Different copies have different spells,' she said. 'All right, all these notes are about shabtis. They're – ancient Egyptian servant-people, little figures that are buried in tombs to do the work of one particular dead person in the afterlife. They have a spell on them to make them do everything their master needs, and that's the one she's looking at. Miss Doggett's translation's bad, but this is definitely the shabti spell, written out over and over again. And she's put in – hah, she's put in her own name as the master. Really! She's got the whole thing absolutely mixed up. This is – nonsense, not ancient Egyptian at all. It's more like voodoo from a story. And those hieroglyphs are all wrong too. They say *Edo Hoggett*, not *Ida Doggett*!'

'*The Shabti Figure replieth: I will do it, verily I am here when thou callest*,' said George, reading over her shoulder. 'What a silly translation!'

'Ugh!' I said. 'But what does it all mean? Daisy, come down from the wardrobe and look at this!'

'HAH!' said Daisy suddenly. She had been balancing on Miss Doggett's chair, reaching up high for something at the very back of the wardrobe. Now she spun round and jumped off the chair with a thump, holding whatever it was aloft. 'Look at this! It seems she was practising her spells on the members of the Breath of Life!'

I got up and looked – and gasped. Daisy was holding yet another scarf that had been wrapped round a set of little dolls, each covered with embroidery. I thought they were only toys at first, until I saw that there was a little fat one with white hair, a tall gawky one with curly hair, a wrinkly one with flaxen hair and a cane . . . and a doll with an impressive bosom and a furious expression on its face – and three pins stuck into its soft doll throat and heart.

12

'They're embroidered with the hieroglyphs from the books!' whispered Amina. 'They – she's using them as her nonsense shabtis! *Oh!*'

As we all stood, gasping from Daisy's discovery, we heard a querulous voice from out on deck. 'Boys!' Mr Young was crying from somewhere nearby. 'Boys! Where are you? *Boys!*'

'I thought he was in his room! *Whose* idea was it to bring him?' asked Daisy crossly.

'He was supposed to be!' said George. 'I thought he'd be there for hours. Here – you hide, and I'll go out and head him off.'

'All right,' said Daisy, nodding. 'Meet back in our cabin as soon as you can get away. We need to have a detective meeting while the facts are still fresh in our minds! And you still haven't told us what you found out about the body. That's crucial!'

'Back as soon as I can,' said George briefly. 'He shouldn't be too difficult to subdue – but hide until you hear us go. If he sees you in here, he'll kick up a stink.'

He ducked out of Miss Doggett's cabin door, and Daisy, Amina and I all bundled into her little wardrobe. Inside it was stuffy and close, almost suffocating, not helped by the fact that Daisy had her hand across my mouth. I breathed through my nose and tried not to cough or think about the time that Daisy and I had been stuck inside à Hong Kong wardrobe, peering out at an even more awful scene.

Amina giggled, and Daisy said, 'Hush, Amina! Don't pinch me!'

Then I felt even more awkward. We had come a long way since Deepdean airing cupboards, I thought.

The voices outside tailed off, and Daisy said, 'Come on! To our cabin!'

Amina took her hand laughingly and towed Daisy out into the cabin. As she followed, Daisy looked back at me, blushing, and I shrugged at her. I did not want to be Daisyish about this. I liked Amina. But all the same – it was an odd new feeling, seeing my best friend bowled over by someone who was not me. I did not entirely enjoy it. Martita had been quite different. There had been no chance of her ever noticing Daisy, not like that. But Amina . . . thinking about it gave me an uncomfortable headache. It all seemed impossibly grown-up.

Daisy would hate me to write that – she would hate me to say any of this – but Daisy is not here to lean over my page and correct my writing as I go. I am still struggling with that. I keep imagining her behind me, but when I turn round there is no one there at all. The room feels very empty, and that is still strange. I never really thought that she might not be with me one day. Daisy always seemed as permanent as myself.

Of course, I have been reminded now that everything changes, and there is really no such thing as solid ground.

But in the cabin that day I did not understand that yet. All I was worried about was the case. I could feel the engine beneath me, and the ship's paddles turning as we set off after the night's pause. We were on our way to Aswan. Time to prove Heppy's innocence was slipping away from us.

PART FOUR

TAKEN AT THE FLOOD

1

When we got back to our cabin, Daisy was jumpy and unlike herself. She kept looking at Amina and twitching away again, catlike.

It was on the tip of my tongue to ask her what on earth was wrong with her, but that was simply too cruel. After all, I knew exactly what it was. We all three stood in rather awkward silence – until the boys came bursting in.

'Ah, *there* you are!' said George artificially. 'Mr Young! We've found them!'

'In our own cabin,' said Daisy, raising an eyebrow. 'How surprising.'

Mr Young stuck his silly, perspiring head round the door. 'Girls!' he cried. 'You're safe! Thank goodness.'

'Are you *our* tutor now?' asked Daisy rudely.

'Miss Wong's father has asked me to help in this time of need,' said Mr Young – which I knew perfectly well was a lie. My father couldn't stand Mr Young any more than we could. 'Now, girls, can I trust you to stay here for a while? Mr Mansour is bringing breakfast round to everyone's cabins, and I suggested to him that you could all take it in here. The boys will look after you.'

'Aren't they *brave*!' said Daisy, still sharp. I elbowed her. 'But what about *you*?'

'I will – er – go back to my own cabin,' said Mr Young. 'It's not safe to be out. Please lock your door once I'm gone, and stay alert. Is that understood?'

'Perfectly, Mr Young,' said George. 'We'll look after the girls. You ought to look in on Miss Beauvais too – Alex escorted her back to her cabin just now, and she's still a bit weak.'

'Good, good, of course,' said Mr Young and, with a haunted glance around him, he withdrew and we heard his feet pattering away.

We waited, and then—

'Hah!' said Daisy. 'I should say you did too good a job of finding yourselves a fool tutor!'

'I know,' said Alexander gloomily. 'At least he didn't lock *us* in!'

'He's too afraid,' said George with a snort. 'He still half believes that Heppy will get out of the cabin she's being held in and kill him for knowing too much about ancient Egypt. He only came out of his room because Mr Mansour unlocked it and tried to give him breakfast. He asked where we were, and Mr Young had to pretend to be taking care of us and go and look.'

I realized then that I was starving hungry – we had woken just after six, and it was past eight now. I imagined crisp pastries, sweet fruits, halwa and honey and dates. I swallowed.

'We can't stop for food!' snapped Daisy – but, when Mr Mansour knocked a moment later and ushered in white-clad servers carrying sweet-smelling trays, piled high, none of the rest of us complained. Even Daisy knows perfectly well that we need bunbreak to help us solve our cases, so she sighed and gestured at our little table. Soon we were munching away.

'What next?' asked Amina, wiping her mouth delicately.

'Detective meeting, of course. Hazel, get out your casebook again. We have plenty to add to it since we spoke last. Body first, if you please. What did the three of you find out?'

'Well, we got into the cold room where it's being kept. And Alexander nearly fainted,' said Amina with a twinkle.

'I don't know why you guys didn't!' said Alexander. 'You're monsters. Go on, George, I can't.'

'Two deep stab wounds around her heart, and one up near her neck, which accounts for most of the blood,' said George. 'She would have died very quickly. We knew she was stabbed already, but *where* she was stabbed is interesting. It's hard to stab someone's heart, you know – all those ribs. Hazel, you're right that it points to a murderer who cared about getting her in the heart, someone from the Breath of Life. And I don't think they could have been so precise in their sleep, either. Another point to back up our theory.

'Apart from those three wounds, there aren't any others. No cuts on her hands or arms. But there was something that we almost missed at first.'

'What?' I asked.

'Bruising,' said George. Alexander made a face. 'On her shoulders and arms, as though someone had leaned against her. And – tell them, Alex.'

'We think they held a pillow over her face,' said Alexander.

'Why do you think that?' asked Daisy, rather scornfully.

'We found a feather on her eyelash,' said Alexander. 'A tiny one, but we think it came from a pillow.'

'Oh,' said Daisy.

'It seems most likely, under the circumstances,' said George, smirking at Daisy. 'Don't you think? There was blood on the pillow in her room, wasn't there? Perhaps that was the one used. Anyway, none of that evidence – that someone covered her mouth with a pillow to keep her quiet, and leaned on her to keep her still – fits with a sleepwalking murder. Go on, Alex, say what you said to me.'

'You know when you're dreaming, and you think you're running, or yelling – and then you wake up and all you did was kick off your sheets and mumble a bit?' asked Alexander, waving his hands expressively.

'Mumble!' said George. 'You've never mumbled in your sleep. You do laugh, though.'

'I have funny dreams! All right, George, *you're* the one who mumbles. I was trying to be nice to you. All I'm saying is, imagine leaning on someone's chest while you hold a pillow over their face with one hand and stab them with the other *in your sleep*. There's no way!'

'We don't know if it's impossible until we try it,' said Daisy. 'Which reminds me, we need to do a reconstruction after this. But – well, good work, I suppose. Though I ought to have been there.'

She glared at George unlovingly.

'Well, you weren't,' said George. 'And you wouldn't have seen any more! The body helps rule out Heppy, and we'll say it to anyone who asks. Add that to what we saw at the crime scene—'

'It doesn't make any sense!' said Alexander firmly. 'I mean, maybe you could argue that Heppy was trying to clean up, not very well – that she automatically wiped off the knife – but—'

'—but it's not very likely,' said George. 'It makes far more sense to assume that the person who wiped the knife was very much awake, and very much not Heppy.'

My breath caught in my throat. Suddenly I wondered whether Mr Young's fear was quite sensible, after all. 'And there's something else,' I said. I told them about what Daisy and I had found at the crime scene. 'We know Heppy didn't wash her hands, because they're still bloody. So we have to assume that the murderer was the one who washed up in the sink after they'd hung up the sheet – silly of them, as it makes Heppy's framing less perfect. But, if they did that, they couldn't have gone through the doorway while the sheet was hanging up, otherwise they'd get bloody all over again. So what if the murderer waited there for her? What if – they did all the things you said, and then stayed there to wait until they'd seen Heppy sleepwalk into Mrs Miller's room and out again?'

I had a terrible, looming image in my head – of a dark figure, standing in silence and watching Heppy push aside the bloody sheet, in her dream imagining it as nothing more than the curtains of the cabin.

Alexander looked sickened.

'It does make sense,' said George. 'That way, they could make sure that Heppy walked into their trap!'

2

'All right, now suspects,' said Daisy. 'What have we discovered about our five possible murderers?'

'Four, right?' asked Alexander. 'We just said that the evidence we've found rules Heppy out!'

'*Five*,' said Daisy severely. 'Yes, we believe that Heppy was framed, and the evidence of the corpse helps, but until she is absolutely ruled out we must keep her on the list. Anything else would not be rigorous. We have to be able to prove to these Parquet people that she didn't do it. Our evidence must be watertight. So – go on. Heppy, Daniel, Miss Doggett, Miss Bartleby and Mr DeWitt. We've told you about the crime scene, but what else have you learned?'

'Well, there's what we found in Heppy's room. Tell them, George.'

'First off, the bed's all disarranged and bloody – it looks as though someone with blood all over them had climbed into bed and gone to sleep. That doesn't prove anything much, of course, apart from what we know is true – that Heppy went into Mrs Miller's room some time in the night and got blood on her, before going back to bed.'

'Then we found her Book!' said Alexander excitedly.

'There wasn't much else to find!' agreed George. 'She's got hardly any clothes in her wardrobe, and the ones she does have are odd sizes. I think she's been given the cast-offs from the other society women. Another reason for her to be resentful! She dresses like an old woman, doesn't she?'

'Hah, she does!' said Amina. 'I was wondering why.'

'So, the Book,' Alexander cut in. 'It's – look, it's just awful. I didn't have much time, but I copied down all the entries I could in shorthand. Here, I'll read from it.'

He flicked his notebook open, cleared his throat and began to read. I was expecting something a little like a diary, but what we heard was much more odd and frightening than that.

December 2nd, 1936

I got up in my sleep and went into Theodora's room

I ate an apple too loudly

I sneezed during morning service

I did not button my cardigan correctly
I made a face that was impolite
I left the window open
I forgot to collect the sheets for washing
I wrote untidily
Signed: Hephzibah Miller
Witnessed: Ida Doggett. Eight black marks to be entered into
    the Book.

December 3rd, 1936
I got up in my sleep and went into Theodora's room again
I moved too quickly and tripped over my skirt
I failed to listen to Theodora
I coughed and frightened Miss Bartleby
I—

'Oh, stop!' I said, and Alexander, looking extremely relieved, stopped and closed his notebook with a sharp snap, as though the words might escape if he did not. 'Horrible! Poor Heppy! I'm not surprised she's so upset all the time.'

'It's awful,' said Alexander, looking as horrified as I felt. 'Whenever someone in the society does something bad, they note it down, and then Miss Doggett collects all the marks in the Book.'

'Yes, yes, very sad, but this shows the pattern Heppy's sleepwalking took!' said Daisy, leaning her chin on my shoulder in her excitement. Every time she spoke, it dug into me.

'Ow, Daisy,' I said. 'You're right, though. What we saw the night before last – this proves it really was a pattern.'

I spoke casually, but I still felt sickened. Listing all of her flaws – some of them so small – seemed dreadfully cruel. No wonder Heppy walked in her sleep. And I had another stab of worry. The blood, and now this Book. It all seemed to point back to where we had begun, to the simplest and most dreadful solution to the crime: that it really had been a tragic accident, and poor Heppy was to blame. She had been pushed too far.

'A pattern someone else could use,' said Alexander gently. I looked up and saw him watching me. Had he realized what I was worrying about?

'Indeed!' said Daisy. 'And we must work out who.'

3

'Let's take Daniel next, as he's got the next cabin along. What do we know about him? We all witnessed him arguing with Theodora last night, so we know that things are not well between them. He's her son, but he's been estranged from her – did he come back with good intentions, or with murder on his mind?'

'We know something about that too,' said George. 'Daniel's cabin is full of *extremely* interesting papers – he's writing a book exposing the Breath of Life as an evil cult.'

I gasped.

'Not really!' said Daisy.

'Absolutely!' said Alexander. 'We read it – I mean, skimmed through it. He's left the manuscript all piled up on his desk, so he obviously isn't worried about someone finding it. Or maybe he even wants them to! It would make sense with what Daniel said last night. The

Breath of Life sounds awful. Theodora doesn't let any member keep ordinary family connections – that's why she hates it when Daniel and Heppy call her Mother. And Theodora's a fraud too: apparently, she breathes into bottles and sells them for bags of cash, saying they'll help you connect with your past lives.'

'Imagine thinking that's true!' said George, grinning. 'Haven't they done any science lessons?'

'Grown-ups are hopeless,' said Daisy. 'I think we've proved that by now. What else? I can tell there's something – you're buzzing with it *most* annoyingly.'

'There is!' said Alexander. 'It's *wizard*. There's a chapter about Daniel's friend Joshua Morse.'

Joshua again! He seemed to be running through this case, almost like one of the characters in it, even though he was dead before we met him.

'It was a few years ago,' Alexander went on. 'He and Daniel were the same age and met in the army, and once the war was over Joshua came back to meet Daniel's family. He got swept up by the Breath of Life – it sounds like they both did, even though Daniel wants to pretend he wasn't ever tricked properly – and they were at its heart for years. Joshua was rich, and his parents were dead, so he gave pots of money to the society, especially once Theodora decided that he was the reincarnation of Tutankhamun.'

'They bled him dry!' said George.

'Anyway, it made Daniel uncomfortable to watch – and I wonder whether it upset him that Joshua was Tutankhamun and not him, even though he never says it. He started trying to make Joshua leave. Joshua wouldn't hear of it for ages, but finally he saw sense, and agreed. They packed their bags and headed for London. And the day after they got there—'

'Joshua died,' cut in George. 'He was only twenty-seven, and he'd always been healthy, so it makes no sense at all. Apparently, he got sick, and the doctors thought it was food poisoning.'

'Food poisoning!' said Daisy. 'Hah! We've seen *that* before, haven't we! *Arsenic* poisoning, more like.'

'That's what I thought,' said Alexander, nodding. 'It fits, doesn't it? And Daniel thought so too.'

'The whole book's about it, really!' George put in. 'Daniel's obsessed with the idea that Theodora ordered Joshua's murder because she wanted all the rest of his money. He left it to the society in his will – a will she helped him make. Daniel thinks that *he* was meant to have been poisoned too, only he was too suspicious to eat any of the going-away meal that the society – and more specifically *Miss Bartleby* – prepared for them. I know Daniel said that he was here for a family reunion, but he's obviously lying. He's here to spy on Theodora, and prove what happened to his friend Joshua.'

'And he decided to take matters into his own hands!' said Daisy.

She was swept up with enthusiasm, but I frowned. I was not so sure.

'Why wouldn't Daniel want to take the evidence to the police?' I asked. 'Why kill Theodora before he proved anything – especially if it was Miss Bartleby who actually cooked the food? And why frame his own sister too?'

'But he thinks Mrs Miller ordered Joshua's death!' said Alexander. 'So he blames her for it. And I know he's acting nice to Heppy, but what if he blames her for not leaving with him? What if he wants to punish her as well as his mother?'

'Excellent point,' said Daisy, rather regretfully – it always annoys her when Alexander says something clever. 'But we're getting ahead of ourselves. Yes, we must find out exactly what happened to this Joshua person, and whether Miss Bartleby, and therefore Mrs Miller, is behind it – but first we must consider our other suspects.'

4

'Miss Doggett's really suspicious,' said Alexander. 'That creepy comment about the gods punishing Theodora! She was arguing with Theodora last night; she's angry that Mr DeWitt has become such a big part of the society; she's jealous that Theodora is Hatshepsut; May overheard her threatening Miss Bartleby; she has expensive taste in clothes and she has a doll that looks like Theodora in her room with pins through it.'

'And she thinks that she can use black magic!' said Amina scoffingly. 'It's so stupid!'

'Yes, but she believes in it!' said Alexander. 'I guess you might kill for something you believe in that much. And she thinks she can control the other members of the Breath of Life – at least, I guess that's what the spell means.'

Daisy had gone quiet. I looked over at her and saw her practically crackling with energy. 'What is it, Daisy?' I asked.

'Oh, nothing much,' said Daisy. 'Except that I know a very important thing.'

'Would you like to share it with us?' asked George. 'Or would you rather keep it to yourself?'

'I was waiting for the opportune time,' said Daisy with dignity. 'And now it has come. The thing is this: while Hazel and I were distracting Miss Doggett on the deck earlier, I pretended to trip in order to stumble against her. She had her bathrobe on so *very* tightly, after all, that I wondered why.'

'And . . .' said George, eyebrows raised.

'*And* Miss Doggett's nightdress has blood on it. Just a few smears on the stomach and chest – or at least that's all I saw. But it does.'

I was electrified. I looked at Daisy, and I felt the spark jump between us. This was enormous.

'And that, combined with what I found on top of her wardrobe, is very interesting indeed. Now we all agree that the doll's injuries were really very similar to Theodora's, don't we?'

Everyone nodded. 'Three wounds around her heart,' said George.

'Yes,' said Daisy. 'And, of course, it might be a coincidence, only I don't believe in coincidences, not when murder is involved. I believe Miss Doggett saw the body and added those pins to the doll afterwards. So when did that happen?'

'After she – oh!' I cried.

'Exactly, Watson! Miss Doggett came out of her cabin, she looked in at Theodora's body, Miss Beauvais fainted and she was taken into Miss Doggett's empty cabin. She was then *still* in that cabin when we went in to examine it, and we also saw Miss Doggett moving about on deck during that time. So we can assume she did not at any point shove past Miss Beauvais, climb up onto the top of the wardrobe and push pins into a doll. So . . . when did she do it?'

'During the night,' I breathed.

'Indeed,' said Daisy. 'Which means that either Miss Doggett committed the murder, or she saw the body after the murder, but before it was discovered this morning. And that – well, that is extremely suspicious, don't you agree?'

I nodded, fizzing with amazement. What had seemed only an hour before to be a very simple mystery was unfolding into something fascinating.

'Then there's Miss Bartleby,' I said. 'And now we know more about Joshua, doesn't it make sense of what she said to us earlier? She's remembering *his* death.'

'Not just remembering, confessing to it!' said Daisy. 'And to Theodora's death too. Not that it's a particularly good confession. She didn't have any blood on her clothes, or any in her room that I could see, and she kept on mixing up the victims. I don't think the police

197

would give her the time of day if we presented her as our main suspect.'

'Maybe she's only pretending to be confused, though!' I said, although I wasn't sure I really believed that.

'Hmm, yes,' said Daisy. 'It's possible. And she could have got rid of her bloodstained clothing in the Nile – May heard a splash, didn't she? We must investigate what that was. Why, anyone could wrap their bloodstained clothes around a – a paperweight, or something, and toss them over the side of the boat.'

'Perhaps we're *supposed* to think that poor Miss Bartleby is upset enough to confess to something she couldn't possibly have done, using incorrect facts, and discount her immediately?' asked Alexander. 'It might all be a clever double bluff.' He paused. 'I'm not sure I believe it, though. I feel sorry for her. She's like my mom's mom – sweet. I bet she bakes cookies.'

We all looked at each other and carefully did not mention his other grandmother, the Countess, who was certainly not sweet at all.

'I think I agree with Alexander,' I said. 'What she was saying to Daisy and me earlier – she seemed so upset. I think she really is mixed up between Theodora's murder and Joshua's death.'

'Remember how she was behaving during the ritual?' asked Alexander. 'She forgot things then too. And she looked really confused about it.'

'So you think she truly can't remember what happened,' said George slowly. 'But does that mean she didn't commit the crime?'

'We can't be sure,' I said, after a pause. 'It's not as though she can't do things – it's only that she forgets them. And if she really does believe that she committed the crime – and I think she does – then we ought not to discount her. We can't ignore a confession!'

'But then what's her motive?' asked Amina.

'Obvious,' said George. 'If she had something to do with Joshua's murder, she might be afraid of it getting out. Perhaps Mrs Miller *was* the one who ordered it, and Miss Bartleby can't live with what she did any more. She's certainly fixated on it!'

'So that's Miss Bartleby,' said Daisy, nodding. 'And then there's Mr DeWitt!'

'But he was on Theodora's side last night!' said Amina. 'Doesn't that – what's the word – rule him out?'

'Not necessarily,' I said. 'He wants to get higher up in the society, that's obvious, and now Theodora's dead he might even be in with a chance of taking it over. He hates Miss Doggett, we saw that, and I think he's quite ruthless.'

'What did you find in his room?' asked George.

Daisy flushed. 'Er,' she said. 'We weren't – we weren't able to—'

'So the great Daisy Wells failed a task!' George cried.

'Oh, do let up,' snapped Daisy. 'We were stopped by the suspect on deck! Then you called us over – we didn't have time to finish our investigation. We—'

'HELLO!' said May from the doorway. 'HELLO, HELLO!'

'Mei!' I cried. 'What are you *doing* here?'

'I got out again!' said May triumphantly. 'When the men were taking away our breakfast things. I've been doing some more detecting. I found blood in the murderer woman's room, and the wrinkly man's.'

'WHAT?' we all said.

'He didn't notice me – he was eating his breakfast,' said May. 'But there's a pair of trousers hidden under his bed with blood on them. I think he's *suspicious*.'

'I'm becoming more and more impressed with the Wongs the more I know about them,' said George. 'Are there any more of you?'

'Teddy,' said May. 'Only he's still a baby, so he couldn't come along this time. Well? Aren't you coming to look? Hurry, hurry, before Father finds me!'

'May!' I said. 'You have to go back to your cabin!'

But then I looked over at Daisy and heard her voice in my head, as clear as anything: *Don't be such a grown-up, Hazel Wong.* I sighed. 'And anyway, how are we supposed to get in?' I asked weakly.

'As to that,' said George, 'I have an idea.'

5

Which was how I found myself hovering anxiously outside Mr DeWitt's closed cabin door, the sun on my back and the churn of water beneath me. We were moving quickly up the Nile, the river wide and sparkling, high lion-coloured hills rising far away behind a green streak of palms.

We had no idea, really, whether George's idea would work. I felt jittery, heart thumping, every inch of my body itching with nerves.

Alexander and George stood side by side, facing the closed door. Amina and I were off to one side, squashed together – and crouched behind our feet, squeezed as small as possible, was May. She shifted against my ankle impatiently, like the little monkey we nicknamed her. Very gently, I pressed my right foot down on her hand to remind her to stay still.

Amina squeezed my arm, I nodded at George who cleared his throat and nudged Alexander, and Alexander gave me an apologetic look that made my heart beat even stronger. Then he turned to George and said loudly, 'Hey! *Don't* touch me!'

'Then keep away from me!' George said. 'I say, I got here first!'

'You did not! Look, this is totally unfair – you KNOW how much she means to me.'

'And I told you in *strict confidence* that I liked her. You pretended to support me! See here – DAISY! DAISY! DAISY! PLEASE!' George began to shout. I could tell he was enjoying himself. Alexander, on the other hand, looked distinctly uncomfortable – or perhaps I only wished he was.

'DAISY!' he cried, and there was a definite pink tinge to his cheeks. 'PLEASE – DAISY!'

They shoved at each other and yelled – and, as we had hoped, there was movement within the cabin. The door snapped open a few inches and Mr DeWitt was standing there, staring out at George and Alexander with an expression of bemused horror.

'What's all this shouting?' Mr DeWitt asked. 'What's wrong? Is someone else dead?'

I thought how odd that statement was, if he truly thought that the murderer was Heppy. She was locked

202

away, after all – the ship ought to have seemed entirely safe.

'They're arguing over Daisy,' said Amina. 'Typical silly boys!'

'It isn't fair!' panted George, lunging at Alexander. 'I love her!'

'*I* love her!' cried Alexander, his voice cracking slightly from embarrassment. Mr DeWitt, though, clearly took it as a sign of emotion. He took a step forward, out onto the deck. I nudged May gently with my toe, and she moved forward to catch the door before it closed all the way.

'Boys, really!' said Mr DeWitt. 'This isn't the time, is it? Not now!'

At that point, Daisy made her dramatic entrance. She came rushing round the side of the ship, looking shocked and sweetly pretty.

'Whatever's wrong!' she cried. 'Oh goodness!'

George and Alexander surged forward, struggling and yelling, and Mr DeWitt moved after them. He was all the way out of the doorway now. I felt May wriggle past me on her hands and knees. I tried desperately hard not to look down.

'Daisy!' George was shouting dramatically. 'I must confess my love!'

'Boys!' Daisy cried. 'Oh, this is dreadful – please don't fight! We must be peaceful in this terrible time!'

I caught Daisy's eye, and some of my disapproval must have shown in my face, for she winked at me and pursed her lips. I knew then that she did not mean a word of what she said – and I also knew that I had to go after May. While everyone on deck was looking at Daisy, I took a deep breath and slipped through Mr DeWitt's doorway.

6

Mr DeWitt's cabin was dark and quiet after the heat and sun outside. It smelled very strongly of cologne, several sorts, which clashed in the air and made me hold my hand up to my nose in disgust.

'Where is it?' I asked May (with difficulty, for I was trying to breathe as shallowly as I could). 'And shh! We don't want anyone noticing we're here.'

'Under the bed!' said May. She dived forward and emerged a moment later with a pair of pyjama trousers, which she laid out on the floor like a proud cat displaying a dead bird.

'I'm going to be a spy one day, you'll see,' she told me.

'You are not!' I said to her. 'Now shush, I want to look at this.'

I was kneeling down to peer at the trousers, and realized that she was perfectly right. There were half-scrubbed-away smears and spots of blood on their hem – blood that had darkened to copper brown. Mr DeWitt had tried to wash them, but he had not done it very well.

'The blood's been there a while,' I said. 'We can't be sure that it's Mrs Miller's, or even from last night.'

I knew as I said it how silly that was. Blood on the bottom of a pair of trousers – where else could it have come from?

The pocket of the trousers was bulging suspiciously, so I wrapped my handkerchief round my fingers and stuck them carefully inside. I pulled out another handkerchief, stained oddly with dark blotches.

'Ooh!' said May. 'What is it? More blood?'

'Not blood,' I said, squinting. '*These* blots are something else.'

'Are they from those?' asked May, pointing to the top of the dresser. 'I saw them when I came in before!'

I looked up at where she was gesturing – and saw a row of little dark bottles, each with a smart white-and-blue label on their side. *Easton's Syrup*, they all read.

'Those are tonics, May,' I said. 'It's the same stuff that Theodora has in her bathroom.'

'Yes, but why are there so *many*?' asked May, sticking out her bottom lip.

The door opened again then, and we both froze.

'It's me,' whispered Alexander. 'How are you doing? Daisy and George are pretending to argue with Mr

DeWitt now, so I've snuck in here. I don't know how long I have, though. What did you find?'

I could feel myself blushing. 'Bloodstains, here,' I said, pointing at the pyjama trousers. 'And a handkerchief with stains – May thinks it's from these tonic bottles, but it doesn't make any sense.'

'Hmm,' said Alexander. He strode over to the row of bottles and stared closely at one of them. 'This says *one to two spoonfuls a day, for health and vitality* – tonics. But why are there so *many*? Even if this trip was three weeks long instead of one, he would hardly get through a single bottle, let alone seven. That's weird!'

I got up and went over to him. I was only going to look at the bottles, really – but then I glanced sideways, and saw that Alexander was smiling at me. In the dimness, his eyes looked very dark blue. I couldn't help it – I smiled back at him.

'So,' he said, picking up one of the bottles and spinning it about between his fingers. It smelled dark and medicinal, quite horrid.

I couldn't bear to remind him what poor detective practice that was.

'So,' I said back idiotically.

'I'm glad we're here,' said Alexander. 'I mean – you know – even though there's been a murder again, like always. It's, er, nice to see you.'

May made a disgusted sound, and hid under the bed.

'It's nice to see you too,' I said, trying to ignore her and also stop my heart from pounding so hard.

'Yeah,' said Alexander, running his hand through his hair distractedly. 'George really does like mummies a lot. And I've always wanted to see the Pyramids. When my parents said they couldn't have me this Christmas – I guess it made sense.'

'Of course,' I stammered. *He came to Egypt to see* you, a little voice in my head whispered. *He wanted to see* you.

The two of us stared at each other. Then May, still rustling about, made a rude noise, and I jumped.

'So, er, how about these bottles of syrup?' asked Alexander, and I could have sworn the tips of his ears had gone slightly pink. 'Not very murderous, are they? I mean, they're just tonics. Just iron phosphate and quinine and – hey, Hazel. HAZEL. Look!'

He stuck out his hand towards me, and I stared at the label of the bottle.

'Iron phosphate, quinine and – *strychnine*,' I gasped. 'But that's a poison! It can kill you!'

'Hazel, this has to mean something, right? Why should Mr DeWitt have so many bottles of this stuff? It has to matter that it's got strychnine in it! And – and maybe that's the reason for the blotches. What if he was straining out the solution to extract the strychnine?'

'Oh,' I breathed. 'I think you're right.'

Then we looked at each other, and I suddenly realized that our heads were still very close together where we had bent over to read the bottle ingredients. I could see the freckles on Alexander's nose, and I felt as though the whole air was electricity.

Then the door banged open again, and from the deck we heard Mr DeWitt shouting, 'Do go away and leave me alone!'

He did not turn to look inside, otherwise he would have noticed us.

'But, sir!' cried George. 'I must say—'

I stepped backwards very quickly and the feeling vanished. Mr DeWitt made a furious noise and strode away. The coast was clear for a moment.

'We should go before he comes back in,' said Alexander, stepping backwards just as quickly as I had. 'Come on, let's hurry.'

And although we had found an astonishing new clue, sending our investigation in a very interesting direction, as we hurried together to the doorway of Mr DeWitt's cabin, I suddenly felt unaccountably furious with myself.

But that was nothing to the feeling I had when I stepped out on deck and heard my father bellow, 'HAZEL!'

7

'There you are!' he cried. 'How is it possible I can lose so many daughters on such a small ship?'

'But you've got Rose,' I pointed out, for Rose was beside him, clutching another book.

'Yes, I do,' said my father. 'But May is quite gone. Have you seen her? She hasn't been – *helping* you, Hazel? When I told you I would not stop your – activities, I didn't mean that you should drag your little sister into them with you.'

I flinched. 'No!' I said, and I heard my voice come out wrong. 'May has nothing to do with this. She must just be – hiding somewhere, pretending to be a pirate.'

'Hazel,' said my father. 'Do not abuse my trust. Having one daughter who finds murders wherever she goes is bad enough, but I think having two would break me.

Perhaps the answer is to remove Miss Wells from the picture? I swear she is bad luck.'

'It's everyone else who's bad luck!' I said, stung. 'Daisy and I *fix* things!' It was terribly bold of me – I knew that my father was already trusting me more than he had ever done – but I could not help myself. It was true, and I wanted him to know it.

'Wong Fung Ying, why can I see your little sister behind you?' asked my father, his voice freezingly calm. 'Wong Mei Li, WHY ARE YOU OUT ON DECK?'

May, safely out of Mr DeWitt's cabin, jumped up. 'I escaped!' she said proudly. 'I wanted to come and see Hazel. I'm sorry. I'll go back with you now.'

'Was this your big sister's idea?'

There was a pause. 'No, Father,' said May, her face shining with earnestness. 'It was all my idea. Hazel told me not to.'

'I hope that is the truth,' said my father. 'I hope so for both your sakes. May, come with me AT ONCE. And, Hazel—'

'Yes, Father?' I squeaked.

'I hope you know what you are doing,' said my father. 'I hope so very much.'

And he stormed off, dragging May and Rose behind him. May looked back at me and stuck out her tongue. And I had a brief moment of – pride, I suppose.

Mr Mansour was in among us all now. 'Please!' he cried. 'Please go back into your cabins, everyone! Please!'

'Of course, Mr Mansour,' said Daisy. 'We're so sorry for the fuss. George and Alexander are sorry, aren't you, boys?'

'We're so sorry,' said Alexander.

'Yes, terribly,' said George insincerely.

'Good. Then off you go,' said Mr Mansour.

'Are we really going back to our cabins?' whispered Amina.

'Of course not!' snapped Daisy. 'We have too much to do – including updating our suspect list, doing our re-creations and getting in to see Heppy. I believe you have the answer to that problem?'

Amina laughed. 'I think I do,' she said. 'Is it always like this, during your cases?'

'Usually,' said Alexander. 'Whenever Hazel's around, something exciting's bound to happen.'

'Whenever Daisy's around, you mean,' I said.

'Nope,' said Alexander. 'I'm pretty sure it's you just as much as it is Daisy.'

And I blushed bright red.

SUSPECT LIST

1. *Hephzibah Miller.* The victim's daughter. She
   was first on the scene, and was found covered in
   blood. She says that she woke up with no idea how the
   blood got onto her, and only realized her mother was
   dead when she went into the victim's cabin. We know
   she is a sleepwalker, and she believes that she
   murdered her mother while asleep. But can this be
   true? It does not explain several things we noticed in
   Theodora's cabin: the cleaned knife, the sheet on the
   floor and the bloody sink. We believe she has been
   framed — but we need to prove that before we rule her
   out.

2. *Ida Doggett.* The second in command in the
   Breath of Life Society. Theodora believed Miss
   Doggett was the reincarnation of Cleopatra, but Ida
   wanted to be Hatshepsut instead, Mrs Miller's
   reincarnation! We witnessed many disagreements
   between the two — they have clearly fallen out since
   Mr DeWitt joined the group. Miss Doggett
   mentioned being pleased that Theodora was dead this
   morning, and blamed the gods for the crime — a
   strange thing to say. She appeared on the scene
   wrapped in a bathrobe — could she have been hiding

blood on her nightdress? This has been confirmed by Daisy Wells — there is blood on Miss Doggett's nightie! From the evidence in Theodora's room, we know that she will have partial control of the society's money now, and she has expensive taste in clothes — could this be a motive for murdering Theodora? From looking in Miss Doggett's cabin, we know that she believes herself a practitioner of magic. She has shabti dolls representing the Breath of Life members — and Theodora's doll has three pins stuck in its heart! We believe Miss Doggett must have seen the body at some point during the night, as there was no opportunity for her to go back to her cabin and do this between the body being found and us discovering the dolls. She also knows Heppy's sleepwalking patterns very well from the evidence of Heppy's Book. But is she the murderer?

3. *Rhiannon Bartleby.* Another member of the Breath of Life Society. Theodora believed she was the reincarnation of Nefertiti. She seems sweet and gentle, but she made a suspicious confession when the death was discovered this morning. From the conversation May Wong overheard, we know that she seems convinced she not only hurt Mrs Miller but also Joshua Morse, Daniel's friend. She seems

to be confused about the details — but does she really not recall exactly what happened, or is she only pretending? Could she have killed Theodora because of her guilt at Joshua's death?

4. *Daniel Miller.* The victim's son. He has been estranged from her, but was temporarily reconciled with his mother to come on this holiday. However, we know he was extremely angry with her last night. He mentioned Joshua Morse, an ex-member who is now dead. In the book he's writing, Daniel seems to blame Theodora for the death of his friend Joshua — did he kill her in revenge?

5. *Narcissus DeWitt.* High up in the Breath of Life Society, and seemingly on Theodora's side. It's clear that he is fighting with Miss Doggett to become second in command. Mr DeWitt was wearing mismatched pyjama trousers when we saw him this morning — why? We have discovered blood on a pair of pyjama trousers, and seven suspicious bottles of Easton's Syrup in his room — these have strychnine in them! We believe he was straining them to get at the strychnine — but what does this mean? Is he the murderer?

PLAN OF ACTION

1. Take a closer look at the scene of the crime.

2. Investigate the other cabins on the saloon deck for clues.

3. Re-create the crime: work out why no scream was heard in the middle of the night and pin down the time of death.

4. Discover ~~who Joshua Morse is and~~ what happened to him!

5. Investigate our suspects, gain their trust and begin to rule them out.

6. Discover more about Theodora Miller. Who was she?

7. Get in to see Heppy!

8

'So, how do you intend to get us in to see Heppy?' asked Daisy.

'It's easy!' said Amina, eyes gleaming. She put out her hand and turned Daisy's wristwatch towards her. Daisy twitched. 'The guard will change over in ten minutes, so we should go now. Only I don't think it should be all of us.'

'Let me guess, you want Alex and me to wait up here and cover for you,' said George.

'Thank you for volunteering,' said Daisy, eyebrow raised. 'What an excellent idea! Now, Amina, tell us your plan.'

'So,' said Amina, twinkling at Daisy, 'when I was scouting around earlier, I heard Mr Mansour talking to the sailors in Arabic. The guard on Heppy's door is to be changed every hour, and they all have to take a turn. And the sailor who's been put on this hour is Muslim, like me. And – well, I think we can use that.'

'How?' asked Daisy.

'Lots of Muslims believe in jinn and afarit, and so, since Theodora was murdered, he's quite probably worried that she might have become an ifrit.'

'What's that?' I asked curiously.

'Hazel! Haven't you read the *Arabian Nights*?' asked Daisy, sniffing in a superior way.

I opened my mouth to tell her crossly that I have read as many books as she has, but then I saw Amina's eyes on Daisy and closed it again with a sigh.

'The afarit are demons or spirits, bad ones. They're powerful and dangerous – and they often try to take revenge on the person who murdered them. So, if someone believed that Theodora might have become one, they'd be nervous in case she came to get Heppy.'

I shuddered. I did not like the sound of that.

'So I think we could try to frighten this guard – Ahmed – away from Heppy's door quite easily if I pretend to be an ifrit. All we need is a sheet and a glass of hibiscus juice.'

We had discovered Amina's fondness for pranks last year – she had disrupted all of Deepdean with them, and for a while we were afraid that she might ruin one of our investigations because of them. But it turned out that Amina's cleverness stopped us going in the wrong direction with our investigation, and in the end her help was exactly what we needed to solve the case. So, although pouring some hibiscus juice on a sheet did not seem obviously brilliant to me, I was willing to go along with it.

'Excellent,' said Daisy. 'Boys, as agreed, you stay up here. You might as well use the time rigging up our first re-creation. We need to prove that May's activity really did rule out anyone from the lower deck. Put up that bell contraption she says she used. Go on, go! Now, Amina, once we've got the sheet and the juice, where shall we meet you?'

'Cupboard on the bottom deck!' said Amina. 'It's obvious enough. I'll get the juice; you get the sheet. Meet you there in three minutes!'

Two minutes and fifty seconds later, Daisy and I were crowding into the little cupboard on the bottom deck, next to the cold storage where Mrs Miller's body was being kept. I shuddered as we crept past it. We were lower than the cabins here, lower than the restaurant, where only the sailors were supposed to be, and this deck was small and dark compared to the grandeur and light above us.

The cupboard was dark and close inside, with a strong smell of damp. Once we were inside, I pulled out my little torch from my pocket and shone it around.

'Very clever!' said Amina, popping her head into its beam. 'Do you always carry one?'

'Always,' I said. 'Daisy insists.'

'I do!' said Daisy. 'Amina, I must say I'm impressed.'

'Thank you!' said Amina with a twinkle. 'All right, spread out the sheet. I'm going to bloody it nicely.'

We stretched out the bedsheet in a billow of clean white, and Amina artfully splattered juice across it. It came out disturbingly red, and I felt a bit wobbly looking at it.

'Excellent,' Amina said. 'Now the cabin they've got Heppy in is next to the stairs, which is useful. When we go back up, I think I ought to be the ifrit. I can speak Arabic and it'll frighten Ahmed more if I curse him a bit. You two can stand behind me and wave your torches on me. It'll look horrifying.'

'We ought to turn off the lights, otherwise it won't work,' I said. The lower deck was a sort of negative of the saloon deck – the cabins were on the outside, and the corridor was in the middle, with a stair going down and up on each end and lit by a succession of lamps both day and night. If they were on, I was worried that our trick would be revealed.

'About that,' said Amina. 'The generator's switch is in this cupboard. Why d'you think I told you to come in here?'

I was impressed, and my face must have shown it.

'Ready?' asked Daisy in a slightly higher voice than normal.

'Ready,' said Amina, nodding.

9

We flicked off the switch, and pushed the door to the cupboard open into velvety darkness. Above us I could hear shouts of confusion (I thought of Pik An, ill in her room, and felt rather guilty), and close by our own shufflings and nervous breathing. At least, I hoped they were ours. Daisy put her hand on my shoulder.

Amina walked in front of us, one careful foot in front of the other to stop herself tripping on the trailing sheet. We had draped it loosely round her and arranged it artfully to show the worst splashes of juice (which really did look uncomfortably like blood).

'Now!' I whispered, once we were in position at the bottom of the stairs. Amina raised her white arms, we flicked on the torches and lit her like a candle from behind. Amina gave a shriek, and rushed upwards, shouting terribly. We flickered the light wildly up after her so it caught her fingers, dipped in the remains of the juice, the whirling white sheet and her rushing form.

It only took a few seconds, and then we heard a terrible scream, a stumbling rush of feet and something falling to the floor. A door slammed further away, and Amina stopped her shrieking, spun round (her face stark and hair wild in the torchlight) and cried down to us, 'He's gone, and he's dropped the key! Come on, quickly, through here!'

She scrabbled for it, clicked the key into the lock and shoved the door open, and Daisy and I rushed up the last few stairs and tumbled inside the cabin.

I had forgotten that this cabin would be dark too, as dark and close as the cupboard, with a nervous voice calling out, 'Who is it? Who are you? Please don't hurt me – please—'

Daisy's torch flashed up to show Heppy crouched against a small bed, her expression terrified. She was still wearing her bloodstained nightgown, and it suddenly made Amina's sheet look like the poorest costume. There was nothing really frightening about it, after all – this was real horror.

'It's all right!' I said, with difficulty, trying to make myself breathe calmly. 'It's just us: Daisy, Hazel and – and Amina. There's been a power cut and we wanted to make sure you were all right.' I was proud of how easily the lie slid off my tongue.

'Who was screaming just now?' asked Heppy. 'Are they all right?'

'The guard was frightened,' said Amina. She had wriggled out of her sheet, and as I glanced at her she kicked it at Daisy across the floor. Daisy caught it with her foot and shoved it behind us. 'So we're here instead. We'll look after you until the lights come back on.'

'But you shouldn't be here,' gasped Heppy. 'I – I'm dangerous! I hurt people! That's why I'm locked away here – I can't be trusted!'

'We think you can,' I said gently. 'We don't think you hurt Theodora, after all, not in the way you said.'

'I don't know what you mean!' said Heppy, holding up her hands. 'I killed her!'

'Are you sure about that?' snapped Daisy. 'What do you remember?'

'I don't remember anything properly! I never do when I sleepwalk! I was having such a terrible dream, though, and when I woke up this morning – oh, poor Mother!'

'Have you always sleepwalked?' asked Amina.

'Since I was little,' said Heppy, nodding. 'Only it's got worse the last few years. I do all the wrong things, and I try to fix them, but it only makes it worse.'

'But,' I started, 'are you sure you're doing things wrong? Only – I mean, the others aren't very nice to you.'

'Oh no, I'm always wrong,' said Heppy. 'That's what Mother said, and she's always right. Mother told me I had to stop sleepwalking, that it was bothering everyone in the society and it was bad of me, but everything we tried made me sleepwalk more. I had Miss Doggett tie me to the bed, only I untied the knots myself and I woke up in the garden. Then I took Moth—Theodora's tonic, but it only made me more jumpy. I even slept . . . *without clothes on* in case it made me too ashamed to go anywhere, but it didn't. It was terribly embarrassing and Theodora had to punish me after that. I thought that perhaps, in another country, the fresh air would help me sleep, but it didn't. I sleepwalked the night before last, right into Mother's room, and moved things about. And then last night – I must have picked up the knife in my sleep and *killed her*!'

'How do you know you sleepwalked the night before last?' asked Daisy sharply.

'I put a piece of thread across the door. It was broken in the morning, so I knew I must have got out during the night. So last night I asked Miss Bartleby to lock me in. But she must have forgotten.'

'What do you mean?'

'She came into my cabin last night, after we'd put Mother to bed. She said goodnight to me, and I gave her the key to my cabin door and asked her to lock it behind her. She took it, and I thought I heard it turn in the lock – but I must have been wrong!'

'Are you saying you were locked in last night?' Daisy whispered the words. She seized my hand and squeezed it so tight in her excitement that I almost yelped.

'I thought so,' said Heppy mournfully. 'But I can't have been, can I? This morning, when I woke up, the door was open!'

10

'But – but—' Daisy was stammering with amazement.

I felt my breathing quicken. Was this the final proof that Heppy was not responsible? But Miss Bartleby was forgetful – we knew that. She might really have forgotten. This could be another false hope. And of course, I realized with a sinking heart, Heppy's door *must* have been unlocked, at least for part of the night. We knew from the evidence that she had sleepwalked into her mother's room, and the bloody sheet, at some point after the crime. So how could we prove that Heppy could not have committed the murder itself?

'Tell us everything you remember about last night,' I said with an effort. 'Please.'

'Why does it matter?'

'We want to *understand*!' said Amina.

'There are things about how Theodora's cabin looked this morning that seem – odd,' I said. 'We're trying to make everything fit. Please, won't you tell us?'

Heppy blinked at us. 'You are strange!' she said. 'When I've told you and told you what really happened. Oh, all right, if you want. Yesterday evening, there was Mother's ritual. I – failed again. I must try to be better, I must!'

'But there's nothing wrong with you!' I cried, frustrated. 'The things you think are so bad – they're all perfectly ordinary. You mustn't listen to the Breath of Life!'

Heppy's face crumpled, just for a second. 'You don't understand,' she said. 'No one can. The whole Breath of Life are my family, not just Daniel and M—Theodora. That's something that Theodora explained to us all. I *have* to listen to them. And I will be better, I must be! If I could stop sleepwalking . . . but anyway Mother held the ritual. It was almost done when Daniel came in to stop it.'

Her face had turned red with anger. 'He doesn't understand!' she said. 'He won't work on himself. His soul will be weighed, and found wanting. He'll *never* learn his reincarnation.'

This was interesting. Heppy would not get cross about Theodora, and her punishments – when really she had every reason to be. No wonder she sleepwalked,

I thought. But all of her anger seemed to be directed at her brother, not her mother.

'What happened next?' I asked.

'Well, I went back to my cabin to calm myself,' said Heppy. 'And then – then I went to help Miss Bartleby get Theodora ready for bed. Miss Bartleby – well – hasn't quite been herself lately. She gets so tired, and sometimes she misplaces things. She doesn't mean it, but it makes Theodora . . . talk sharply to her. She only needs prompting – the way I do – but, all the same, sometimes she responds poorly to it. She hasn't learned yet. So I help. Miss Bartleby tucked her in tightly, and I read to her – some passages from the Book of Life; it always soothes her. Once she was asleep, Miss Bartleby and I left. I asked her to come back to my cabin and make certain it was locked. She agreed – I remember giving her the key, and hearing the click of the lock outside as she turned it. Then she said goodnight, and went away, and I got into bed and fell asleep. And when I woke up the door was open, and I was covered in blood and – oh, MOTHER!'

Her voice rose in a wail.

'But I don't understand!' said Amina. 'You were locked in when you went to sleep, but you weren't when you woke up. That means somebody else must have unlocked your door. What if – what if that person is framing you?'

But Heppy was shaking her head.

'No, you don't understand,' she said. 'It was *magic* – don't you see?'

The three of us exchanged mystified glances. 'I don't think we *do* see,' I said carefully.

'Dark magic,' said Heppy, almost with satisfaction. 'Miss Doggett was telling me about it. I must have cast one of the spells she was talking about in my sleep to unlock the door from the inside. Then I walked to Theodora's room and killed her. I did it, and now I deserve to be punished!'

'But – but – magic isn't real!' I said.

Heppy looked at me pityingly. 'Nonsense,' she said. 'No one else was responsible. They couldn't be.'

And then the door to her cabin opened and Mr Mansour barked, 'Young ladies! OUT!'

11

Mr Mansour was furious.

'You cannot be in there!' he told us, flapping his hands to shoo us down the hallway. Ahmed was standing, glowering at us, his shoulders as wide as possible to show that he had not really been afraid. 'All of this running around, disrupting the other passengers – that is not how to behave! You girls are trouble. You are not – what's the word – *ladylike*. The pranks, the fights – on my way down here, I walked through some strange string contraption that rang a bell, which I assume was your doing.'

Daisy nudged me, and I elbowed her back. There was another part of the mystery closed. The boys' reconstruction had been completed successfully. Mr Mansour had not noticed the string and bell until he had set it off. May had been right – we could trust her story. Our suspects really were limited to the five members of the Breath of Life.

'And now I find you in with the prisoner!'

'But, Mr Mansour!' I said. 'Heppy just told us – she said that Miss Bartleby locked her in her cabin last night. If she did, the crime is impossible – she *couldn't* have got out on her own. That means someone else must have unlocked her door – someone framed her for this crime! Everyone in the Breath of Life knows she sleepwalks. You've got it all wrong!'

'It's true!' said Amina. 'It is, I heard her!'

I expected him to ignore us. Daisy and I are used to grown-ups sniffing at us, thinking that we are only babies or foolish little girls. But Mr Mansour stopped in his rush and turned on us.

'Miss El Maghrabi, Miss Wells, Miss Wong,' he hissed, so close I could smell the oil he put on his moustache and see the fine little threads of blood that ran through the whites of his eyes. '*I am doing my best.* I have never – I have *never* had a journey like this. I have a *murder* on my hands. I *must* keep the rest of my passengers safe, and that means asking you not to behave like you believe yourselves to be female Sherlock Holmeses. Since you will not stay in your cabin, I have decided to gather everyone together on the top deck. Please come up as soon as possible. If we all remain calm and stay together, this experience will be over quickly and quietly.'

'All right!' said Daisy cheerfully, pushing in front of me as I gaped at him. 'We're terribly sorry, Mr Mansour.

We didn't mean to upset you. We'll go and get our things, and be up on the top deck in five minutes. Come along, Hazel, Amina. Let's go.'

Mr Mansour eyed her suspiciously.

'We really don't want to upset you, Mr Mansour,' Daisy carried on. 'We have something important to tell you, but it can wait until we're up with the others. We're sorry to have worried you.'

'Er – thank you, Miss Wells,' said Mr Mansour.

'Daisy!' I hissed. 'What are you doing?'

'Don't speak, Hazel,' said Daisy, and when she turned to me I could see that, oddly, she was beaming. 'Oh, come along, we have to get to our cabin as soon as possible! We have to collect some things – your father doesn't have our passports, does he?'

'Our passports?' I asked, bewildered. 'They're in my case. But why do we need those?'

'Proof,' said Daisy confusingly. 'Like in *Murder on the Orient Express*. You'll see.'

'See what?' asked Amina. 'Daisy, what are you going to do?'

'Really!' I said. 'You can't just keep things from me any more.'

'I'm not!' said Daisy. 'But there's no time, Hazel. I'm thinking too fast to talk about it yet. I'll show you when we're in our cabin. Come on! It's the only thing left that might work – really the only possible plan. And it's an excellent one. Come on, come on, you'll see!'

For what felt like the hundredth time in our strange detective careers, I let her drag me forward by the wrist. I could not think what she was planning. From the look on her face, I could tell it was quite audacious – but, all the same, I never guessed exactly how audacious it would be.

PART FIVE

CARDS ON THE TABLE

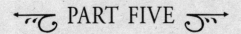

1

What Daisy had to do in our cabin was quick, and we got up onto the upper deck, among delicate potted ferns and dainty white chairs, only a minute late. Far-off calls to prayer were floating across the wide bright water to us, and I could see the spire of a minaret through the palm trees.

Most of the *Hatshepsut*'s passengers were already there, waiting, though I could not see Miss Beauvais or Pik An. Mr Mansour gave us a very angry glance and moved away to the front of the deck. I looked at Daisy, and she nodded at me fiercely. I knew what we had to do – I was holding part of the plan squeezed tightly in my fist – and it made me feel dizzy with nerves. Could we pull it off? Surely not! *But if anyone can, it's us*, I told myself. *We're the Detective Society and, no matter how difficult things seem, we never lose.* That thought was like a hand on my shoulder, a warmth on my back. I smiled at Daisy, and we moved forward together, Amina just behind us.

Miss Doggett was standing, stork-like, beside the railings, now wrapped in a patterned shawl, a look of furious concentration on her face. Opposite her, his hair shining brassily in the sun, was Mr DeWitt, leaning on his cane and glaring at Miss Doggett. Miss Bartleby was huddled in one of the cane chairs, squeezing her hands together in her lap and whispering something to herself that was not loud enough to be heard by anyone else. Daniel was just behind her, pacing anxiously, his fists clenched.

My father looked over at us, and when he saw us he gave a sharp nod of his head. There was no doubt about his meaning – I led Daisy and Amina across the top deck to sit next to him, May and Rose.

'Remember, Hazel!' Daisy whispered to me. 'It's imperative that you wait until—'

'QUIET,' said my father, and I took Daisy's hand and squeezed it. Mr Mansour stepped forward to speak.

'Good morning, honoured guests. Once again, I apologize for this inconvenience. I had hoped that keeping the suspect safe in a cabin on the lower deck would be enough to restore calm, but I see that this is not the case. Therefore I have called this meeting to allay suspicions one more time. It seems clear what happened, after all. Mr Miller, you are her brother?'

'Yes!' said Daniel crossly. 'That is, not by birth. Theodora adopted us all when we were very young. But the three of us grew up together—'

'Three?' asked Mr Mansour, puzzled.

'Our brother Gabriel died at Passchendaele.'

'I'm sorry,' said Mr Mansour. 'My brother died at Rafa.'

'He was Mother's favourite,' said Daniel with a shrug. 'And as our father had already been lost at sea, Theodora was left with only Heppy and me, and we weren't much consolation, I think. She was – angry that we were the ones she'd been left with. She said more than once after they died that she wished *we* had gone, not them. That's when she began to tell us to stop calling her Mother, and when this idiotic society of hers began.'

'It is not idiotic!' snapped Miss Doggett. 'Earthly bodies may fade, but spirits live on. Theodora knew perfectly well that Gabriel and Alfred's souls may have flown out of their bodies, but they will return. No one is truly lost, and we are all part of the great wheel of existence. Even Joshua—'

'Nonsense!' shouted Daniel. 'It's all utter nonsense, and I'm ashamed that I ever listened to it – and brought poor Josh into it. If I hadn't, he'd still be alive.'

'JOSHUA BROKE THE FAITH!' cried Miss Doggett. 'He deserved everything he got!'

The two of them glared at each other, panting.

Mr Mansour jumped in. 'Please, please – I understand tempers are high. I am attempting to calm them by laying out the truth as clearly as possible. I was simply going to ask Mr Miller if he knew whether Miss Miller walked in her sleep often.'

'We all know about that, poor child,' said Mr DeWitt, nodding.

'Yes, indeed,' said Miss Bartleby. 'Poor Heppy, she is plagued with it.'

'We – we even saw her do it, the night before last,' said Amina. The rest of us all stared at her, and I saw her realize that she had admitted to being out of bed in the middle of the night. 'From the cabin, I mean,' she added, rather weakly.

'Hephzibah sleepwalked because her ba – her soul, in your parlance – was troubled,' Miss Doggett put in. 'She was a very damaged, unquiet girl, and she has caused the society much heartbreak over the years. It had become so bad that we – Theodora and I – were concerned that, if she did not work hard, her soul might be too heavy in the weighing to merit reincarnation at all. That is what happens to the very worst people, you know. The universe has a way of purging its dross.'

'So you – were not surprised at what happened?' asked Mr Mansour, rather nervously. 'Is Miss Miller really so bad? She seems quite – ordinary to me.'

'That is simply because you do not know her well enough. She's a real troublemaker. And yes, I was not surprised that she attacked Theodora.' Her lip curled here. 'Again, I say that the universe has a way of purging itself of its dross.'

'Do not speak of Theodora like that!' cried Mr DeWitt. 'Poor lady, she was the best of us!'

'Her ba was unworthy, if anyone's was!' snapped Miss Doggett. 'She was no more the reincarnation of Hatshepsut than – than that little child is!'

She pointed a shaking finger at May, who glowered at her.

'I'm not Hatshepsut – I'm Ching Shih the pirate queen!' she said.

'MAY WONG,' said my father threateningly. 'QUIET.'

'I – well – now, onto the matter of the knife,' said Mr Mansour, floundering rather. 'It was taken from our dining room last night. Did any of you see it?'

'Goodness, never!' said Miss Bartleby, shaking her head definitively.

'What are you *talking* about, Rhiannon?' said Miss Doggett. 'We used it in our ritual in the saloon. You brought it! But I don't know how it ended up in Theodora's room – Heppy must have taken it. Yet another example of her degenerate character.'

Miss Bartleby's face went very still, for just a sliver

of a second. Then she said easily, 'Why of course we did. What was I thinking? I simply – didn't assume it important.'

I squeezed Daisy's hand. '*L-Y-I-N-G?*' I tapped out in Morse code on her palm, and Daisy wrote back with a simple '*Y-E-S*'.

'So – so who was with Theodora after this ritual? Who saw her last?'

'Heppy helps her prepare for bed,' said Miss Bartleby. 'I do too. I took Theodora to her room, and then – and then Heppy came in, and read to her. I left her cabin just before midnight, and she seemed quite well, then.'

And again I saw an expression on her face that told me there was something about this story that was causing her worry.

'Everyone went to bed as normal?' Mr Mansour asked.

'Yes, absolutely,' said Mr DeWitt.

'I was asleep all last night,' said Daniel.

'And I was meditating in my cabin,' said Miss Doggett, po-faced.

'*L-Y-I-N-G,*' Daisy and I both tapped out on each other's hands at the same time, our fingers getting tangled up in our haste. I slid my eyes sideways at her and saw that she was smiling at me. It was almost time for our announcement. I felt prickly with nerves, but also strangely calm and floating. It was no good trying to stop it now. It would happen.

'Well, all right – I think that is clear enough. And you were all woken by Miss Miller's screaming this morning. Now—'

And that was when Daisy got to her feet. 'Excuse me,' she said.

'Miss Wells, please don't complicate things,' said Mr Mansour. 'Unless you have something to say that has a bearing on the investigation?'

'I should say I do!' said Daisy. 'We have not been entirely clear with you. We may appear like schoolgirls on holiday, but that is, in fact, a ruse. We are policewomen and, although we have been trying to keep a low profile, the time has come to reveal ourselves. Show them our credentials, Miss Wong.'

I stood up too, and now I opened my hand to show the things that were pressing deep creases into my palm – the badges Inspector Priestley gave us two years and eight cases ago.

Of course, they are simply shiny toys that Daisy and I keep for sentimentality's sake, but none of the people on the *Hatshepsut* (apart from George and Alexander) knew that, and as they flashed in the sun they looked most impressive. I was almost taken in myself.

My father made a furious noise. I stared at him, willing him not to ruin the moment, and he shook his head in disgust. I felt ashamed, but we had to keep going.

'*Official* badges of the British police force,' said Daisy. 'We are two of their youngest and most promising officers.'

'But,' Mr Mansour cried, 'you are girls! Girls cannot be in the police!'

'Nonsense,' said Daisy. 'Women have been working with the police for years. Haven't you heard of Maud West? And there are plenty of women officers too these days.'

'This is ridiculous. You're lying!' said Mr DeWitt.

'You can call our supervisor once we get to Aswan,' said Daisy with a shrug. 'We have a personal line to him at all times.'

'But they *are* schoolgirls!' I heard Mr Young say plaintively in the background. 'I'm sure they are!'

'Ridiculous,' snapped Daisy. 'We can show you our passports. We are policewomen and, since I do not see anyone else on this ship with more authority, we must be allowed to take over this case.'

2

'I cannot allow it!' said Mr Mansour. 'You are young women! And, besides, the case has been solved. It has been clear from the very start that Miss Miller was responsible.'

'Perhaps,' said Daisy. 'Or perhaps not. Miss Bartleby, may I ask you a question?'

'Of course, dear,' said Miss Bartleby vaguely.

'What did you do last night, after the ritual?'

'I put Theodora to bed, of course. Heppy helped me. We always do it together. I tuck her in tightly, and then Heppy reads to her, and then we leave.'

'Very good,' said Daisy. 'And then you went back to Heppy's room?'

'Why, of course!' said Miss Bartleby. 'We spoke together, and then I went to bed.'

'And did she ask you to do something?'

There it was again – the haunted look in Miss Bartleby's eyes. 'Indeed, she did,' she said. 'She – ah – asked me to brush her hair.'

'And?'

'And she – asked me – asked me to lock her in,' said Miss Bartleby.

'AH!' said Daisy. Miss Bartleby's face flooded with relief.

'Yes, I did do that! I locked her in and said goodnight and went to my own bed.'

I had another stab of doubt. Miss Bartleby was so vague, so suggestible. We had seen her forget things in the ritual last night, and she had been so confused when we had spoken to her this morning. Could her evidence be worth anything now? Could we really use this to build our case? But then—

'See here,' said Mr Young. 'Er. I think I may know something about this.'

We all turned in surprise to look at him. He was sitting anxiously, drawn into himself.

'I – well, I decided to take a turn around the deck last night, just after twelve. The lamps were still lit, and the whole thing was really quite pleasant.'

'Wonderful for you,' said Daisy shortly. 'What happened next?'

'Well, I was up by the saloon when I saw someone coming out of the port cabin closest to me and I heard someone else call after her. It was – well, it was *you*, Miss Bartleby, and Miss Hephzibah Miller's voice calling. She said – and I didn't mean to overhear, you understand, it simply happened – she said, "Lock the door after yourself, please, Miss Bartleby." Miss Bartleby agreed, put the key in the lock, and turned it. She went away to her own cabin – I saw her go in. Then I walked past Miss Miller's door. The key was turned in the lock. So I can confirm that Miss Miller was locked into her room last night.'

'Mr Young!' cried Daisy. 'Whyever didn't you say this before?'

'I – er – I thought,' said Mr Young, ducking his head and rubbing his neck awkwardly, 'I thought that, well, I thought it wasn't relevant. I'm not – I'm not used to this sort of thing.'

'I see that,' said Daisy, through her teeth. 'Well. You have given us the most important piece of evidence yet. Don't you see? Don't you all see? If Heppy Miller was locked into her cabin – a fact confirmed by two people – she could not have sleepwalked into her mother's cabin to murder her. She has been framed!'

3

'Yes, but,' said Mr Young, turning pinker than ever, 'she, er, *did* get out, didn't she? If you're so clever, how d'you explain *that*?'

'Easily,' said Daisy. 'Someone turned the key and unlocked the door – *after* Miss Bartleby locked it at midnight, and *before* this morning. Someone wanted Heppy to sleepwalk through the crime scene, and someone knew that she would. Someone on this ship – someone whose cabin is on the saloon deck. And I *am* clever, thank you very much. I should like you to remember that.'

'We both are,' I put in. 'We're policewomen, aren't we?'

Daisy turned her eyes on me, almost laughing. I fought the urge to smile back.

'This – this is nonsense,' stammered Daniel. 'You are *girls*! You aren't the police!'

'I agree,' said Mr Mansour. 'I cannot simply trust that—'

'They certainly *are*,' snapped my father. I jumped, startled. What was he—?

'I was afraid this would happen,' my father went on. 'That my daughter would be disrespected and disbelieved just because she is a young woman. I tried to dissuade her from pursuing this career, but she – well, she is just as stubborn as I am. She *would* do it, and I have given up the argument. Take it from me: these girls are exactly who they say they are.'

'Mr Wong!' gasped Mr Mansour. 'Are you – are you certain?'

'I am,' said my father, through teeth that I could tell were slightly gritted.

'Thank you, Mr Wong,' said Daisy, curtseying. My father eyed her as unlovingly as ever. He might be willing to back us up, but I knew (with a warm glow, as though I had swallowed a candle flame) that it was all for me, and not for Daisy. 'Now that's cleared up, may we be allowed to carry on with the case? As I think we have proved, there is more going on with this mystery than initially meets the eye. Mr Mansour?'

I could see Mr Mansour wrestling with himself. He looked at my father, and then doubtfully at us. And then—

'There are still several hours before we reach Aswan, and the police there,' said Mr Mansour, twisting his hands together in thought. 'But until then I – well – I don't like it.'

'You don't have to like it!' said Daisy.

I nudged her. 'When we arrive in Aswan, we'll tell the Parquet what we've found and then step back,' I said to Mr Mansour. 'We promise!'

Mr Mansour looked at my father one more time. My father nodded, and Mr Mansour threw up his arms.

'I suppose I have no choice,' he said. 'But it is not how we do things here in Egypt!'

'See here!' cried Daniel. 'This is ridiculous! Have you all taken leave of your senses? These are two little girls! They have no authority! They've barely stopped playing with dolls!'

I felt my cheeks heat up.

'We're not so many years younger than your sister,' said Daisy. 'And *you're* prepared to believe that she committed a murder last night. If she's old enough to be accused of one, we're old enough to prove she didn't do it. And what's wrong with being a little girl? Hatshepsut was twelve when she became queen of Egypt.'

'I expect people complained about her too,' said Daniel.

'I expect she chopped off their heads,' said Daisy calmly. 'Never underestimate a young woman, Mr Miller.'

Daniel was left gasping at that.

'Now Miss Wong and I need some time to confer in our cabin. Miss El Maghrabi, you may accompany us. Mr Mansour, please make the saloon bar ready for us to use – and we would like a late lunch served to us. We will be speaking to everyone with a cabin on the saloon deck. Is that clear?'

'Perfectly, Miss Wells,' said Mr Mansour. 'I shall make sure it is done.'

I looked round at our suspects. Daniel was furious – that was easy enough to see. Miss Bartleby was fluttering anxiously, one hand on her stomach. Mr DeWitt was watching Daisy with a curious twisted smile on his face, and Miss Doggett was glaring at her, so poisonously that I had to take a step backwards.

Daisy had her head thrown back, shoulders set, smiling slightly like the statues of Sekhmet we had seen in the Cairo museum. She did not seem to be afraid at all – but suddenly I got a chill. We had never announced ourselves like this to our suspects before. They had never known we were on their trail. Whoever the murderer was, they knew that we meant to uncover the truth. Would we be safe?

4

Daisy, Amina and I all piled into the cabin that Daisy and I shared. After a moment, there was a knock, and George and Alexander stuck their heads round the door.

'We gave Mr Young the slip,' said George. 'He thinks we're washing before lunch. Daisy, how dare you!'

'I think I was brilliant,' said Daisy with a shrug. 'I've got us on the case, haven't I?'

'Yes, but only *you*!' said George. 'We still have to pretend to have nothing to do with detection at all.'

'It isn't *my* fault that Mr Young knows how old you are,' said Daisy. 'Who'd believe that schoolboys could be detectives, after all?'

'It's not fair,' said Alexander.

'Oh, we'll let you assist us,' said Daisy. 'Remember, just the way you did with Dr Sandwich on the Orient Express!'

'Daisy, this isn't revenge for that, is it?' I asked. In our Orient Express case, Daisy and I had to pretend to be ordinary schoolgirls while Alexander helped with the official investigation. I know it rankled with Daisy, then – I ought to have known that she had not forgotten it.

'Don't be silly, Hazel!' said Daisy – proof, if I needed it, that it was exactly that.

'Of course you can help us,' I said to Alexander and George. 'We're sorry – or at least I am!'

'Traitor!' Daisy whispered in my ear.

'Let's have a meeting,' I said. 'While we're all here. We need to think through what's happened just now. We know, properly, that Heppy really is innocent.'

'I never thought Mr Young would be useful!' said George.

'He's a really bad tutor,' said Alexander.

'But an excellent witness!' said Daisy. 'I must say – and I do hate to – that we owe you boys for bringing him onboard. He's the perfect witness at the perfect time, and his story proves that Heppy really was locked in her cabin last night. She couldn't have got out unless someone opened the door for her – and, since we know she *did* get out, it follows beautifully that someone did just that.'

'Poor Heppy!' I said. 'She really does think she did it. We couldn't persuade her otherwise.' My heart ached for her every time I thought about it.

'How *did* you get in to see her?' asked George curiously.

'Oh, Amina came up with a brilliant plan,' said Daisy.

'It was just a prank,' said Amina. 'Easy, really.'

'It was wonderful,' said Daisy, and Amina glowed.

'So Heppy's cleared,' said George. 'All right. We're left with four suspects. Which one of them did it?'

'I think we should do a re-creation before the interviews,' I said. 'We still don't know exactly how the murder happened, after all.'

'Exactly what I was going to say, Hazel,' said Daisy, and I could tell she was a little put out not to have suggested it first. 'A re-creation, before we eat. We can use this cabin as Theodora's, even though it isn't a perfect copy – it's on the wrong side of the boat, after all.'

'When has perfect mattered?' I asked. 'We once did a re-creation with a doll's house!'

I only realized after I had said it that I'd admitted to the boys that Daisy and I had recently played with dolls. I ought to have been embarrassed – but I found I was only proud of our ingenuity. Daisy and I do anything we need to in order to solve a case, and that is all there is to it.

'Very clever,' said George. 'All right, how do we organize this one?'

'It's easy enough,' said Daisy. 'After all, we're only testing whether we can kill someone without them making any noise.'

5

'Daisy!' I said, aghast. 'We can't *kill someone*!'

'Well, I know *that*,' said Daisy. 'And I didn't mean that at all. *George* understands, don't you?'

'We need to do a test of noise,' said George, nodding. 'We need to prove that a pillow over Theodora's mouth could have kept her quiet enough – after all, Daisy said that she only heard some thumping, no screaming at all. And, while we're at it, we need to work out whether it would have been possible to quiet her and stab her at the same time.'

'Are you sure we really need to do this?' asked Alexander. 'We don't want anyone to get hurt.'

'Of course we need to!' said Daisy fiercely. 'We must know everything. We need a *complete* picture, otherwise we won't properly understand the truth. Detection *has* to be perfect. We have to see it *all*. If you don't understand that, you don't understand anything! See here, if you're going to be wet about it, *I'll* be the victim. Someone come and kill me.' As she spoke, she clambered up onto her bed, threw herself down on her back and squeezed her eyes shut. She looked rather like a princess in a fairy tale, with her hair streaming down around her shoulders and her hands on her chest.

'I'm not doing it,' said Alexander. 'No way! You could get hurt! George, *don't*!'

George sighed. 'I – see here, Daisy, are you certain about this?'

'OF COURSE I AM!' said Daisy, sitting up with a snap. 'Will SOMEONE come here and MURDER ME?'

Amina and I looked at each other.

'I don't want to do it,' I said helplessly. 'I don't think this is a good idea, Daisy.'

'Oh, all right, I will!' said Amina. 'But I agree with the rest of them. Daisy, this is stupid, and dangerous. Do you want to get hurt?'

'I want the truth!' said Daisy. 'Come here at once!'

Amina walked across the cabin on light feet and knelt down beside Daisy. 'I really am sorry about this,' she said quietly – and then quick as a flash she pulled Daisy's pillow from under her and pressed it over Daisy's face. Daisy made a furious muffled noise like a swarm of wasps.

'I can't hear you,' said Amina sweetly, leaning on her chest. 'Speak up.' I had the rather uncomfortable feeling that she was enjoying herself.

'*MMMMPH!*' said Daisy. Alexander, George and I looked at each other doubtfully.

'Go into Amina's cabin!' I said to them. 'See if you can hear anything!'

George nodded, and he and Alexander ducked out of our room into cabin ten next door. They were back a minute later.

'We couldn't hear much,' said Alexander. 'A few noises that could be the thumpings Daisy heard, but nothing I'd worry about if I woke up and heard them in the middle of the night.'

'And now I stab her, I suppose?' asked Amina. 'I have one hand on the pillow over her face, and then the other holding the knife, and I'm leaning on her chest to hold her down. Oh, this is awkward! Here, give me something to stab with.'

I passed her my pencil. Amina waved it about over Daisy's chest. 'See here, this is quite difficult!' she said. 'Daisy, stop wriggling and flailing your arms about!'

'Shan't,' said Daisy thickly, through the pillow.

'Rude!' said Amina, twinkling down at her.

'Wait!' I said. 'This isn't right.'

'It's the body, isn't it, Hazel?' said George.

I nodded at him. 'There weren't any wounds on Theodora Miller's hands or arms!' I said. 'She couldn't have been flailing like Daisy is, otherwise she'd have been all cut about there as well, and she wasn't.'

'OH!' said Daisy, muffled. 'Stop it, Amina – let me go!'

Amina lifted up the pillow, and Daisy's flushed face came into view.

'I know why she didn't fight!' she said. 'She was tucked in! Remember, Hazel, what Miss Bartleby said? She always tucks in Theodora tightly? If she was all wrapped up in her sheet like a mummy, she might not have been able to get her arms out quickly enough to defend herself when she was attacked. And if the pillow was held over her head firmly – Amina, excellent work, but you didn't press hard enough—'

'—I didn't *really* want to kill you!' exclaimed Amina.

'—then she might very well have died without anyone hearing her cry out. But I do believe we've shown that the murderer had to be awake to do everything that we know they did. It's hard work to stop a murder victim making a noise! Excellent work, Detectives!'

'Hold on,' I said. 'That isn't the end of the re-creation.'

'Nonsense, Hazel,' said Daisy.

'We've proved how Theodora died, but not what happened next. So, Daisy, you lie there, tucked in. You're dead. I'll be the murderer this time.'

258

'Bossy!' muttered Daisy.

'Quiet!' I said. 'You've been murdered.'

Suddenly I was enjoying myself.

'You've changed, Hazel!' hissed Daisy as I bent over her. I stuck out my tongue at her, and she narrowed her eyes at me. Amina moved away rather reluctantly.

'So, I'm the murderer,' I said. 'Mrs Miller's dead. I tuck the pillow back under her head, pull off the sheet – and I have to hold it carefully, don't I, to make sure the blood doesn't go on my clothes? It was so high up around her neck that it and the pillow would have caught all the blood until now. I think I can do it – but I'm getting some on my hands.'

'Which you'll have to wash in the sink later,' said George. I nodded at him.

'All right,' I went on. 'So I'm carrying the sheet across the room, and now I reach up to the curtain rail, and – oh!'

I am taller now than I used to be, but I have come to terms with the fact that I will never be very tall. As I stood in front of the door, and tried to get the sheet over the rail, I realized that I could not reach high enough and still hold it away from my body. I did not want to raise the sheet over my head, for fear of getting invisible blood on myself.

'What do I do?' I asked.

'Get the chair,' said Amina. 'No! It'll drip!'

'And there wasn't any blood on Mrs Miller's chair, was there?' said Daisy, watching with interest from the bed. 'I remember that from the crime scene.'

'Reach higher!' said Alexander.

'I can't!' I said, frustrated. 'I'll get blood everywhere and I still won't be able to get the sheet over the rail.'

'Here, let me,' said Amina. She stepped forward. With her extra few inches, she could tip the top of the sheet neatly over the railing.

'Mr DeWitt is the same height as Amina,' said George thoughtfully. 'And Miss Doggett's taller. So's Daniel. But Miss Bartleby—'

'She's almost the same size as me!' I exclaimed. 'She could only do it with a chair, and the murderer couldn't have used the one in Mrs Miller's room, like Daisy said. They're too heavy to move about easily too, so they couldn't have got one from another cabin or the deck without May hearing. So—'

'So I think,' said Daisy, leaping out of bed, 'we can rule Miss Bartleby out! Come along, Detectives, we must go and prepare the saloon, and ready ourselves for the next part of our investigation!'

6

I stepped outside our cabin to see that we were still sailing past high yellow cliffs and a line of thick green trees. The river here was set about with low islands, with lush grass on them. I saw goats on one, and then something I thought was a dark branch, until it moved its heavy crocodile tail.

On the east bank I saw people in white clothing walking at the edge of the water, a plough being pulled by an ox, the tops of houses behind the trees. It was all so peaceful and everyday – and a world away from our reality. We were on a ship where a murder had happened – as far away from the order of life on the banks of the Nile as we were from the moon.

I felt a hand on my arm – Alexander.

'Hey,' he said quietly. 'Are you all right? Are you ready?'

I felt the warmth of his hand through the fabric of my blouse, as though his fingers were on fire. I met his eyes for a moment, and said, 'Yes, I am.'

'I think you're incredible,' said Alexander – and I could not look at him any more. I ducked my head, and turned back to the door of our cabin – to catch sight of something I had not expected. I did not mean to see it, I really didn't, though that has not stopped me feeling guilty about it.

Amina and Daisy were standing close together, their heads tilted towards each other, murmuring to one another. Then I saw Amina shake back her long dark hair, lean upwards and touch her lips to Daisy's. The look on Daisy's face – bewilderment and utter delight – made me turn away at last, cheeks burning. This was something I ought not to have intruded on.

I felt awkward, and – although I do not like to write it – itching with something close to jealousy. Was that how easy it was? Why could I not simply step forward and kiss Alexander?

'What's wrong?' he asked from behind me.

'Nothing,' I said quickly. 'I thought I forgot my casebook, but it's in my pocket. Er – would you take notes in the interrogations? I might be distracted.'

'Of course I will,' said Alexander. 'Hey, will you give me some of your paper? Mine's in my cabin.'

As we walked towards the saloon, I tore out a few pieces of paper from my casebook and then handed them to Alexander. I blushed as I did it – it felt so personal, like giving him a part of myself – but Alexander simply smiled sunnily at me. It was the sort of romantic gesture that was only romantic in my head, I realized, and I was cross with myself all over again.

'Hello,' said Daisy, catching up with us. Amina was just behind her and, if I did not know every inch of Daisy's face as closely as I knew my own, I would not have noticed anything odd about her. But I could see how she was blazing with excitement, struggling to keep herself in check. 'Are you ready, Hazel? We can't get this wrong, you know. We have to be perfect.'

'I know we do,' I said, still prickly because of everything that was going on inside me. 'Daisy, you don't have to lecture me!'

'Touchy!' said Daisy. 'What's up with you, Hazel? Never mind. Boys, you'll be our assistants. George, go and get our first subject as soon as we're ready, and bring lunch. Alexander, you're recording the interviews, I see.'

'Stop it, Daisy! You're not the queen!' I said. 'We're all working together.'

'Yes, of course we are, Hazel,' said Daisy, and then she winked at me. I sighed. I did not feel ready at all. I felt like nothing more than the little girl who had discovered Miss Bell's body on the Gym floor, all those years ago. But then—

—I still can't explain what it was: the heat, my confusion, the ancient Egyptian stories swirling in my head about parts of souls flying out of bodies in different directions, but I got a strange, vertiginous, flashing moment where I saw myself from the outside, a girl who was standing up straight, her shoulders set, determination on her face. That girl looked important, like a person who mattered, like a detective. And I realized that I knew what to do. I could be a real detective. I could solve this case. Daisy and I could do anything, so long as we were together.

7

'Well!' said Daisy to Narcissus DeWitt, once we were settled in the saloon half an hour later. Amina and I had moved the chairs about, and draped two of the nicest with scarves so they looked rather like thrones. Daisy and I sat in them, Daisy in a fresh white dress and me in my nicest floral print, legs crossed at the ankles and hands severely folded, trying to look like grown-up ladies and policewomen all at once. Amina stood behind us. Daisy turned to look at her, and I had to nudge her to keep watching Mr DeWitt. The lamps had all been draped with more scarves to make the room soft and mysterious, and Amina had sprayed some of her perfume in the air. The saloon smelled light and floral.

Mr DeWitt sat on the smallest cane chair we could find, low down and uncomfortable. His position looked as though it hurt him – his face was more creased up than ever. He held his cane across his knees and clung on to it with both hands.

Alexander was standing beside the doorway, papers from my casebook under his arm. He looked nearly threatening – his head almost touched the lintel and, despite what Daisy says about him, he has lost quite a lot of his stretched-out wristiness – until he saw me looking at him and ducked his head, running his free hand through his hair awkwardly and almost stabbing himself with his propelling pencil. Daisy reached over to pinch my leg, and I tried not to jump.

'Mr DeWitt,' said Daisy. 'Welcome.'

'Thank you for coming,' I put in. Daisy looked at me sideways in muffled annoyance. She always hates pleasantries – despite everything, I have never been able to explain to her why they are necessary during a case.

'Yes, indeed,' Daisy went on. 'As you know, Mr DeWitt, there has been a terrible crime. We do not believe the truth has come out yet, but these interviews will help change that. Are you happy to speak to us about what occurred last night?'

'Of course, Miss Wells,' said Mr DeWitt. He tried to smile conspiratorially at her, but Daisy froze him out with her blue eyes, and Mr DeWitt faltered.

'Tell us your movements last night,' I said, summoning up everything I could remember from Aunt Lucy's lessons. 'It's important you don't miss anything out. Every detail may be vital.'

'Ah, yes, right away. I would just like to say that I've always supported women. I campaigned for votes for women, of course. I think it's wonderful that you girls have decided to become policemen.'

'Police*women*,' said Daisy severely. 'Yes, yes, aren't we brilliant? Last night, if you please.'

'Certainly, certainly,' said Mr DeWitt, shifting in his seat. 'It's quite simple really—'

'Then *tell us*.'

Mr DeWitt frowned. 'I was here, in the saloon, with Theodora and the others, for the planned ritual.'

'What was the ritual?' I asked. Of course, we had seen it, but we did not need to let Mr DeWitt know that.

'Not for you to hear about,' said Mr DeWitt. 'It's a deep mystery. All you need to know is that it took the form of a test. I passed it, as did Rhiannon, and Ida and Heppy failed. I remember that Heppy was extremely upset and out of sorts, even more so than usual, and she talked back to Theodora. I left the saloon when it was over – it must have been about eleven p.m. I went back to my cabin, read for a while and fell asleep. I saw no one, I heard nothing, and the first I was aware of the crime was this morning when I was woken by Heppy's screams. I don't believe there's anything more to this than a tragic accident – Heppy was still angry at Theodora, and she took out her rage at her in her sleep.'

'But she was locked in!' I exclaimed.

'We all know that Miss Bartleby is unreliable,' said Mr DeWitt with a shrug. 'She forgets things. And as for the evidence of Mr Young – well, he must have been confused, or perhaps he has been briefed by someone.'

'By which you mean us, I suppose,' said Daisy. 'We're not liars, Mr DeWitt. Unlike you.'

Narcissus DeWitt flinched. His face looked pinched up and as ancient as a tortoise.

'Me? A liar?' he cried.

'Indeed,' snapped Daisy. 'You're lying to us. You say you went into your room just after eleven, and you didn't come out again until you heard Heppy scream. Unfortunately for you, I remember the scene quite distinctly. You came out of your cabin after Miss Wong and I had already arrived. You never went into Theodora's room. Is that right?'

I caught the thread of her thought, then, and met her eye.

'That's absolutely right,' said Mr DeWitt.

'But it can't be,' I said. 'If you never went near the body, as you say, then there shouldn't be any blood on a pair of your pyjama trousers. And there is, isn't there? How do you explain that?'

8

'How – how do you know that?' gasped Mr DeWitt. 'You – how dare you go into my cabin!'

'We have our ways,' said Daisy. 'But you don't deny that there are bloodstained pyjama bottoms in your cabin, do you?'

'I – I—' Mr DeWitt stuttered into silence. 'This is monstrous! You can't just accuse me—'

'I don't see why we shouldn't,' said Daisy coolly. 'We caught you in a lie, didn't we? You haven't yet given us an explanation for the bloodstains. And there are other suspicious items in your room too. Why do you need seven bottles of Easton's Syrup for a week-long cruise? What were you planning to do with them all?'

Mr DeWitt began to wheeze. He doubled over in his chair, gasping, and fell to his knees. Spit trembled on his lips and his eyes streamed. I jumped out of my chair and ran to him. Alexander left his position at the door and knelt down beside us, his arm on Mr DeWitt's back. Amina's hands were over her mouth.

'Mr DeWitt!' I cried. 'Mr DeWitt, are you all right?'

'He's just shamming,' said Daisy.

'He isn't!' I said indignantly. 'Daisy, don't just sit there!'

Daisy got up and came to stand over us. 'Mr DeWitt,' she said clearly, 'are you dying?'

Mr DeWitt wheezed.

'He's quite clearly not dying,' said Daisy to the room. 'Mr DeWitt, do calm down, otherwise we shall never get to the bottom of this. Explain yourself!'

'Alexander, bring him some water!' I said. 'Amina, help me get him back up into his chair.'

We hauled Mr DeWitt, still gasping, back up onto his chair, and Alexander put a cup of water to his lips. He sipped, coughed and wiped his eyes.

'There,' said Daisy. 'What did I tell you? Come along, Mr DeWitt, *explain*! What did you do?'

There was a pause.

'I didn't kill her!' cried Mr DeWitt at last. 'You have to believe me – I didn't.' His eyes were streaming again, but I did not think it was just from his coughing. 'There's been a terrible mistake – it's all just a coincidence – you have to believe me—'

'Good grief, what happened? Come on!'

'Look, I – I did go to bed last night, but then I woke up again. I looked at my wristwatch, and it was just after two. And I – er – I wanted to look in on Theodora. See how she was sleeping. So I got up and went out on deck.'

The words were pouring out of Mr DeWitt now in a torrent. Alexander was scribbling notes furiously. I glanced at Daisy and saw her intense expression, the wrinkle appearing at the top of her nose.

'It was a clear, cold night. The moon was high above the deck. And I saw Heppy coming out of Theodora's room.'

'Don't lie to me!' said Daisy fiercely. 'Are you sure?'

Mr DeWitt shifted again in his seat. 'I saw her back and the curls of her hair in the moonlight,' he said. 'I thought she was just having one of her episodes. I – er – didn't want to wake her. She gets upset when she's woken. So I waited until she'd gone back into her cabin, and then I went in to Theodora. Her door was open, and the curtains on the door too. I tripped over something on the floor, and almost fell over it – and then I realized my feet were wet. I looked and I could see there was something dark on them. And then I bent over Theodora, and she was dead. Her eyes were open, and there was blood all over her nightgown – her sheet was bundled up on the floor. That was what I'd fallen over. I panicked. I went running into her bathroom and tried to wash myself clean – I don't know if I got it all – and then I ran out of there back to my cabin. I changed into fresh pyjama bottoms, scrubbed off the bloody ones and bundled them under my bed. I hoped no one would notice. I – er – they're my favourite pair, so I didn't want to throw them away. And that's how I know that Miss Bartleby and Mr Young are lying. Heppy could not have been locked in her room. She *did* sleepwalk, and she murdered Theodora. I didn't kill her, I swear it. She was already dead when I got there!'

9

There was a pause. My mind was rushing.

'Very well,' said Daisy at last. 'Do you have anything else to say?'

'No,' said Mr DeWitt. 'That's everything.'

'Wait!' I said. 'Mr DeWitt, you still haven't told us one important thing.'

I saw Daisy glance at me, and nodded reassuringly. Something in May's story had come back into my head.

'When did you throw the bottle into the Nile?' I asked. 'Before or after you went into Theodora's room?'

'I – I—' Mr DeWitt's jaw worked. 'Oh, curse it! Afterwards. I should have thrown in the handkerchief too, but I forgot it, and then I was afraid it would float. But there was nothing in that bottle, nothing at all, and I'll stick to that.'

'Of course there wasn't,' said Daisy, eyebrow raised. 'Go on, then, you may leave. Alexander, show him out.'

'Thank you,' I added, as Mr DeWitt struggled to his feet with almost indecent speed, pushing himself up with his cane so quickly he nearly toppled over.

'And fetch me Miss Bartleby,' said Daisy. 'At once, if you please.'

'*Was* he lying?' I asked into the silence, as soon as Mr DeWitt had been led out of the room.

'Most certainly,' said Daisy. 'Didn't you think? Simply deciding to go into Theodora's room at two in the morning, while she was asleep! That's nonsense. Either they were having an affair, or your theory about the strychnine is correct.'

'An affair!' I gasped. 'But they're both so old!'

'Yes, well, grown-ups are dreadfully disgusting. We know that by now, Hazel. I don't believe in the affair theory at all, not when we have those bottles as evidence, and the stained hanky you found, but I wanted to mention it. So Mr DeWitt was on his way to do something awful – probably intending to plant the bottle of doctored tonic that would poison Theodora – when he stumbled across a frame-up in progress. This helps us narrow down the timings, doesn't it? We now know that the murderer had committed the crime and unlocked Heppy's door *before* two a.m. That was the time she sleepwalked the night before, wasn't it? That's her pattern. The murderer must have known to use that! So the crime was done between twelve, when Mr Young confirmed that Heppy was locked in, and two.'

'But that's if Mr DeWitt's innocent, isn't it?' asked Amina, behind us. 'What if he's guilty? He might have murdered Theodora, unlocked Heppy's door and let her walk into the crime scene. If he killed her, it explains the blood on his pyjamas.'

'I'm not sure,' I said slowly. 'I saw those stains – they were just around the hems of the pyjama bottoms. That fits with Mr DeWitt's story – that he tripped over the sheet *on the floor*. If it was already down there when he got in, that means Heppy must have gone into the cabin before him.'

'*Oh*,' said Daisy. 'Oh *bother*! I do believe you're right.'

'And it explains the stains we found in the sink – if Mr DeWitt washed himself off in a panic, getting fingerprints and blood all over the taps. They never fitted with the framing – now we know why.'

I could imagine it – shaking hands, the cold of the water and the swirling dark stains, knowing that there was a dead body a few feet away. I shuddered.

'Does that rule out Mr DeWitt?' I asked, to quiet my mind. 'Whatever he was hiding, he told the truth about going into the cabin – the crime scene proves it. And he's the person who made the splash May heard – the last noise she heard. So that tells us that everything happened *before* two.'

'Hmm,' said Daisy. 'Bother it, it does seem that way. But we can only be absolutely certain once we've completed our interviews.'

'George is here,' Alexander said from the doorway. 'He's got lunch.'

'Oh, excellent,' said Daisy. 'Let him in. You bring us Miss Bartleby – and *don't* let her talk to the other suspects.'

'Alex will be perfectly fine,' said George, coming in with a tray piled high with food. 'He's a good detective. And he doesn't work for you, no matter how much you wish he did.'

'Oh, shush, you,' said Daisy, eyeing George with a cross expression.

'No,' said George cheerfully, putting down the tray with a crash. It was piled high with creamy hummus and baba ganoush, flatbreads freckled from cooking and crisp pickles. 'I won't. It's not good for you. You keep forgetting that there are *two* detective agencies trying to solve this case. Alex and I aren't your minions, and we don't have to do what you say.'

'You got lunch for us, didn't you?'

'Only because I'm not *quite* heartless enough to let you get poisoned.'

'You don't think someone would!' I gasped.

'Why not? Saying you're detectives is dangerous. It'd be much easier for quite a few people on this ship if you and Daisy just went away.'

'Including you!' said Daisy.

George grinned at her. 'We like each other enough to tell each other where we're going wrong,' he said. 'If I poisoned you, I wouldn't have nearly as much fun.'

'I do not like you!' spluttered Daisy. 'How dare you! You are a nuisance!'

'The good news is that I watched the cook make up this tray and there's no poison in any of it,' George went on. 'You can eat it – but tell me what you've found out while you're eating.'

We explained. George whistled. 'So we can rule him out!' he said.

'I think so,' I said, nodding.

Alexander stuck his head round the door of the saloon. 'I've got Miss Bartleby,' he said.

He beamed at me, and I beamed back. Daisy pinched me and settled herself, her mood quite gone.

'Bring her in,' she said grandly. 'Hazel, compose yourself.'

And I was cross with her. I remember that now, and feel so guilty. I was cross with Daisy on her last day.

But of course I did not know that then.

10

Our interview with Miss Bartleby did not go at all like Mr DeWitt's. She perched herself on the little chair and smiled cheerfully round at all of us.

'Well,' she said, 'isn't this nice?'

'Miss Bartleby, we're here to ask you about the murder,' said Daisy, sitting forward in her chair.

Miss Bartleby's face fell. 'I don't know anything about that,' she said. 'Don't ask me, please. We agreed we wouldn't say anything.'

'I'm afraid we have to,' I said gently.

'We agreed we wouldn't say anything!' cried Miss Bartleby. 'That poor boy – I never meant to – there was something wrong with the meat, I'm certain of it!'

I got the most uncomfortable feeling. This wasn't right of us, I knew it. We had already worked out that Miss Bartleby could not be behind this crime. 'Miss

Bartleby,' I said, 'that isn't – it's not Joshua's death we're talking about. It's Mrs Miller's.'

'*Hazel!*' hissed Daisy.

'No, dear,' said Miss Bartleby. 'Theodora is quite well. You're confused.'

'Miss Bartleby, really! Mrs Miller is dead. She's been murdered. It happened last night, and we need you to tell us what you know about it.'

Miss Bartleby stared at me. 'But it can't be!' she said. 'Surely Theodora can't be dead! I remember it quite clearly – I put her to bed the way I always do! I tucked her in! She's quite well – she must be!'

My breath caught. Tears were rolling down Miss Bartleby's cheeks.

'It keeps happening!' she said. 'It keeps happening, and I try to stop it. I didn't mean it . . . I never meant to. Please!'

I stood up. I suddenly decided that this could not go on. 'Miss Bartleby,' I said, 'we're sorry. It's all right. You can go. Thank you so much.'

'Hazel!' cried Daisy, but I shook my head at her.

'It's all right,' I repeated. 'You can go. Alexander, help her.'

Alexander moved forward and took Miss Bartleby's arm. She leaned on him as she got to her feet, her face still wet with tears.

'I never meant to,' she whispered, as she was led away.

'Hazel!' said Daisy again, as soon as she was gone. 'How dare you! She was about to tell us something important!'

'She was not!' I said. 'Daisy, she was getting mixed up about the time again. I know she's an important witness, and we have to interview everyone, but it's not fair of us to press her. She knows what happened to Joshua, that's clear, but she doesn't know anything more about Mrs Miller's murder. She's not well in the head at all. We shouldn't keep bothering her like this.'

'But she might be lying!' cried Daisy. 'This might all be a clever ruse!'

'It's not a ruse and you know it,' I snapped at her. I was furious. 'She couldn't reach the curtain rail, so she couldn't have committed the crime. And she genuinely can't remember things.'

'I think Hazel's right,' said Amina. 'My great-aunt – she was like that. She would get so confused, and ask me the same things over and over again. She thought I was Mama sometimes.'

I nodded. I remembered the fear in Miss Bartleby's face. And I knew that we were right to rule her out.

11

Daniel came in. He looked furious.

'See here,' he said. 'This is all nonsense! Why has anyone let you do this? You're children!'

'How dare you!' said Daisy. 'I am a policewoman. More respect, please!'

'You are not!' said Daniel. 'You're children. I'm sure of it. You're no older than those boys you've got being your heavies.'

'I simply won't dignify that with a response,' said Daisy. 'We are here to solve Theodora Miller's murder. Will you help us or not?'

Daniel's shoulders slumped. 'This whole trip – it's like a bad dream,' he said. 'It's all absolutely ridiculous. I never should have come. I thought I could finally get some answers about Josh, and make Mother see sense, but it's – it's just not *worth* it. Nothing is. I swore when I left – after what I knew she had done to Josh – that I wouldn't come back, and I should never have broken my vow.'

'But you wanted to see Theodora,' I said. 'You couldn't stay away from her.'

I looked at Daniel and saw a person who felt utterly abandoned, by his best friend and by his mother. And although the dead are dead, and will never come back, you never quite lose the flame of hope in your soul where living parents are concerned. I know this perfectly well. No matter how dreadful they are in reality, the vision never stops rising up that one day they will come to you with their hands held out and apologize for every wrong they ever did you, if only you could discover what to say to turn the key to their heart.

'I didn't want to be right about Josh,' said Daniel. 'I was hoping she'd tell me I was making it up.'

'But she didn't deny it,' I said.

'She didn't,' said Daniel. 'I went to her about it, and she just smiled up at me with that – that inscrutable look she puts on. And she said, "Some unpleasant things are necessary, Daniel. You mustn't think of it any more. Go to bed." It was – it was monstrous! I couldn't believe it.'

'So this was last night?' asked Daisy. 'What time? Hurry up! Come on!'

'I – before that idiotic ritual of hers.'

'No, it wasn't,' said Daisy silkily. 'I was watching her last night – policewomen are always watching, you know. She went straight from dinner to the ritual – the ritual that you interrupted the end of. She asked you to come and speak to her later – so, did you? Did you come back while she was alone in her room, after Heppy and Miss Bartleby had left?'

'I – I – no! This was earlier, I tell you!' Daniel stuttered.

'You're quite clearly lying. You said she was looking *up* at you. Was she in bed when you spoke to her? Did you kill her? Did you make her pay for what she did to Joshua?'

'No!' gasped Daniel. 'All right, it was in her cabin. I waited until Heppy and Miss Bartleby had gone, and that Mr Young fellow had stopped wandering around, and I went in to see her.'

'What time was that?' I asked.

'About – oh, about half past twelve, I suppose. I spoke to her, she said those things to me – she didn't even get out of bed – and then I left. I was quite done with her. But I didn't kill her. How dare you suggest it! You're just children – I won't stand for this any longer!'

And with that he leaped up off his chair and stormed out of the saloon.

'Well,' said Daisy, after a pause, 'I would say that was quite interesting, don't you think?'

'He didn't have blood on his slippers this morning,' I said, remembering.

'Yes, but that doesn't mean anything. He might have been barefoot, or committed the murder in another pair. We know he was on the spot last night, Hazel – he really might have murdered her!'

12

Mr Young was next – for we had agreed that we should speak to everyone who had been on the saloon deck last night, and Mr Young had already given us some very useful evidence. He was a most frustrating interviewee, though. He repeated his story about seeing Heppy locked in, then said that afterwards he had returned to his room and gone to sleep. 'I sleep lightly,' he said vaguely. 'I'm sure I heard someone running about on the deck several times in the night. I thought it might be robbers, so I locked my door from the inside.'

Did he know Theodora and the Breath of Life before this journey? No, he had never heard of them. 'I don't think they know much about ancient Egypt,' he said. I glanced up at Alexander, behind him, and saw him grin. I covered my mouth to hide my smile.

It was clear that Mr Young was quite uninterested in the Breath of Life, and quite unable to help any more.

We sent him away and called in Miss Beauvais. But Miss Beauvais, when we tried to question her, simply wept and shook her head. She was no use at all.

After her – and I quailed at this – were my family.

The thought of speaking to my father about the murder made me feel prickly all over. I put out my hand to squeeze Daisy's shoulder. She turned to look at me.

'Buck up, Watson,' she murmured. 'Remember, you are terribly important, and you can deal with anything. And now *do* look serious, will you?'

I took a deep breath and pulled my spine up straight, shoulders back, trying to make my body look as though it knew exactly what it was doing. It is hard for me to do this, still – even years of friendship with Daisy, and training at Deepdean and the Rue Theatre, have not been enough to truly make me confident. I still feel as if I am acting a part, and not acting it very well. I am privately convinced that one day I will be found out.

I looked at Daisy, chin up, neck straight, eyes a little veiled by her lashes, every inch a golden heroine, and for a moment felt quite desperately inadequate.

But then – well, then I remembered what I have learned since I first arrived in England. There is no one way for a heroine to look or be, whether or not Daisy herself will ever accept that.

So, by the time my father came into the room, I had put all my silly thoughts out of my head. I was ready to show him how grown-up I really was these days.

May came rushing in first, as always, Rose behind her with my father. I looked at Rose's serious little face, the way she was glancing up at him, and realized something about my little sister that I ought to have seen before. I had thought she was being timid and bookish, so far away from home, but it was not that at all. Rose was trying to keep close to Father to take care of him. She was only afraid of what might happen to him, not of what might happen to herself.

And I felt guilty. Looking after my father should be my job. I should be looking after them all – being the good eldest daughter – but instead I was off helping Daisy with this case.

'I'm sorry!' I said, startling everyone.

'Hum!' said my father. 'You should be. I lied for you, Wong Fung Ying – I lied to adults! I hope you have a good solution to this awful business, otherwise we shall all look very foolish.'

'I think Hazel's amazing!' said May.

'And as for you, Wong Mei Li, do not speak any more! You've already been naughty enough. Getting away from me three times! At least I have one dutiful daughter,' my father said, putting his heavy hand on Rose's shoulder. Rose stared up at him anxiously, and then at me.

'Father, we only need to ask you if you saw or heard anything last night,' I said. 'You or Rose.'

'Why not May?' asked my father suspiciously. 'Has she already told you? Has she been helping you? Hazel, you promised!'

'No, no, I – I didn't ask her to! But she did tell me, and it was very helpful. Father, she proved that no one on our side of the saloon deck could have committed the murder – she gave you an alibi!'

'WELL!' said my father. 'I suppose that's not a bad thing. But, May, you will be in very deep trouble once we are back on dry land.'

'Yes, Father,' said May happily.

'Now, Rose, can you help Hazel in any way?' asked my father. 'Hazel, once your sisters were in their cabin, I read for twenty minutes and then fell asleep. I don't believe I heard anything or saw anything that might be relevant, I'm sorry.'

'I – er – no, nothing,' said Rose.

'Are you sure, Ling Ling?' I asked.

Rose blushed. 'Will I get in trouble?'

My father sighed. 'No, you will not be in trouble, Rose,' he said.

'Oh. Then I saw May go out of our room. She thought I was asleep, but I wasn't. I woke up because she bumped into my bed. She was taking all her blankets with her.'

'Hah!' said May to herself crossly. I could tell that she would not make the same mistake twice.

'Anyway, I couldn't get back to sleep properly after that,' said Rose. 'I was worried about her. In *Peril in the Winter Term*, a girl crept out of her dorm at night and got pneumonia and almost *died*. I knew May was out on the deck, so I kept watching her. Every time I heard a noise, I'd go and look out, to make sure no one else was there. But it was only her, every time.'

I beamed. May's story had been helpful – but here was the final confirmation of it. 'Brilliant, Rose!' I cried.

Rose blushed. 'I did hear some other sounds, from the other side of the boat,' she said. 'Once or twice. Just little bumps and thumps. I thought someone might have fallen over their slippers on the way to get a glass of water, something like that. But it wasn't May, so it didn't worry me. I went back to sleep.'

'What time were the sounds?' I asked eagerly.

'One was at half past twelve, and another was around two,' said Rose. 'I remember I looked at the clock on the wall both times. That's all I know, though.'

'That's more than enough!' said Daisy. 'Really! The Wong family are the most excellent witnesses.'

And both May and Rose smiled at that. Despite himself, even my father looked pleased.

'May I have a moment with my daughter?' Father asked, as May and Rose turned to go.

'Oooh, Big Sister, you're in *trouble*!' May whispered to me. Father glared her into silence and motioned me outside. I took a deep breath of river air, squinting against the afternoon sun. I felt suddenly utterly terrified. I could not look Father in the face.

'Wong Fung Ying, stop staring at your feet,' said my father crossly. 'Are you May's age?' And then, in a softer voice, he added, 'Hazel, I am not going to tell you off. You aren't a child any more. I only want to ask you – are you sure you know what you're doing? Are you sure this is right? I worry for you, my good girl.'

I looked up then, the light and the water splitting and dazzling in my eyes, and saw him frowning, his face creased with concern. 'I think so,' I said. 'I don't know, but we have to do it. No one else will.'

My father sighed and put his hand on my shoulder. 'You know, I never thought you'd be the one to give me trouble. May, absolutely, but you – you were always so quiet, before I sent you off to England! But I suppose I should have known. You are too much like me sometimes. If you're sure what you're doing is right, you'll never give up. And you're sure.'

'I am,' I said, nodding up at him.

'Well then,' said my father, 'that's all I wanted to know.'

13

Miss Doggett was our last suspect, and she came into the saloon with an angry look on her face. She did not like that she had been kept waiting.

'Welcome,' said Daisy, as sonorous as a bell – and, of course, I knew then that she had kept Miss Doggett until last on purpose.

'Hello again, Miss Wells,' said Miss Doggett, glaring. 'Hello, Miss Wong.'

'As you are aware, we are working to uncover the truth about Theodora Miller's murder,' said Daisy. 'What do you know about it?'

'I know that some people are better off dead,' said Miss Doggett. 'I know that Heppy killed Theodora in her sleep. I don't know why you insist on complicating matters.'

'But we've proved she didn't!' I said. 'She *can't* have!'

'My colleague is quite correct,' said Daisy, laying a calming hand on my arm. 'Hephzibah Miller is quite innocent, and we shall say so to the Parquet. The question becomes, then, who *could* have done it? We have it on good authority that no one on the starboard side could have committed the crime.'

'So you rule yourselves out, then!' cried Miss Doggett. 'Most convenient.'

'We do not commit murders, we solve them,' said Daisy. 'I do wish I did not have to keep on explaining this to people. I do not intend to let you know who gave us this information, only to tell you to trust that it is good.'

Daisy, I thought, was sounding more and more like Inspector Priestley in her interrogations.

'Now, when did you go to Theodora's cabin last night?'

'I did not go to Theodora's cabin. After the ritual was over, I went back to my own cabin and went to bed.'

'Don't lie to me, please. I know you did.'

'I told you—'

Daisy pressed her fingers down on my arm, and I knew what she was getting at. 'We know you did,' I repeated, 'because of what we found in your cabin.'

'You – when did you go in there? You had no right! I shall complain to Mr Mansour!'

'Your cabin was searched less than an hour after Theodora had been found dead by Heppy,' continued Daisy. 'You had not yet been back in – we saw you out on deck at the time, still in your night things – but when we went in we found several dolls that were clearly meant to represent the members of the Breath of Life. And the doll that looked like Theodora—'

'—had three pins in it!' I finished off triumphantly. 'You must have seen the body at some point in the night, otherwise you wouldn't have been able to re-create the way it looked so accurately. So we know you're lying.'

Miss Doggett flinched and clamped her hands down round her knees firmly. It might have been for emphasis, and it might have been to stop them shaking. 'I – I – that is purely a coincidence. I was praying. When I pray, my ba leaves my body and flies like a bird out around me. Last night it went down the saloon deck to Theodora's cabin, and it saw her lying there, the sheet tucked up around her neck, with three great wounds in her chest and neck. I was not sure, then, whether this was truth or prophecy, and I am still unsure, but I – recorded it. I drove pins from my sewing kit into Theodora's doll. And then this morning I woke up and saw – what we all saw. I believe magic was at work last night.'

'What if we don't believe in magic?' asked Daisy fiercely. 'What if we take this as an admission of guilt?'

'Take it however you like,' snapped Miss Doggett. 'I don't have to speak to you, you know.'

'Of course you don't,' said Daisy. 'You don't have to say anything about Theodora, and you don't have to say anything about Joshua Morse, either. But I do wonder why your nightdress had blood on it this morning.'

Miss Doggett cried out, and jumped to her feet. 'How dare you!' she shouted. 'You have no right! You wicked girl. You – you ought to beware. There are forces in this world – forces that should not be played with. I know ancient magic, and I can use it. I've done it before. If you don't leave us alone, you'll regret it. Just you wait.'

And, with that, she darted from the saloon, shoving past Alexander.

'Well!' said Daisy briskly. 'Wasn't that illuminating?'

'No!' I said. 'Daisy, that was horrid!'

'Oh pish!' said Daisy. 'Nothing we haven't heard before. It won't come to anything.'

But, as I stared at Daisy, I was not so sure. Magic might not be real, but murderers certainly are. And murderers do not tend to stop until someone stops them.

14

'So what does it all mean?' asked Amina, once Miss Doggett had gone.

'It means that we're getting closer to working out who committed the murder!' said Daisy, getting up with a bounce. 'Ah, that's better! It's tiring being a grown-up. You have to sit so still.'

'I thought you couldn't wait to be one,' I said, rather sarcastically.

'Don't, Watson, it doesn't become you. All right, all right, let's sum up! What first?'

'Clues,' I said at once, ignoring Daisy's groan of 'Hazel!' for Alexander's quick, surprised grin. Daisy always preferred to take each suspect first.

'And we had plenty of them!' said Alexander. 'The sheet, the bloodstains, the pins – and the timings! Here, look, I made a note of the timeline.'

'We don't need that!' said Daisy. 'We've never done one before.'

'Then it's about time you did,' said George. 'Even the best detectives can get better.'

The two of them eyed each other for a moment, and then Daisy stretched out an imperious hand. 'Show me,' she said.

We all crowded round Daisy, looking over her shoulder at Alexander's scribbled notes.

WHAT HAPPENED ON THE NIGHT
OF THE MURDER

1. 11 p.m. Ritual broke up. Daniel confronted victim and victim told him she would speak to him later. Victim went back to her room with Miss B and the knife (confirmed by GM, AA, HW, DW, AEM).

2. 11:02 p.m.–11:20 p.m. Victim in room with Miss B (confirmed by her – we have no corroboration, but victim seen alive afterwards so irrelevant).

3. 11:20 p.m.–midnight. Victim in room with Miss B and Heppy (confirmed by both RB and HM). Miss B tucks her in, Heppy reads to her and then they leave. Miss B locks Heppy in her room (witnessed and corroborated by Mr Y)

and goes back to her own room. May Wong leaves her cabin (confirmed by RW).

4. 12:30 a.m. Victim argues with Daniel (according to DW).

5. 12:30 a.m.–2 a.m. Murder takes place.

6. 12:30 a.m.–2 a.m. Miss D claims she has a vision of Mrs M lying stabbed in her bed, the sheets up around her neck.

7. 12:30 a.m.–2 a.m. The murderer unlocks Heppy's cabin door again.

8. 2 a.m. Heppy seen sleepwalking away from NdW towards the other end of the saloon deck, port side. NdW then went into the victim's room and found her dead. NdW tripped over the sheet on the floor, and the blood was still wet. NdW threw bottle into Nile.

9. 6:05 a.m. Victim discovered by Heppy waking up.

'This is imprecise,' said Daisy.

'So it is,' said George. 'But it lists the main points. Well done, Alex. We know that Theodora was murdered between twelve thirty a.m. and two a.m. – quite close to two a.m., if we take into account the evidence of the blood on the sheet. It was still sopping wet when Mr DeWitt tripped over it. And, when we look at those separate events, we can see two of the four different times May was woken up – at twelve thirty, when Daniel was in Mrs Miller's cabin, and just past two, when Mr DeWitt fell over the sheet and then threw the bottle into the Nile. So the other two must have been part of the murder!'

'Isn't Miss Doggett's account one, though?' I asked. 'She must have been into Theodora's room at some point – what she said about Theodora being tucked in doesn't make sense otherwise!'

'Well, she's either a witch or she's lying about not being there,' said Daisy with a shrug. 'And, since there's evidence that she was in Theodora's cabin, I would guess it was the latter. So that's one of the other times May woke – and it might be the moment of the murder itself!'

'You think she murdered Theodora and pretended to have a vision about it?' asked George.

'I think she certainly was there,' said Daisy, the thinking crinkle appearing at the top of her nose. 'I don't believe in magic, after all. And the detail about the three wounds, and the sheet – wait a moment! Hazel, as usual, has got to the crux of the matter. The sheet was on the ground when Mr DeWitt came in, and was still there when Heppy found her this morning – no one but the murderer should have seen the body while it was covered by the sheet!'

'So what does that mean?' asked Amina.

'It means that we are very close to being able to work out who the murderer was,' said Daisy. 'We have only two credible suspects left: Daniel and Miss Doggett.'

'All right,' said George. 'But which of them was it? I think we ought to do a re-creation of the night to make sure.'

SUSPECT LIST

1. ~~Hephzibah Miller.~~ ~~The victim's daughter. She~~ ~~was first on the scene, and was found covered in~~ ~~blood. She says that she woke up with no idea how the~~ ~~blood got onto her, and only realized her mother was~~ ~~dead when she went into the victim's cabin. We know~~ ~~she is a sleepwalker, and she believes that she~~ ~~murdered her mother while asleep. But can this be~~ ~~true? It does not explain several things we noticed in~~ ~~Theodora's cabin: the cleaned knife, the sheet on the~~ ~~floor and the bloody sink. We believe she has been~~ ~~framed – but we need to prove that before we rule her~~ ~~out.~~ RULED OUT. From the evidence of Miss Bartleby and Mr Young, we know that she was locked in just after 12, yet at some point during the night her door was unlocked. Therefore someone let her out, intending to frame her – and that person is the murderer!

2. Ida Doggett. The second in command in the Breath of Life Society. Theodora believed Miss

Doggett was the reincarnation of Cleopatra, but Miss Doggett wanted to be Hatshepsut instead, Mrs Miller's reincarnation! We witnessed many disagreements between the two — they have clearly fallen out since Mr DeWitt joined the group. Miss Doggett mentioned being pleased that Theodora was dead this morning, and blamed the gods for the crime — a strange thing to say. She appeared on the scene wrapped in a bathrobe — could she have been hiding blood on her nightdress? This has been confirmed by Daisy Wells — there is blood on Miss Doggett's nightie! From the evidence in Theodora's room, we know that she had partial control of the society's money, and she has expensive taste in clothes — could this be a motive for murdering Theodora? From looking in Miss Doggett's cabin, we know that she believes herself a practitioner of magic. She has shabti dolls representing the Breath of Life members — and Theodora's doll has three pins stuck in its heart! We believe Miss Doggett must have seen the body at some point during the night as there was no opportunity for her to go back to her cabin and do this between the body being found and us discovering the dolls. She also knows Heppy's sleepwalking patterns very well from the evidence of Heppy's Book. But is she the murderer? NOTES:

Miss Doggett believes herself to be a black-magic practitioner! There are lots of strange books in her room, and we also found dolls of all the Breath of Life members. Does she believe she has influence over them? She claims that she had a vision of Theodora's dead body — a vision that is suspiciously accurate. So, did she see the murder — or did she commit it?

3. ~~Rhiannon Bartleby. Another member of the Breath of Life Society. Theodora believed she was the reincarnation of Nefertiti. She seems sweet and gentle, but she made a suspicious confession when the death was discovered this morning. From the conversation May Wong overheard, we know that she seems convinced she not only hurt Mrs Miller but also Joshua Morse, Daniel's friend. She seems to be confused about the details — but does she really not recall exactly what happened, or is she only pretending? Could she have killed Theodora because of her guilt at Joshua's death?~~ RULED OUT. A re-creation proved that she is too short to have hung up the sheet — and interviews with her prove that she is too confused to have planned this crime.

4. *Daniel Miller.* The victim's son. He has been estranged from her, but was temporarily reconciled

with his mother to come on this holiday. However, we know he was extremely angry with her last night. He mentioned Joshua Morse, an ex-member who is now dead — we must learn more about him. In the book he's writing, Daniel seems to blame Theodora for the death of his friend Joshua — did he kill her in revenge? NOTES: From Daniel's writings, it is clear that he believes Joshua was poisoned. We know that Daniel went in to speak to Theodora at 12:30 a.m. on the night of her murder. Theodora did not deny Joshua's killing, and Daniel seems to still genuinely believe that she was responsible. But did he kill her in a fit of rage? He was the last person to admit to seeing her alive, after all . . .

5. ~~Narcissus DeWitt.~~ High up in the Breath of ~~Life Society, and seemingly on Theodora's side. It's~~ ~~clear that he is fighting with Miss Doggett to~~ ~~become second in command. Mr DeWitt was~~ ~~wearing mismatched pyjama trousers when we saw~~ ~~him this morning — why? We have discovered blood on~~ ~~a pair of pyjama trousers, and seven suspicious~~ ~~bottles of Easton's Syrup in his room — these have~~ ~~strychnine in them! We believe he was straining them~~ ~~to get at the strychnine — but what does this mean?~~

~~Is he the murderer?~~ RULED OUT! Narcissus has admitted to going to Theodora's room on the night of her murder, just after 2 a.m. He says that he saw Heppy leaving the cabin, and then walked in to find Theodora already dead, the bloody sheet on the floor. He fell over it, and ran to wash his feet in Theodora's sink – explaining the bloodstains and bloody prints that Daisy Wells and Hazel Wong found there the next morning. He also threw a bottle overboard, a sound heard by May Wong. We believe that Narcissus was planning Theodora's death by poison – but he was not guilty of stabbing her.

PLAN OF ACTION

1. Take a closer look at the scene of the crime.

2. Investigate the other cabins on the saloon deck for clues.

3. Recreate the crime: work out why no scream was heard in the middle of the night and pin down the time of death.

4. Discover who Joshua Morse is and what happened to him!

5. Investigate our suspects, gain their trust and begin to rule them out.

6. Discover more about Theodora Miller. Who was she?

7. Get in to see Heppy!

8. Complete Daisy's plan!!!

9. Re-create the night of the murder.

10. Reveal the murderer!

15

'All right,' I said. 'Let's see. There are five of us, and six people who need to be in the re-creation. So – what do we do about that?'

'I could be two people,' said Daisy at once.

'You can't!' said George. 'We need to make sure that everyone is in the right place, and if you're two people you can't be.'

'There aren't five of us!' said Amina. 'There are six! You've forgotten May.'

'I have not!' I gasped. 'May is not a detective. She might *think* she's one, but—'

'If she's not a detective, I'm not, either,' said Amina. 'This is my first case, isn't it, but you've let me help? May's exactly the same. I know she's little, but she can't do much about that.'

'But she's six!' I cried.

'She found the bloodstains, didn't she?' said George. 'And she helped us in other ways. She's done a lot for this case. I know she's your little sister, Hazel, but she's a good detective – or she will be one, some day soon.'

'A new generation of the Detective Society, when we're all grown up!' said Amina, laughing.

'That's a terrible idea,' said Daisy. 'It implies that we will one day be too old for the Detective Society, whereas that will never be the case. I shall be Detective Society President until I'm one hundred, and I shall turn the Detective Society into an organization greater and more respected than even the Pinkertons – the real ones, not *your* version,' she said with a toss of her head in Alexander and George's direction. 'But I grant you, we can use May. Someone go and get her.'

'HELLO!' said May, sticking her head out from under the bed.

I shrieked. 'How long have you been there?' I asked her furiously.

'Just now,' said May. 'I told Father I needed the loo and I ran for it. I'm ready to help with the creation thing you're doing now.'

'*Re*-creation,' I said. 'And – oh, May! You have to be careful!'

'Why? You aren't careful, and you're all right. I want to be a detective like you, Big Sister. Only I don't need

306

your Detective Society. I shall invent something even better.'

'How dare you!' said Daisy. 'Shrimps these days are getting far too bold. If you heard us, May, then you know what you need to do. You must be one of our suspects and do exactly what we say.'

'All right,' said May. 'I want to be Heppy, though.'

'*Fine*,' I said.

'I shall be Theodora, of course,' said Daisy. 'George, you be Mr DeWitt.' They grinned at each other, highly amused. 'Hazel, you be Miss Doggett, and Amina, you be Miss Bartleby. And Alexander—'

'OK, I'll be Daniel,' said Alexander.

'So,' I said, 'shall we start with the end of the ritual?'

We stood in the saloon. Outside, the sun was low to the west, its rays almost horizontal, and the ship was shivering and juddering as it moved through the water. Our journey was almost over. We would be pulling in to Aswan in little more than an hour, and the problem was not yet solved. We would have to present our solution to the *Hatshepsut* very soon. My heart raced.

'So we begin,' said Daisy, raising her arms dramatically. 'It is past ten, and Theodora – me – is holding her ritual. Amina, you're Miss Bartleby, George, you're Mr DeWitt, Hazel, you're Miss Doggett, and May, you're Heppy, so you're all my acolytes. We're all in the saloon. Alexander, you're Daniel, so you go outside and wander about in a rage for a bit.'

'What's acolyte?' asked May.

'Follower,' said Daisy. 'Be quiet. Now is the moment when Alexander, as Daniel, BURSTS through the door and argues with me. Hello, Alexander, very good. Everyone is very upset. It's eleven p.m. What happens now?'

'I take you to your cabin,' said Amina. 'We're using your cabin as hers, aren't we?'

'Yes, we are – go on, then,' said Daisy. They beamed at each other, and I knew perfectly well why she had chosen Amina to be Miss Bartleby. 'Everyone else, please follow the movements of *your* suspect on the night of the murder. Remember, every minute is ten minutes in real time. Keep a close eye on your wristwatches if you please! Hazel, where is your wristwatch?'

'I gave it to May,' I said.

'I've got a spare one in our cabin,' said Alexander. 'D'you, er, want to come get it?'

'Oh, er, all right,' I said, blushing.

'GOOD LORD, HAZEL, HURRY UP!' said Daisy. 'You don't want to miss anything.'

Flushed with shame, I rushed out of the saloon after Alexander. It was even worse when we arrived in

Alexander and George's cabin. It felt so strange and wrong to be here – seeing George's clothes pressed tidily and hanging in their wardrobe, shoes together beneath his bed, and Alexander's scattered chaotically across the floor and the dresser, mixing with pots of brilliantine and toothpaste and half hiding a pile of magazines and notebooks and pencils and thick, serious-looking tomes. The room smelled of soap and paper and that funny boy smell that somehow is nothing like a Deepdean dorm.

'Oh,' said Alexander, ducking his head and running his hands through his hair awkwardly. 'I'm sorry. I'm usually not this messy. Hold on, I'll get it for you.'

'It's all right,' I said, my voice sounding very strange all of a sudden. 'I don't mind!'

I stood and stared as Alexander dug in his chest of drawers. I found I was sweating at my elbows and knees. Desperate for something to do, I began to shuffle through the pile of books.

'Got it!' said Alexander, wheeling round and holding out a heavy silver watch. 'It's my dad's. I don't like to wear it, but you can borrow it. And look – Hazel. While you're here. There hasn't been much time – I mean – I've been trying to talk to you, but I just – I just think that you're the most—'

I did not seem to be breathing properly. Alexander was looking me in the eyes, not glancing away, and—

'Oh, look at this book!' I gabbled, snatching up one at random and brandishing it in Alexander's face. 'How interesting!'

I felt the tension in the air fall and shatter like a cup on the floor. Alexander's shoulders slumped.

'Oh,' he said. 'Yeah. I guess. It's got the case of that sleepwalker in it, actually, the one I told you about. OK, let's go find the others. We don't want to be late.'

He walked away, out of the cabin, and, although I knew that I ought to be thinking like Miss Doggett to help solve the case, for several seconds I could not move at all.

In the event, we were a little late. I only managed to stumble back out onto the deck, and towards Daisy's room, as Alexander's wristwatch told me that it was ten to two in our reconstruction.

'Hurry up, Hazel!' Daisy hissed from her bed. I did not even want to look at her. My head was swimming. 'So, you're having your vision of me, stabbed to death. But are you murdering me, or am I already dead?'

'I don't know,' I said dully.

'Hazel, whatever is wrong with you? What's that book? Here, give it to me—'

'HELLO!' said May, from the doorway. 'I'm sleepwalking! Look, I found this funny bit of bent-up wire – is it important?'

'Oh, for heaven's sake! Watson, go and hide – May can't see you. May, where did you find that?'

'Heppy's room,' said May. 'What is it?'

'Shouldn't I be coming in now?' asked George, from behind May. 'I need to fall over the sheet, don't I?'

'You're all doing this quite *wrong*! This doesn't work!' bawled Daisy, sitting up on her elbows and letting the sheets fall off her. 'Stop crowding the cabin! Good grief!'

'IS MY YOUNGEST DAUGHTER IN THERE?' roared my father from the deck outside.

May squeaked and tried to burrow into the bed next to Daisy.

'This is chaos!' complained Daisy, who was holding May's wire in one hand while she flipped through Alexander's book with the other. 'None of you are taking this seriously—'

And then she froze.

'Good grief,' she said again, looking down at her lap. 'I – this has not been entirely in vain. Excellent news, Detectives. I believe I know what happened last night, and who the murderer is.'

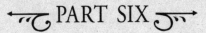

PART SIX

DEATH COMES
AS THE END

1

It was just after five o'clock, and the sun was almost down, dropping liquid gold down through the sky and sliding below the high dark hill that had come into view on the west bank in front of us. The palm trees below it were a long dark scribble, and we were suddenly surrounded by feluccas sailing for the shore. Voices singing the call to prayer began to float across the water, and lights were sparking up ahead of us and to our left. This was Aswan, at last, and our journey – and our case – was almost over.

On deck, the air was shivery and dark, but we were in the saloon again, surrounded by soft lights and velvet seats. This time, though, we were not alone.

All the passengers of the boat had been called in, and were sitting in lounge chairs in a semicircle, facing us. I looked at them and saw an unnerving range of emotions on our suspects' faces. Miss Doggett was furious, vibrating with quiet, ferocious rage. Daniel was puffed up with anger that I thought was really more like terror, while Mr DeWitt was trying to hide his nervousness behind a proud front. Miss Bartleby, though, was scattered like clouds, her hands plucking at her skirt. Mr Mansour stood behind them, next to Heppy, who had been brought up from her prison cabin and was hunched in her seat, her eyes red.

There was Mr Young, looking peaky and unsettled, Miss Beauvais looking despairing and my father sitting with Rose and May on either side of him, hands protectively on their shoulders. May wriggled crossly under his palm, and I really saw, then, that my father has given up on holding me down. He may not like what I do, but he has accepted it. Pik An had come up from her cabin too, still rather green and bilious-looking, but better, and was sitting near my sisters. Next to her, Amina, Alexander and George sat in a group, watching us rather enviously.

'I have called this meeting—' Daisy began importantly.

'*We* have called this meeting,' I said. Daisy glared at me, but I stared back at her without blinking, and at last she lowered her eyes and sniffed.

'*We* have called this meeting to discuss what happened last night,' I said.

'Yes, indeed!' said Daisy. 'We have interviewed all the relevant parties, and we are now ready to present our conclusions.

'LAST NIGHT,' she began, 'a terrible wrong was perpetrated. Theodora Miller was murdered. The crime looked simple. We all thought the explanation was clear – that Heppy Miller sleepwalked into her mother's room and killed her. But, in fact, this crime was much more complicated than it first appeared. A deviously brilliant mind was behind it – a mind currently in this saloon.'

I saw several people flinch.

'So what did happen last night?' asked Daisy. She was enjoying herself, I could see. Daisy loves an audience, and here she was the centre of attention. Her eyes blazed blue, her hair crackled pale fire – she was absolutely Daisy, absolutely my best friend.

I keep on remembering her like that.

'We all know that Theodora held a ritual before bed last night,' I said – I could feel that Daisy wanted me to speak. She did not even need to look at me. 'Daniel Miller came in at the end of it, and the two had an argument. Then Theodora Miller was led away to her cabin – cabin seven – by Miss Bartleby. Miss Bartleby prepared Theodora for bed, and as she did so was joined by Heppy. Miss Bartleby tucked Theodora in and Heppy read to her until just before midnight, and then they walked back to Heppy's cabin – cabin one. Heppy asked Miss Bartleby to lock her in, and Miss Bartleby did so, something confirmed by Mr Young. The boat was then largely quiet.'

'Until, of course, we were all woken up just after six this morning by screaming,' Daisy said. 'Heppy had discovered Theodora lying dead in her bed in cabin seven. Heppy was herself covered in blood. It seemed, as I have said, very simple. Heppy had sleepwalked into Theodora's cabin, killed Theodora and then gone back to her own cabin. She only realized what she'd done the next morning.

'But, you see, that story did not quite fit the facts. First of all, the bloodstains on Heppy did not match the crime scene. Theodora had only been stabbed a few times, in the throat and around the heart, and she must have been covered with her sheet when it happened – we heard from several people that Theodora liked to have it tucked tightly, high up around her neck. It ought to have caught all the blood, meaning that Heppy should have been hardly bloody at all, and it ought still to have been on the bed. But instead it was on the floor, on the other side of the cabin, and Heppy's hands and nightie were covered in blood. There was blood on the sink in Theodora's bathroom too, which didn't fit with Heppy's story.'

'Then we went to talk to Heppy,' I went on. 'And she told us that, because she knew she might sleepwalk, she had asked to be locked in her own cabin by Miss Bartleby, from the outside. Then she went to sleep – but when she woke up the cabin door was open, the key still on the outside. That was when she discovered that she was covered in blood – and that she had sleepwalked that night, after all. So we realized that, for Heppy's door to be open, someone must have unlocked it *after* Miss Bartleby and Mr Young saw it locked up.'

'Yes!' said Daisy eagerly. 'Someone who knew Heppy sleepwalks, usually at around two a.m., and that she always goes into Theodora's room when she does so. Someone was trying to frame Heppy. So who else could it be? We knew from the evidence of a witness that only someone with a cabin on the port side of the saloon deck could have committed the crime.'

'What witness?' asked Daniel, interrupting rudely.

I saw May bounce and twist in her seat.

'*Someone*,' I said. 'We aren't at liberty to say.'

My father pressed down on the top of May's head until she subsided crossly.

'We also deduced that, because it must have been someone who knew that Heppy sleepwalked, it had to be a Breath of Life member, or ex-member, which meant—'

'—Miss Doggett, Mr DeWitt, Miss Bartleby or Mr Miller!' said Daisy at once. 'We had our suspects. But who fitted the facts? We had to dig deeper. And what we discovered was *extremely* interesting.'

2

'This really is all nonsense,' said Daniel. 'Are you going to admit that you're not policewomen at all? You're little girls – you're the same age as these boys!'

'I *did* think they were at first,' said Mr Young plaintively.

'We are absolutely NOT the same age as the boys!' cried Daisy. 'You can look at our passports, if you like.'

'Oh really?' asked Daniel. 'May I? As it happens, I've done a spot of spying myself. I've been into your cabin and I have your passports here.'

He put his hand in his pocket and pulled out two passports. My heart clenched. 'Just look at them! These are not young women – these are little girls, not even out of school yet. See!'

As I watched, he thrust the two passports in Mr Mansour's face.

'How dare you!' cried Daisy, panting with rage. 'How dare you break into OUR cabin!'

'Ah, you don't like it much, do you?' crowed Daniel. 'Mr Mansour, just look at these. They were clearly both born in 1920 . . . something!'

Mr Mansour peered at the pages Daniel had thrust under his nose. The whole saloon had gone shiveringly still, or perhaps it was only the inside of my own head.

'Hmm,' said Mr Mansour at last. 'It is not very clear, is it? There seems to have been some water damage.'

'We were caught in the rain at Paddington Station,' said Daisy, pink with outrage.

'LIAR!' cried Daniel.

'Curious but not definitive,' said Mr Mansour. 'And if the two young ladies say they are from the police, and Miss Wong's father confirms it, then I must listen to him.'

My father merely turned his gaze on to Daniel and nodded. I knew it was because he could not bear to lie again, but to Daniel it must have seemed like yet another confirmation.

'You – you're all quite mad! This is nonsense!'

'*Do* be quiet,' said Daisy. 'We must get on with revealing the murderer. As we were saying, we had narrowed down the suspects to four. Now we must return to what we discovered in Theodora's cabin, and examine it more thoroughly.'

'There were some very odd things,' I said in answer to her nod. 'It wasn't only that the sheet was on the floor, it was – well, the *detail* of it. Daisy, you explain.'

'Blood!' said Daisy. 'The thing about blood is that, when it's fresh, it's a liquid, so it tends to drip and move about.'

Miss Bartleby said, 'Really! Ugh!'

'And that's what the blood on the sheet in Theodora's room had done. The sheet was all covered in long drips. Which, when you think about it, quite goes against the laws of physics. You see, the sheet was on Theodora's bed when she was murdered, and then it ended up crumpled on the floor. There shouldn't have been any time when it was hanging up – only from the evidence of the drips, we can tell that there was. So why on earth would someone – the murderer – hang up a sheet and then throw it back down onto the floor?'

'We worked it out when we looked at the curtains in the door of Theodora's cabin,' I said. 'There were one or two little smears of blood on them, and more on the curtain rail. But we guessed that the sheet might have brushed up against them—'

'Not guessed,' said Daisy. 'We never guess. We *looked rationally* at the stains, and then at the sheet, and *deduced* that the sheet must have been hung up in the doorway immediately after the murder. After we'd worked that out, the reason why came quite quickly on its heels. Watson, do the honours.'

I took a deep breath. I could feel the eyes of everyone in the room on me, and I realized that I am almost used to this now. I always think of Daisy as the one who is the centre of attention, but the truth is that these days I don't mind attention at all. 'The murderer hung up the sheet so that Heppy would push through it, thinking it was just the curtain to the room, and cover herself in blood,' I said.

Several people exclaimed. I saw Mr DeWitt look horrified.

'This whole murder was very cleverly planned,' said Daisy. 'Planned to look as though Heppy murdered her mother in her sleep, when really that wasn't the case at all. The murderer killed Theodora when they were very much awake, and then spent time carefully staging the scene. They hung up the sheet, knowing perfectly well that Heppy would soon walk through it. She would only notice the blood when she woke up – and, of course, her first assumption, and the assumption of everyone else, would be that she killed her mother.'

Heppy sobbed quietly.

'And that's what we all thought, didn't we?' I went on. 'That's what Mr Mansour assumed, and why he locked her away. But, as soon as we realized what the sheet really meant, we saw how useful Heppy's arrest was to all of our suspects.'

'How could you say that?' gasped Miss Bartleby. 'Poor sweet Heppy! I was devastated!'

'Were you!' snapped Daisy. 'Shall we take you first, since you've so helpfully volunteered?'

3

'Daisy,' I said, laying my hand on her arm. I had a worm of discomfort in my heart. What we knew about Miss Bartleby – I did not think it should be shared. But Daisy narrowed her eyes and shook me off.

'The truth is important,' she said. 'We have to do this!

'You were with the victim last night,' Daisy went on, turning back to Miss Bartleby. 'We all know that. You helped her get ready for bed – you and Heppy. Did you argue with Mrs Miller? Did you decide to go back later, when you knew she was asleep, and kill her, unlocking Heppy's door afterwards, so that she would sleepwalk into her mother's room and be blamed for it?'

'No!' said Miss Bartleby, raising a shaking hand to her mouth. 'I would never! I loved Theodora!'

'Perhaps you did,' said Daisy. 'Perhaps that's the truth of it. Perhaps you loved her enough to commit a murder on her behalf – because that's what happened to Joshua Morse, isn't it? You killed him for her?'

'NO!' cried Miss Bartleby. Her eyes were bright with tears now, her little mouth trembling. 'I – it – I don't – I don't remember. I don't remember, *please*.'

'Daisy!' I snapped. This was too much. I did not want us to shame Miss Bartleby like this.

'We'll leave Joshua's death for now,' said Daisy, eyeing me reluctantly. 'And – well, for this crime, we came to the conclusion that you did not kill Theodora. You're far too short to reach the top of the curtain rail, for one thing. There was no blood on your clothes this morning, and no blood in your room – it seems quite clear that you are entirely innocent. So, regretfully, we must turn away from you. You did not unlock Heppy's door last night. But, again, we know that someone did, for we have a witness who saw Heppy leaving Theodora's room at two a.m. this morning. Mr DeWitt, please let everyone know what you told us earlier.'

'Ah,' said Mr DeWitt, straightening his spine. 'Well. I happened to be awake at two—'

'Why?' asked Daisy sweetly.

'I, ah, couldn't sleep. So I went out of my cabin and saw – well, I saw Heppy walking away from me. She had clearly been into Theodora's cabin, so I decided to look in on Theo, to make sure she was all right.'

Mr DeWitt's story had already changed somewhat, I noticed.

'I looked inside, and saw her lying there – dead! I rushed in, tripped over the sheet on the floor and realized it was covered in blood. I had to – I had to clean myself in Theodora's sink – I thought – I didn't want to, I mean, I didn't want to be caught up in anything nasty.'

'Alas, you were, anyway,' said Daisy. 'So, if you're telling the truth, you saw Heppy leave at two, and then went into cabin seven to find Theodora dead in her bed, the sheet already on the floor. I assume it was lying in the middle of the floor when you fell over it, and you kicked it to the right in your haste – that's where it was found in the morning. That part of your story does have the ring of truth to it – the sheet itself and the sink corroborate it – but could you have killed Theodora, hung up the sheet, waited for Heppy to walk through it and *then* did everything you say?'

'But I didn't!' spluttered Mr DeWitt. 'I didn't! I swear it! I—'

'I don't believe *you*,' snapped Daisy. 'But what I *do* believe is the evidence of your trousers, and the Easton's Syrup.'

Mr DeWitt froze.

'Hazel,' said Daisy. 'Explain.'

'We went into Mr DeWitt's cabin today and noticed something interesting,' I continued. 'There was a pair of discarded pyjama bottoms, with blood around the hems. Exactly where it would get if Mr DeWitt had tripped over the sheet while wearing them. There was no blood anywhere else in the room, but there *were* seven empty bottles of Easton's Syrup on his dresser.'

'The thing about Easton's,' said Daisy, 'is that it's a pick-me-up that's used quite widely. It's supposed to be terribly good for you – but it does have quite a lot of strychnine in it. Strychnine is a poison. There's not enough of it in Easton's to hurt you if you shake up the bottle properly, but if you only drink the dregs you can be very badly affected. I heard about a woman who died of it! And, of course, if someone carefully strains the contents of several bottles and decants the distillation into one, the resulting mixture would be absolutely deadly. So why did Mr DeWitt have so many bottles? It seemed quite obvious. He was planning to poison the only other person on the ship who we knew took Easton's: Theodora.'

'You can't prove that!' shouted Mr DeWitt. 'I take that tonic regularly. I – I—'

'You'd be a fool to deny it! The tonic and the trousers prove your innocence of this crime,' snapped Daisy. '*That's* what you were doing last night, isn't it? You were going to put the doctored bottle in Theodora's room and kill her that way. But, when you woke up to carry out your plot, you stepped into the middle of quite a different one. You realized someone had already done the job you had set out to do. In a panic, you threw the doctored bottle over the side into the Nile – our witness heard the splash. But you forgot to throw away the cloth that you'd strained the tonic through, and so it was easy enough to work out what happened.'

Mr DeWitt was papery white, his face leathery with fear.

'I didn't kill her!' he whispered. 'It wasn't me!'

'Yes, we know,' said Daisy severely. 'I've just said: you did not commit this murder. You are the reason for the bloodstains in the bathroom, and the sheet on the floor where we found it, but we must look elsewhere for the criminal mastermind. We are getting close to the truth now – but who is it?'

4

'So we've ruled out Mr DeWitt,' said Daisy. 'And that poisoning story got me thinking again about another poisoning we've heard about on this trip – that of Joshua Morse.'

'Joshua was NOT poisoned!' cried Miss Doggett. 'He died of gastric flu!'

'How dare you!' shouted Daniel. 'How can you still deny what happened!'

'NOTHING HAPPENED!' screamed Miss Doggett.

'Now that's not true,' said Miss Bartleby decisively. We all turned to look at her. She was sitting up in her chair, lips pursed and brow wrinkled.

'Rhiannon dear, we don't talk about this! Remember?' hissed Miss Doggett.

'I know you've told me so before,' said Miss Bartleby. 'But I *do* remember, sometimes, and I'm remembering now. I didn't serve the tea that day, because you said *you'd* do it!'

'Rhiannon!' snapped Miss Doggett. 'You're confused! I haven't liked to say it, but you're not in your right mind any more. You forget everything!'

'I know I do,' said Miss Bartleby, her lip trembling. 'I *know*. But sometimes things come back to me, just for a while. And I know, I know *now*, that I wasn't there that day. But *you* were, Ida.'

'YOU ARE CONFUSED!' bellowed Miss Doggett. Several people flinched. 'You – you – your word means nothing. I hope you know that. There's no proof. Joshua Morse died of a stomach complaint, and that's all there is to it.'

'It was *you*!' whispered Daniel, staring at Miss Doggett. 'When all along – all along – I was so sure that it was Mother. She never denied it, but I should have known – I should have known. Why, Theodora called you Cleopatra – and Cleopatra was a poisoner!'

'Yes, Theodora never denied Joshua's murder,' Daisy cut in. 'And that gave *you* a motive, didn't it, Daniel? By your own admission, you went to her room at half past twelve. You were the last person to see her alive. So – did you kill her?'

'No!' said Daniel. 'I swear it!'

'I don't think much of that,' said Daisy. 'I suspect you've at least entertained the idea before, haven't you? You said that you came on this ship to try to reconcile with your mother, but I don't believe that. I think you were out for revenge. It's true that you didn't have any blood on you this morning – but you might have thrown away your clothes. If you went in to see your mother at twelve thirty, and we know that Heppy sleepwalked at two a.m., it's possible that the blood might have been dry by then – but the night was cold, and so we can't be sure of that. So it could very well have been you – until we take into account something that Miss Doggett told us.'

'Pardon?' said Miss Doggett.

'You said,' Daisy told her, 'that you were praying in your cabin, and you had a vision of Theodora with three stab wounds in her chest and throat. That is why you weren't surprised this morning – because your magic powers had already shown her death to you.

'Now, did you truly have a magic vision? I don't believe so at all. It's nonsense, pure and simple. So, how could you have known *in what part of her body* and *how many times* Theodora was stabbed *before* Heppy discovered her body this morning? Logically, there's only one answer to that. You saw her body. Either you killed her, or you walked into her room after she had been murdered and saw her then.'

The whole saloon had gone quiet, watching Daisy, who waved her hands in the air as though she was pulling her story out of it.

'I asked myself which one it was, and I was not sure. But then – Hazel, will you tell everyone exactly what Miss Doggett said to us about the sheet? Because I think it's very interesting indeed.'

'Miss Doggett said that Theodora was lying with three stab wounds in her chest and throat, and the sheet tucked up around her neck, as it always was,' I said.

'*Tucked up around her neck*,' said Daisy, deathly quiet. 'So, when Miss Doggett saw the body, Mrs Miller was dead, but the sheet had not yet been taken off it and hung up in the doorway. And who would have seen *that* image, apart from the murderer?'

5

'So we know who committed the crime!' cried Mr Mansour, relieved.

'We do,' said Daisy. 'We absolutely do. I am not quite finished, though. Miss Wong and I have mentioned how we discovered the evidence of the sheet, and the curtain rail. We know that Theodora was murdered, then the sheet taken off her body and hung up in the doorway so that Heppy would walk into it. It was diabolically clever – and very difficult to pull off – but it must have happened that way. The evidence of the cabin proved it. To test it, we attempted one last re-creation, and I discovered some things that showed me the answer to this puzzle. Miss Wong, please lift that cloth up and bring me the items under it.'

'Of course, Miss Wells,' I said. All eyes were on me as I leaned forward and twitched Daisy's scarf off the little side table. Under it was Alexander's book and the wire

May had found. I handed them both to Daisy, and she lifted them up like trophies.

'Excellent,' she said. 'And now, Miss Wong, tell us what you saw during the re-creation.'

'Er,' I said awkwardly. 'Well – there was a small mix-up at the end of it. I was Miss Doggett, and when I arrived in the cabin we were using as Theodora's I got confused with the person playing Heppy, and the person playing Mr DeWitt.'

'Exactly!' cried Daisy. 'And since we are seasoned detectives, and we always know exactly what we are doing, we realized that this mistake was, in fact, nothing of the kind. It was telling us that some of our suppositions were incorrect. But what were they? This book, and this wire, provided the answer.'

'I want to protest!' said Miss Doggett. 'You are impugning *MY* reputation! I never – I would never commit murder! I have no need to stoop to such a thing!' Her jaw was set. 'I am a magical practitioner! My spells work!'

'Now that's a lie,' said Daisy. 'It's very clear that a spell didn't kill Joshua: arsenic poisoning did. You are guilty of that murder, I think, though as you have just said I don't have proof. And a spell didn't kill Theodora, either. She was stabbed in the heart. But do wait and listen before you jump to conclusions. You haven't heard what these things are yet.'

'So what are they?' cried Daniel. 'Get on with it!'

'A good detective is never rushed,' said Daisy. 'And as to what they are – this is a book of famous American trials. Did you know that in 1846, Albert Tirrell was found not guilty of murdering his girlfriend, Maria Bickford, because he was sleepwalking when he did it? And this – why, this wire could be used for anything, but I have bent enough hairpins out of shape in my time to know that they make the most cunning little lockpicks. Mr DeWitt, you didn't murder Theodora Miller, and neither did you, Miss Doggett. Your stories, that you went into Theodora's cabin and found her dead, are quite true. What you didn't know is that you *both interrupted someone else's murder.*'

Everyone started slightly.

'But – but—' Mr Mansour stuttered. 'But you've ruled everyone else out already, Miss Wells! So do you mean that Miss Miller *did* sleepwalk into her mother's room and kill her?'

'Ah, not quite,' said Daisy. She was enjoying this, I could see. My heart was beating fast in my chest. I think I saw what Daisy was getting at, but—

'That wouldn't fit the facts!' said Alexander. 'She couldn't have done that!'

'Alexander is quite right,' said Daisy. 'Heppy Miller didn't sleepwalk into her mother's room last night. Heppy Miller didn't sleepwalk at all. Because she was quite wide awake when she stabbed her mother to death.'

6

Several people gasped.

'Don't be stupid,' said Daniel. 'Heppy could never do *that*. She's a basket case, but she wouldn't stab anyone in cold blood.'

'Yes, yes, that's quite nonsense,' said Daisy, flicking her fingers dismissively. 'That's what you all think, though, isn't it? Heppy the Breath of Life's scapegoat, Heppy the pathetic child, who can take heaps of insults without breaking. And that's what we thought too, didn't we, Hazel? We thought that she was a poor girl who was the victim of a frame-up. It all made sense – why, the murder was far too elaborate to have been committed by a sleepwalker, and we know Heppy sleepwalks almost every night. We knew that her door had been locked from the outside, at Heppy's request, and then we discovered that it was later unlocked from the outside again. So we were sure: Heppy was being set up. And we ruled her out.

'But we didn't ask ourselves one key question – how did we know that the murderer and the person who unlocked Heppy's cabin door were one and the same? Then I saw this piece of wire, and I wondered . . . what if that was the wrong way round? What if Heppy had unlocked her *own* cabin door from the *inside*?

'We *believed* that somewhere between half past twelve and two a.m. someone crept into Theodora's room, stabbed her to death through her sheet, took the sheet, hung it up, left the cabin, went to Heppy's cabin, unlocked her door and *knew* that she would very soon get up and sleepwalk at two a.m., as she usually did, into her mother's cabin soon enough to step through the blood while it was still wet, and leave again before anyone else came in. When you lay it out like that, it's absolute nonsense. It relies on so many things happening that would be absolutely out of any murderer's control – or out of their control *unless they were Heppy*.

'But, if it was Heppy, why, it would be the easiest thing in the world to commit a fake sleepwalking murder. Kill Theodora, wipe the knife, drop it and simply walk back out onto the deck. Like Albert Tirrell, she would be arrested, tried and let off, since she was a known sleepwalker and she had apparently committed this crime while asleep. I ought to have realized that it was odd that she was so insistent that she had done it. She was quite sure – because she *had* to be. She wanted a quick, simple arrest, and she was more and more frustrated when we kept on trying to prove that this crime was anything but simple. I also ought to have noticed how resourceful Heppy is. All of the ways she tried to prevent herself sleepwalking, the string she tied over her door – it's the mark of a restless, frustrated, clever kind of mind, the sort of person who might have planned such a diabolically brilliant crime.'

'But I don't understand how the sheet fits with all of this!' said Daniel.

'Well, I assume it wasn't part of the original plan. Miss Doggett's surprise appearance must have ruined things somewhat. Heppy had just stabbed her mother, holding a pillow over her face to muffle her voice, when she heard a noise outside. She fled to the bathroom, leaving Miss Doggett to find Theodora's body. Miss Doggett, in shock, tore off Theodora's sheet to make sure she was really dead, getting blood on her nightdress – blood I noticed this morning – and throwing the sheet to the floor. Then she ran away to stick pins in her doll and imagine that she had magic powers – and, to Heppy's quick brain, this seemed an opportunity to be seized. Not only did Miss Doggett have blood on her, meaning that the police might pass over Heppy and accuse *her* of the crime instead, but she had made the scene of the crime bloody. Heppy could use that to make the sight everyone would see the next morning even more dramatic and shocking. So she hung up the sheet on the door rail and shoved her way through it, pushing it away behind her. This covered her with blood and knocked the sheet to the ground – where it was tripped over by Mr DeWitt. That is why we had *three* people with blood on them this morning!

'Mr DeWitt said that he saw Heppy's figure walking out of Theodora's cabin away from him, and then he went inside and tripped over the bloody sheet, getting stains all over his own hands and feet. That ought to have told us how very fresh the blood still was – and also told us how unlikely it was that there was time for a murderer to commit an entire crime and have Heppy fall into their trap before anyone else went in to see Theodora. The murderer *was* spotted by one person: Mr DeWitt – yet we at first believed that Mr DeWitt had seen the person being framed for murder, rather than the murderer themselves. We believed the complicated explanation, rather than the obvious one! Or rather we believed the explanation that was put in front of us. But, when you strip all of the complexity away, what's left is so simple and beautiful. It all makes sense! Oh, I do like it when things make sense.'

'But I – this isn't right!' wailed Heppy. 'I don't remember anything! I don't!'

'Oh, do stop lying and pretending to be silly,' snapped Daisy. 'I believe that you are a sleepwalker, but you made

340

sure not to fall asleep last night. You committed this crime when you were quite awake. You had motive – all of those horrible things that Theodora shouted at you all day long – you had opportunity and you had the means too. You were very clever about it – if I was any less brilliant a detective, I might have missed what was going on. But, unfortunately, I did not. You are the only person who could be guilty.'

'No,' said Heppy. 'No, no, NO. I – I can't – I can't let you do this. I can't be found guilty like this, I can't, I CAN'T! Leave me ALONE!'

'We can't do that,' I said. 'We have to tell the Aswan police.'

Heppy *screamed*.

I clapped my hands over my ears, and people stepped away in horror. I keep on remembering that moment. I think that if only I had been quicker – if I had taken hold of her – but whatever I imagine I know what the truth is. That no one was quick enough to stop Heppy as she flung herself forward, snatched up my little sister May, and rushed through the open saloon door out onto the deck.

7

Daisy cried, 'STOP HER!' and darted after Heppy. I had one foolish moment when I could not move at all – and then I went running after them both in a whirl. I only remember jagged glimpses – May beating at Heppy with her little fists; Heppy's curly hair under one of the deck lights; the water swirling below us; the glitter of the approaching city.

My father was bellowing at Heppy, and Mr Mansour was pleading with her, but Heppy dragged May along the deck to the very back of the ship, where the paddles were stirring up white water. She hooked her fingers in May's collar and swung her up, dangling her out over the churn.

She did not look like Beanie at all now, I thought – she never had, really.

'Don't come any nearer!' she choked out. 'I'll throw her in! I swear it!'

'LET ME GO!' screamed May. 'I'LL KILL YOU! I'LL BITE YOU! I HATE YOU!'

'Quiet, Mei!' called my father, his voice thin with terror. 'Please, Miss Miller – please put my daughter down. She can't swim.'

'Then you mustn't come any closer!' called Heppy. 'If you do, I'll throw her in. I'm – I'm sorry, but all I want is for you to tell the police that I was asleep. That's all. It's easy!'

'We can't do that!' cried Daisy. 'We have to tell them the truth!'

Mr Mansour and my father were frozen, and so was I. I could not risk it – I could not be the reason May was hurt. And I could not even allow myself to imagine something worse than May hurt.

'Hazel! Hazel!' whispered Rose, tugging on my arm. 'What if – what if we distract her, and May and I swap places?'

'Don't be silly!' I said. 'She'll see you! We can't get close to her, Ling Ling.'

'Yes, but we look alike, especially to European people,' said Rose. 'I know May thinks she's brave, but I can be brave too, I swear it, and I can *almost* swim. It's like in *The Twins at St Marian's*, when the twins swap so that the one who isn't good at Games can still win glory for her school. Only not twins, or Games exactly. Please, Big Sister.'

'No!' I said, louder than I meant to. 'It won't work, and anyway I won't let you. I – if anyone needs to swap with May, I will.'

While we were whispering, the light had dropped still further. Everyone's figures were dim now, the water dark and the last streaks of colour leaving the sky. A bat swooped overhead, and there was the shocking roar of a train from the far bank. Heppy startled a little – and, before any of us knew what was happening, Daisy was on her, reaching out for her arm, poised against the thin polished wood of the railing. I remember seeing her hair down around her shoulders as she struggled, her face fierce and intense.

'Get down!' cried George. 'She'll fall!'

But, even as he said it, Daisy had her fingers round May's dress, and had hurled her onto the boards of the deck.

'You coward!' she shouted at Heppy. 'Kidnap me if you must kidnap someone! May is a child! This is absolutely unsporting!'

'Get BACK!' wailed Heppy. 'Please!'

And then Daisy turned to us.

She may have been about to ask for help – though that would not have been very Daisyish. She might only have been doing it for effect. She might have been looking to see whether Amina was watching.

But that movement made Heppy jump, and overbalance, and drag Daisy over with her.

I remember Daisy saying, 'Hazel' – quite clearly – though no one else says they heard that.

And then she was gone.

There was a scream and a splash and someone behind me shouted, 'They're in!'

We all rushed forward to lean over the railing. I saw a hand, the spread of a skirt, a frantic, gasping mouth. Were they caught up in the paddles? Were they safe?

'Someone go in after them at once!' cried my father. 'Hurry!'

'Can Daisy swim?' asked George. 'Can she?'

'I don't know!' I gasped. 'I don't know, I don't—'

The truth is that I cannot swim properly, and we have never had lessons at Deepdean. But, I thought, this was Daisy. She knew everything. She was strong, and brave. She had gone paddling on the beach this summer. Surely she must be able to—

'Heppy can swim!' said Daniel. 'I taught her myself!'

And there was a curly head, bobbing up and striking furiously away from the boat.

'GO AFTER HER!' bellowed Mr Mansour. 'SHE'S GETTING AWAY! You, there – you dive for Miss Wells!'

But, although one of the crew tore off his shirt and dived in, and then George followed him, they came up alone again and again.

After that, things begin to go murky in my memory. I remember Mr Mansour saying, 'There are crocodiles . . .', I remember SS *Hatshepsut* pulling up in Aswan and everyone being rushed off the ship. I remember being in a hotel, or perhaps someone's house. I remember being told that Heppy was still missing, and not really minding about that, although I could tell that I should.

I remember everyone telling me how sorry they were. I remember thinking that no one was sorry enough. I remember getting on the aeroplane, Amina crying and begging to come back to England with us, and her parents saying no, and me feeling both unable to comfort her and awfully glad that I would not have to deal with her grief as well as feel my own.

And I remember waking up one morning in Fallingford, the day after Daisy's memorial service, and realizing at last that I really am quite alone.

Daisy is gone, and she is not coming back.

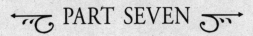

PART SEVEN

CURTAIN

1

And now I have put down almost everything. I could not begin writing up the case properly until yesterday, which is unusual for me. I feel very tired. I keep thinking about the little stone beneath the big oak tree in Fallingford's grounds. It is so small, but it feels bigger than anything else in the world.

And I keep reading the note that I found in Daisy's things, when I was packing them to come back to England. It was only a silly scrap of paper that I had given her a few days before, to make her practise her codebreaking. She must have been about to hand it back to me, for skirting it, curling round my words, were the hasty dots and dashes of Daisy's Morse code, looking as bold and impatient as her.

-../ ./-/ ./-.-./ -/ ../ ...-/ ./ .../ ---/ -.-. / ../ ./-/ -.--/ .. -./ ---/ .--./ ./ ...-/ ./ .-/

Detective Society Forever.

It was as though we were together on the page, like Daisy had put out her hand and taken mine and told me that everything would be all right in the end.

By now it is Christmas Eve, although, as I have said before, no one feels very festive. My father, who came with us back to England, is trying to behave like an English gentleman. Daisy's parents are not here – I am not sure if they don't want to be or they can't bear to be – but a telegram was sent to say that my father was welcome to use Lord Hastings' gumboots. He takes Rose, Millie and Toast Dog on long walks around the Fallingford grounds (May refused, and so did I – I can tell that he is trying to cheer me up, and I am not interested in it), and he comes back covered in mud because the gumboots are too big for him.

Bertie is back from Cambridge with Harold, and he is furious.

'How dare she!' he says, again and again, his eyes red. 'I taught her to swim in the (unprintable word) lake myself, that (unprintable word). How dare she!'

He is even angrier because Uncle Felix and Aunt Lucy are not here, either. They missed the memorial service yesterday, which hurt me just as much as Bertie, even though I did not shout about it. They only sent a telegram saying that they would be unavoidably detained in London until tonight.

'This family is finished!' Bertie said. 'No one cares!'

'I care,' said Harold gently. He put a calming hand on Bertie's arm, and Bertie shook it off furiously.

'YOU don't make up for the rest of them!' he said, and he went to his room and played his ukulele until Hetty burst into tears and begged him to stop.

I try to understand. I suspect that Uncle Felix, like Daisy's parents, cannot bear to be at Fallingford when Daisy is not, and I agree with him. I would rather be anywhere else – only if I was anywhere else I would feel even worse.

This morning, Lavinia, Kitty and Beanie arrived. They have been staying with Lavinia for Christmas this year – Kitty's mother is on bed rest while she waits for the baby to be born, and Beanie's mother is in hospital for a different reason. They all look very sad, though Kitty perked up when she realized George and Alexander were here with us too.

'Ooh,' she said. 'We'll get to meet them at last!'

That made me more miserable than ever. It was so unfair that Kitty should be able to think of anything other than Daisy.

'I never stopped you meeting them before,' I said crossly.

'Hah!' said Kitty. 'That's a lie and you know it, Hazel Wong.'

At lunch she chatted charmingly with Alexander, who only said, 'I guess,' in response to her questions, and seemed very interested in his slightly burnt piece of roast chicken (all Mrs Doherty can do is sit in the kitchen with Chapman and cry, so all the food is burnt). Then Kitty turned to George, at her other side, and found that he was deep in conversation with Lavinia about communism.

'As soon as I'm eighteen, I'm going to fight in the Spanish Civil War,' said George. 'Would you come with me?'

'*Obviously*,' said Lavinia. 'But why wait until we're eighteen? School's stupid and we're hardly learning anything. We could go now.'

They shook on it, beaming at each other, and I saw Kitty pout.

'I'm going to marry that girl,' said George to me, after pudding was cleared and we were sitting together in the window seat in the music room.

'Who – *Lavinia*?' I asked, astonished.

'Why not Lavinia?' said George with a grin. 'I like her. She's fierce. And she's different. She believes in the same things I do.'

'Oh,' I said. Was falling in love as easy as George and Lavinia made it seem – or even Daisy and Amina? At that, I thought of Daisy again, and plunged back down into blackness.

'See here, what's up with you and Alexander?' asked George, as though he were reading my thoughts. 'I was certain, on the ship – did he really not do anything?'

'He tried,' I said dully, taking my scarab beetle out of my pocket and spinning it between my fingers. It has got to be a habit of mine. 'I – well, it was my fault. It's too late now.'

George made a scornful noise. 'It's never too late!'

'Yes, it is,' I told him. 'Nothing matters now, does it?'

'Doesn't it?' asked George, turning to look at me. 'Of course it does. You're still Hazel Wong, aren't you? You're still the most brilliant detective I've ever met.'

'I'm not,' I said, tears burning behind my eyes. 'That's Daisy – *was* Daisy.'

'Nonsense, Madam President,' said George, and he strode out of the music room, shutting the door behind him hard as he went.

Which I think was the first time I realized that, without Daisy, I am the leader of what is left of the Detective Society.

2

I was expecting Alexander – and rather dreading it – but the person who came in next was Mrs Doherty, wiping her eyes and blowing her nose.

'Hazel dear!' she cried. 'I have – there's a problem. I've lost my brooch.'

'Oh,' I said politely. 'I'm sorry, Mrs Doherty.'

'But you see, I was wondering if *you* could help,' said Mrs Doherty. 'Since – since – oh, you know. Daisy – Daisy gave it to me for my birthday, five years ago. She saved up for it with her pocket money.'

I was about to say no. The thought of detecting without Daisy, on a case that was so much about her, made me feel faintly sick. I needed Daisy. Nothing worked properly without her. Without her, I was nothing but a shrimp. It was Daisy who made me special. But the expression on Mrs Doherty's face was suddenly so similar to mine, when I look in the mirror every morning now, that I couldn't bear to.

'Of course, Mrs Doherty,' I said. 'What does it look like?'

Alexander came into the music room, then, and looked startled and embarrassed. 'Oh hey, I didn't realize—' he began.

'Alexander,' I said, 'can take notes. Alexander, could you? Mrs Doherty's lost her brooch.'

'Oh – sure,' said Alexander. 'Hang on, let me get my notebook out.'

And so Alexander scribbled shorthand notes as Mrs Doherty described her brooch to us. 'It's shaped like a crescent moon, with little paste gems. It was on the sideboard in the kitchen just before lunch!' she said. 'I took it off to stir up the Christmas pudding – I didn't want it falling into that and being mixed up with the sixpence! – but then when I turned round again it was gone. I think – I think someone might have taken it.'

'Who else was in the kitchen?' I asked.

'Hetty,' said Mrs Doherty. 'But she would never! She's a good, bright girl and, between you and me, *don't* tell Master Wells, she's been on her best behaviour, saving up for – well, *a secretarial course*. But that doesn't mean that she—'

'Of course it doesn't,' said Alexander, but I glanced at him and saw that he was concerned. Surely Hetty couldn't have done it, not just for the money? But if not – then who?

I marched out into the hallway. May and Rose were there, May teasing Millie as Rose lay cuddled against Toast Dog, reading.

'May, Rose!' I said. 'We've got a game for you. We're hunting for a – well, a brooch. It has blue and red stones, in a crescent-moon shape, and if you can find it you'll win a prize.'

May looked at me suspiciously. 'This is detection, isn't it!' she said.

'No!' I said. 'Well, perhaps. But there really is a prize!'

'BRILLIANT!' said May, and she pounded off up the stairs, Rose just behind her.

So this was what it was like to be Daisy, I thought. You say whatever you want, you do things without having a proper plan, and people just listen to you as though you're being sensible. I ought to have done it years ago – only it was hard to, with Daisy already being so Daisyish next to me.

'What's the prize?' whispered Alexander to me.

'Shh! I don't know!' I whispered back, and Alexander laughed. I had made him laugh, I thought, and for the first time since Daisy had gone I felt myself glow, just a little.

3

The hunt for the brooch went on all that afternoon –
and, as the day drew in and the clouds lowered around
Fallingford and it began to snow, things almost started
to seem cheerful inside. I felt as though we were all
playing a festive game. Even Bertie put down his ukulele,
wrapped himself up in a scarf and hat and went to check
the plant pots outside on the terrace with Harold.

Only Kitty would not join in. She sat on the first-floor
landing, reading a ladies' magazine.

'It's childish,' she said when I went upstairs to see if
she was all right. 'We're almost sixteen!'

'*I'm* only six!' said May, running past.

'And I'm twenty,' panted Hetty, pink-faced from
chasing May in circles round the front hall, 'and, if I'm
still not too old to be childish, then you certainly aren't.'

They dashed away again, but I sat down next to Kitty.
'What's up?' I asked. 'Is it the baby?'

'Nothing,' said Kitty. 'Nothing! I don't care about the baby, and I wish people wouldn't keep asking me about it.'

'Is it – boys?' I asked, my heart beginning to race.

'UGH!' said Kitty. 'Hazel, I ask you, how is it possible that Lavinia – who has bushy eyebrows and an unflattering figure – has managed to get herself a boyfriend in two hours flat? It took me *months* to get Hugo, and last week he – he jilted me, and now no one will even *look* at me!'

Her voice rose in a wail.

'I don't think you should say that about Lavinia,' I told her. 'There's nothing wrong with her figure or her eyebrows. George likes her because she's' – I almost said *nice*, but then realized it was not really a good description of Lavinia – 'interested in the same things he is.'

'So to get a boyfriend I need to pretend to care about COMMUNISM?' squeaked Kitty.

'No!' I said. 'You don't care about communism, so you shouldn't pretend to. All I mean is, if George likes communism and you don't, then you probably don't really want to spend your life with him. You should find someone who likes – er – magazines and fashion and things.'

Kitty sighed. 'I just want someone to look at me,' she said. And I suddenly got a hunch, a tingle of my old detective sense back again.

'Kitty,' I said, 'is that why you took Mrs Doherty's brooch?'

'NO! That is – she wasn't using it!'

'Kitty!'

'But she wasn't! It's far too pretty for her. I thought that if I wore it this evening Alexander might notice me – but it isn't any good, I know that. He's only interested in you.'

My heart jumped up into my throat in the most peculiar way.

'No, he isn't,' I said.

'Hazel,' said Kitty, 'I'm not stupid. Even if you and D—I mean, even if I hadn't learned how to be a detective, I'd still have *eyes*.'

'Stop it!' I said. 'It's nonsense. Just tell me where you've put the brooch.'

'It's in my room,' said Kitty with a sigh. 'Beanie's and mine, under my pillow. And you know I'm right!'

But I was already halfway up the stairs.

Kitty and Beanie's room was on the top floor of Fallingford, dark and chill. Things creaked around me as I walked down the corridor to their room, and once I would have shivered – but, since Daisy, I couldn't be bothered. There was nothing so frightening as losing her, and that had already happened.

I pushed open the door and stepped across the quiet carpet towards Kitty's bed.

'Hazel!' said a voice. I clapped my hand over my mouth to stop myself screaming.

'ALEXANDER!' I hissed. 'What are you DOING here?'

'Sorry,' said Alexander. 'I should've told you. But I just thought – Kitty's been behaving weirdly all day, and she came in late to lunch. I wondered if maybe she—'

'It *was* her,' I said. 'I've just spoken to her. The brooch is under her pillow.'

We both reached towards it together, and our hands touched.

'Hazel,' said Alexander again.

'I'll just take it and give it to Mrs Doherty,' I said quickly. 'We don't even need to tell her who—'

'Look, Hazel, could you just stop for a second?' asked Alexander. 'I keep trying to talk to you, but you've been ignoring me. I – er – I—'

I looked up at him and saw him staring at me. Even through the dimness, I could see his freckles, and we were standing close enough for me to catch the faint warm smell of him.

And I was suddenly so tired of waiting. So I stood up on my tiptoes and I kissed him.

He made a surprised gasping noise, but then he leaned forward and kissed me too, and I felt as though I was floating above my own head, because it seemed so unlikely that I was kissing a boy, and he was kissing me back – and then I jumped backwards in sheer panic as I realized that it was quite true.

'I – I have to give this back to Mrs D,' I stammered. I was squeezing the brooch into my palm so tightly that it was digging into my skin. 'I'm – I'll see you tomorrow, all right?'

'All right,' said Alexander, and I could see that he was beaming at me.

As I ran downstairs, I couldn't stop smiling.

4

That night I was dreaming I was solving a case with Daisy. It was so vivid – I felt her hand on mine, her breath in my ear, I saw the face she made when I got something right before she did – that when I woke up I turned to her bed, my mouth open to tell her about it.

But the bed next to mine was empty, neatly made and still, and I felt as though I had lost her all over again. All I had was my scarab beetle and Daisy's coded note in my hand, by now quite soft from folding and unfolding.

It took me a moment to realize that something else had woken me. I sat up, eyes still smarting, and saw a figure standing at the foot of my bed. It was Aunt Lucy. So she and Uncle Felix were here at last.

'Is it Christmas?' I asked foolishly.

'Not quite yet,' said Aunt Lucy. 'Shh. I need you to get up immediately and come with me.'

'Is something wrong?'

'We have a case for you. Very hush-hush, of course, but you're the best person for it.'

'But I'm only fifteen!' I said foolishly again, for when had our age ever stopped us?

'Not for long,' said Aunt Lucy. 'Children do tend to grow up, and that is what you are currently doing. And I think – well, I think you have a long career ahead of you, Hazel Wong, if this mission goes well. Put on your slippers and your dressing gown and come with me. Hurry up!'

She spoke like a Deepdean mistress, and I found myself dressing with hurried fingers. There was something strange about this, something I could not quite make out. I felt horridly anxious, or perhaps excited, or both.

We walked through the dark corridors of Fallingford together, Aunt Lucy moving with confidence ahead of me. Once we disturbed Toast Dog, lying halfway up a flight of stairs, but he just grumbled contentedly and went back to sleep.

'An absolute failure of a guard dog,' said Aunt Lucy to herself.

'Where are we going?' I asked.

'Shush!' said Aunt Lucy at once. 'The library. Now, not another word.'

Across the big front hall we went – and by now I really felt back in my dream. I was thirteen again, and solving our second case. Suddenly everything was easier and simpler, and Daisy – Daisy – and then I blinked and I was fifteen, and following Aunt Lucy, and Daisy was dead.

And then Aunt Lucy pushed open the door to the library, and I got a blast of warmth and light that staggered me.

The fire was bright and roaring, and so the books and the deep, worn armchairs looked soft and mysterious, lit clear and dark in shifting patterns by the flames. There was Uncle Felix, standing up to greet us, red fire glinting in his monocle lens, very tall and dapper and golden as always.

'Merry Christmas, Hazel,' he said seriously. 'Now, Lucy and I have a proposition for you. We will put it to you in a moment – but first we need you to stay here while we go and get something.'

'Why?' I asked, bewildered.

'Sensitive case notes, you know,' said Uncle Felix easily, waving his hand – and I got another rush of misery, for he looked so like Daisy as he did so. 'Just sit here for a moment and wait, there's a good girl.'

I bristled at that, for I am not a good girl, not at all, and Uncle Felix knows that perfectly well. But he was already escorting Aunt Lucy to the door, and before I could say anything it had closed behind them. I was left alone with the fire in the hearth, spinning my scarab beetle in my hands.

I sat and stared into the flames. I ought to be pleased – I knew that. I was being invited into Uncle Felix and Aunt Lucy's world – a world I had been fascinated with for years. I had solved a case today all by myself, and Alexander and I had – I could not even quite say it in my head yet. It was too new and exciting.

But, all the same, I felt as though half of me was gone. It should not have still been shocking to me, but it was. Every day I woke up and felt *surprised*, as though someone had jumped out at me with a painted sign that said DAISY'S DEAD! Sometimes I had a lovely second on waking where I forgot, and then I caught the memory and it dragged me down deep, so heavy that it was hard to get out of bed.

What was I supposed to do without Daisy, really? Who was I without her? I supposed I was beginning to learn. I closed my eyes.

And then I realized that I wasn't the only person in the room any more. It was the way the space behind me felt, the hush of a door opening and closing, the pad of a foot.

The person moved very quietly, like a burglar, and I suddenly thought that this might be a test. Was I supposed to attack them? Disarm them? But I didn't know how to fight at all, and I had no weapons, anyway.

Or was it only Uncle Felix, back again? He did move quietly – but this person felt smaller than him, in a way I could not explain.

I held my breath. I felt my hands trembling, and clutched them still against the arms of my chair.

The person came closer, and closer. They were just behind me. I could not turn round.

And then a hand came down on my shoulder.

I burst into tears.

5

'Good lord, Watson,' said Daisy, reaching out to click her scarab beetle against mine. 'I thought you'd be pleased to see me.'

'You – you – you,' I gasped, unable to catch my breath. 'But you DIED, everyone said you DIED, you let me believe you had DIED. It's been TWO WEEKS, Daisy, I thought you were DEAD.'

'Heroines don't die, Hazel – you know that perfectly well,' said Daisy.

I turned round furiously, wiping at my cheeks. 'YOU LEFT ME!' I shouted. 'You didn't TELL ME! I thought I was going to have to live WITHOUT YOU! And you AREN'T a heroine, you're a real person!'

'I'm sorry,' said Daisy. In the firelight, I could see that she was thinner, and there was a new scar on her temple. Her eyes looked suspiciously shiny. 'If it helps, that evening I thought I was going to die too. I've never – I've never felt anything like it. Heppy tried to drown me, Hazel. She held me down in the water. I had to go limp to trick her. And then, when I came up for air, I – a branch hit me, and knocked me senseless. I only woke up when I was being pulled out of the river into one of those felucca boats. I had a terrible job convincing them to keep quiet about finding me in case I was still in danger – thank goodness Amina has been teaching me a little Arabic. I got back to Aswan, and when I heard they'd caught Heppy I was going to announce myself, but then I thought of Miss Doggett. We hadn't officially solved the Joshua Morse case yet, after all – we didn't have solid evidence. I accused her of murder and then let her get away! So I decided that Daisy Wells needed to be dead, at least until Uncle Felix and Aunt Lucy could gather the information to finish Miss Doggett's case, and be certain that Heppy would stand trial as a waking murderer, not as a sleepwalking one. I pretended to be someone called Leonora Regler, and sent a telegram to my uncle, Victor Regler, at one of Uncle Felix's addresses. I waited for him and Aunt Lucy at the Cataract Hotel, so I was quite comfortable and safe until they arrived to help me. We finished both cases a few days ago, and we flew home as soon as we could.

'But now there's another matter that needs my help – it's to do with a foreign minister, and his great-nephew.

That's what – well, what we're hoping you might be able to help with. We only arrived an hour ago, and Aunt Lucy came to get you. I asked to see you first, if that matters.'

'It doesn't matter! I mean, it does, but – I thought you were dead!'

'You've said that, Hazel.'

'Oh,' I said. 'Oh – DAISY!'

And I flung myself on her.

'I missed you, Watson,' said Daisy, into my hair. 'You know, I think you've got taller!'

'Not in two weeks!' I protested.

'Perhaps I just missed it, when you were around me every day. See here, Hazel – I'm sorry I tricked you. Aunt Lucy didn't want to do it, but Uncle Felix and I persuaded her. But the thing she asked you is real. Stop crying and listen to me properly.'

I took a deep, ragged breath.

'I'm going to stay dead for a while. Not for ever – but it's quite useful for Felix and Lucy to have a secret operative. I'm going to help them carry out missions for the government now, and not wait until I leave Deepdean.'

'But what about Deepdean? What about Kitty, and Beanie, and Lavinia? And what about – Amina? The new term starts next week, after all. She'll be back for that.'

'I took a leaf out of your book and wrote Amina a letter,' said Daisy, her cheeks pinking. 'Not signed, but she'll know it's from me. And the others – well, I think we can trust them to stay quiet for a few months. But this goes no further! I can't have the whole fifth form in on the secret. I assume you have written up the notes to our last case under the assumption that I am dead? Circulating that casebook might be rather helpful to throw possible enemies off the scent.

'But that is hardly the most important question, Hazel – do focus. We were wondering if you wanted to help me in my work, just during the holidays. After all, who would suspect two young women of being spies? We're really perfect for the job.'

'Would it be dangerous?' I asked.

'Of course,' said Daisy.

'Would we have to keep it secret?' I asked.

'From everyone else, certainly,' said Daisy. 'It'd be even more deadly secret than the Detective Society.'

'But we wouldn't have to give up the Detective Society!' I said anxiously.

'D'you think I'd have accepted if we would?' asked Daisy. 'It might have to change a little, since I can't exactly be at school for a while, but Detective Society Forever, you chump.'

'About that,' I said. 'I made myself President while you were – gone. I'm sorry.'

Daisy made a face. 'I rather think I asked for it,' she said. 'But I suppose – why shouldn't there be two presidents in future? I would be the first president, and the best one, but you could be one too, while I'm away doing other important things.'

It was so utterly Daisyish that I laughed. 'All right,' I said. 'Co-presidents.'

'You haven't said if you'll accept Uncle Felix and Aunt Lucy's offer,' said Daisy, and I could hear worry in her voice.

'Will I be with you if I do?' I asked.

'For ever and ever, Hazel Wong,' said Daisy. 'I promised a long time ago never to let you down or die and, as you see, I keep my promises. So what do you say?'

'All right, then,' I said. 'I accept.'

Amina's Guide to Egypt

Dear Hazel,

I got your letter yesterDAy. Thank you, It waS too kind of You. Here Is the List of reLevant Words you Asked for, for the account you're wrITing.

See you next term.
ALL MY LOVE,
AMINA x

- **Amoona** – my nickname!

- **Amun Ra** – an ancient Egyptian sun god, particularly worshipped in Luxor.

- **ankh** – a looped cross that symbolizes life.

- **ba** – the part of a person's soul that leaves their body when they die and then returns to them in the afterlife. It's usually shown looking like a bird with a human head.

- **baba ghanoush** – a delicious savoury paste made from aubergines.

- **Cleopatra** – a very famous female pharaoh. She died quite horribly, by snake bite.

- **felucca** – a type of sailing boat you see on the Nile.

- **galabeya** – an Egyptian man's dress.

- **habibti/habibi** – 'darling' in Arabic. Habibti is for a girl, habibi for a boy.

- **halwa** – a delicious sweet, very dense and chewy.

- **Hatshepsut** – a female pharaoh, supposed to be the daughter of Amun Ra.

- **hibiscus** – a beautiful red flower that can be used to make tea or juice.

- **Horus** – an ancient Egyptian god who usually looks like a hawk. The son of Isis and Osiris.

- **hypostyle hall** – a large covered hall with columns in a temple.

- **ifrit/afarit** – an ifrit is a demon or unhappy spirit. Afarit means more than one ifrit!

- **inna lillahi wa inna ilayhi raji'un** – this is what Muslims say when we learn that someone has

died. It means: 'We belong to Allah and to him
we will return.'

- **Insha'Allah** – this is an Arabic word that means
something a little like 'god willing', and
Egyptian people use it all the time!

- **Isis** – an ancient Egyptian goddess, the mother of
Horus and the wife of Osiris.

- **jinn** – a magical spirit from Islamic mythology.

- **Nahdat Misr** – a sculpture by famous Egyptian
sculptor Mahmoud Mukhtar. In English it's
called Egypt's Renaissance.

- **Nefertiti** – the wife of the pharaoh Akhenaten.

- **Osiris** – an ancient Egyptian god, the Lord of
the Underworld. Husband of Isis and father of
Horus.

- **pharaoh** – the ancient Egyptian word for
king.

- **piastre** – Egyptian money, like a penny in Britain.

- **Rameses II** – a very famous pharaoh who
put up statues of himself all over the Nile valley.

- **Reincarnation** – the idea that the dead come back to life as different people after they die. Ancient Egyptians didn't believe in this at all, even though the Breath of Life think they did!

- **Sekhmet** – an ancient Egyptian female god with the body of a woman and a lioness's head.

- **Set** – an ancient Egyptian god, the brother and murderer of Osiris. He usually looks like a made-up beast, but is sometimes shaped like a hippopotamus.

- **shabti** – small figures made out of stone or clay that stand for servants in the afterlife.

- **shukran** – the Arabic word for 'thank you'.

- **Thutmose III** – a pharaoh who ruled after his stepmother Hatshepsut.

- **Tutankhamun** – a pharaoh who died young. His tomb was discovered mostly untouched in 1922, which made him very famous and a lot of European people very interested in ancient Egypt!

Author's Note and Acknowledgements

This book, unsurprisingly, began with Agatha Christie. Her *Death on the Nile* (and the 1978 movie starring Mia Farrow and Peter Ustinov) was absolutely foundational for me, and I've known for a long time that I wanted to send Daisy and Hazel on their own Nile adventure as my tribute to an author and a story I adore. By the way, the part titles are all taken from of Agatha Christie books, so well done if you spotted that!

Theodora and the Breath of Life found their beginning in Bedford, when Rachael Rogan told me about the absolutely incredible Octavia, a woman convinced she was the Messiah. I read about Octavia and her Panacea Society in *Octavia, Daughter of God* by Dr Jane Shaw, and their story has influenced this one – though, of course, the Breath of Life members are not based on any real people.

For a long time, I sat with those two ideas – a religious society and the Nile – until my family friend Judith Ross asked me one evening if I would ever write a book about a sleepwalking murder. The whole plot of *Death Sets Sail* flooded into my head at that moment (I went very quiet as a result) and I absolutely knew that I had worked out a fitting end for Daisy and Hazel's adventures.

I first visited Egypt with my family as a seventeen-year-old, only a little older than my characters. I thought I still remembered it clearly, and so convinced myself that I did not need to visit Egypt during the writing of *Death Sets Sail*. My first draft proved me wrong. A thousand thanks to my husband, David Stevens, for pushing me to go on the trip that made this story work, and for acting as photographer, secretary, research assistant and general cheerleader during the week that I discovered I had imagined the Nile the wrong way up and a different shape.

In January 2020 we sailed up the Nile from Luxor to Aswan on the MS *Tulip* – thanks to our brilliantly knowledgeable guide, Waleed, and to the passengers and crew I met during our trip. We visited the sites Daisy and Hazel go to during their Nile trip, the Karnak and Edfu temples – the Temple of Karnak also features in the 1970s *Death on the Nile* film, if you want to know what it looks like. We also went to the Temple of Hatshepsut, which was sadly not in a good enough state in the 1930s to make it part of the book – but I did put in Hatshepsut herself, a fascinating female pharaoh who, like Octavia thousands of years later, called herself the daughter of a god to prove herself a suitable leader. Hatshepsut was succeeded by her stepson, Thutmose III, who spent a lot of time trying to erase her from the historical record (never trust family members!), but luckily it didn't work. Hatshepsut and Thutmose III are also the ancestors of another pharaoh you might have heard of: Tutankhamun (yes, that one!). Was he murdered? Maybe, maybe not. His body isn't in good enough condition for us to be able to tell. But it's definitely true that he was succeeded by his regent (the man who ruled for him when he was a child), Ay. This isn't a very usual arrangement – and it definitely gives Ay a great motive for bumping him off.

By the way, unlike Daisy, I was not offered any mummified fingers or mummified animals to buy at any point. That isn't acceptable any more (and never should have been)! Please don't take artefacts from cultural sites. But I spoke to someone who had been offered such a thing in the 1960s, and I'm fascinated (and disturbed) by how normal it used to be for tourists to buy real objects from ancient Egyptian sites.

I got a lot of details about Egyptian crime-solving in the 1930s from Sydney Smith's *Mostly Murder*, a very lucky charity-shop purchase, and I pulled details about strychnine poisoning and Easton's Syrup (a real thing, can you believe!) from *Forensic Medicine* by Keith Simpson, one of the most disturbingly useful books I own. The aeroplane route the girls take is almost all correct for the 1930s – though I did add a made-up Alexandria to

Cairo leg. The case of Albert Tirrell is true, and Maud West is an entirely real and extremely interesting female detective who I discovered in Susannah Stapleton's excellent *The Adventures of Maud West, Lady Detective*.

And now the thank-yous!

Thanks to the people who read early drafts of this book and worked with me to make my Egypt, and my Egyptian characters, feel vivid and real: Amina Youssef and her father; Rebecca Porteous and Ali Fahmi (and S.F. Said, for introducing us); and Laila Rifaat and Ahmed, Jamila and Amina Gaafar, who showed us round Cairo and gave my Amina her home. You never realize how very much you don't know until you try to write about a country and culture not your own – everything I got right is because of them; everything I got wrong is absolutely my fault.

Thanks to my other readers: Anne Miller (much nicer than the Millers in this book, I promise!), and my favourite Daisy/Amina shippers, Charlie Morris and Wei Ming Kam. Thanks to John J. Johnston for gently pointing out where I'd made up facts about ancient Egypt, and Adiba Jaigirdar for putting me right on jinn and reincarnation.

My mother, Kathie Booth Stevens, has been listening to my stories since I could speak, and has been reading drafts of *Murder Most Unladylike* books since 2011. She told me to keep going when I thought I would never be published, she has talked me through every wobble and every small author disaster and she has never wavered in her belief in me. I hope she's forgiven me for making this book 'too sad', because I can't think of anyone who deserves the dedication more than she does.

Thanks to my friends, especially Non Pratt, Authors Assemble and the Pugs, for being so supportive and understanding. Thanks to my publisher, Puffin, and the brilliant Team Bunbreak: my editor Natalie Doherty, who always knows the right thing to say, my publicist (and possibly sister!) Harriet Venn, my super-organized marketeer Sonia Razvi, Fritha Lindqvist, always calm and collected, Chloe Parkinson, Louise Dickie, Francesca Dow, Jan Bielecki, Steph Barrett, Jane Tait, Wendy Shakespeare, Toria Hegedus and Marcus Fletcher. Thanks to Nina Tara for another glorious cover – I feel so lucky to have her iconic artwork on all of the *Murder Most Unladylike* books.

Thanks to my excellent agent, Gemma Cooper, who seven years ago saw something in a dreadful 80,000-word draft with no plot that made her sign me up as a client. I'm so lucky she took a chance on me! I think it turned out pretty well, all things considered.

Finally, if you've made it this far, thank you to you, my reader. Whether you're a bookseller, a librarian, a teacher, a parent, or someone Daisy or Hazel or May's age, thank you for being part of this incredible journey and believing in my world and my characters. Your support turned a three-book series into a nine-book one and changed my life for ever. I feel so thankful that I've been able to tell Daisy and Hazel's story the way I wanted to, and to watch my fans, and my detectives, grow up together into wonderfully impressive people. As Daisy is fond of saying, I can't wait until they're twenty. Just imagine what they'll be able to do then . . .

Oxford, February 2020

A Q&A WITH
ROBIN STEVENS

Death Sets Sail is the final adventure for Daisy and Hazel. How did you feel about writing it?

Incredibly emotional! Daisy and Hazel have been in my head for ten years – writing this book was like saying goodbye to my dearest friends. I felt a lot of pressure to make sure their last adventure was their best one ever, and it took me longer than usual to get the story right because I just didn't want it to end!

Of all the books in the series, which is your favourite? And which did you find most challenging to write?

I love all of my books – though I have to say that this one might have ended up being my very favourite. *Death in the Spotlight* and *First Class Murder* are also very special to me because I'm so proud of the twists in them. I find the books set in countries I didn't grow up in, like *A Spoonful of Murder* and *Death Sets Sail*, very challenging from a research perspective – I know that they'll be read by people who live there, and so I work as hard as I can to make my versions of their homes and cultures seem recognizable. It's a tough thing to do well, but I try my best.

Apart from Daisy and Hazel, who is your favourite character and why?

Some characters take a while to get right, and some just leap into my head with very distinct personalities. George was one of those characters, and May was another. Her voice has always been very clear to me – I love her boldness and naughtiness, and when I was thinking about a new series set in the world of Murder Most Unladylike she seemed like a very obvious main character. She's got a lot to say – and so do her new friends. I can't wait to introduce you to them . . .

What would you say to any readers who want to be writers like you?

It's a very achievable dream to have! Anyone can tell a story, and to become a good writer you just need to be reading and writing as much as you can – and if you love stories you should be able to have a lot of fun as you do it. Write without worrying about grammar or spelling, and read without worrying about whether you're reading 'important' things, or reading in the 'right' way. Ebooks, audio books, comic books, magazines, fan fiction – it's all reading, and it's all going to make you better at knowing how to shape a great story. Finally, remember that editing is important. My first drafts are nowhere near as good as my final drafts – a great author knows how to rewrite, not just write.

What do you think Daisy and Hazel will do next?

Become the world's greatest detectives, of course! The Second World War is going to make that a little bit more difficult, but I know they'll rise to the challenge. I've always been convinced that Hazel would be a great fit at Bletchley Park, while Daisy would be an excellent field operative. Learning about real historical heroes like Noor Inayat Khan, the Oversteegen sisters and Virginia Hall help me imagine what they might do – true stories are often just as incredible as fiction!